DEMON
SHADOWS

Mike Sirota

Originally published by Bantam Books, New York, NY

Atoris Press edition 2011

Demon Shadows. Copyright © 1990, 2011 by Mike Sirota

ISBN: 978-0-9840072-0-2

Cover design by Karen Phillips

Library of Congress Control Number: 2011916331

Thanks to
Jeff Sherratt and
Michele Scott, good writers
and great friends, for helping
me begin this new adventure.

CHAPTER ONE

Excerpts from John Thorburn's diary, 1845 - 46, published in *Trails of Promise — The Way to California*:

> *November 18, Tuesday — First chance to write since a week ago, when we came to the lake. The snow was deep; we couldn't make it through the pass, even though the summit is only two miles from here. Tried again yesterday, but there was a terrible wind and it began to snow, so we came back. Only the Lord knows if we will be able to cross these Sierra mountains.*
>
> *November 23, Sunday — Snowing four days now. The Stillwell families are in an abandoned cabin on the lakeshore. It is a pathetic shack, with a roof of pine branches. The other cabins we built are not much better. Two are near the Stillwells. Ours is along a creek some distance away. I think that is best, because of all the arguing that goes on among us. We are sharing the cabin with the McClains, an agreeable family.*

December 6, Saturday — The first storm lasted seven days. This new one has gone on for three. Hard wind from the west. Very cold, snow up to the roof. Our food supply is low. The McClain baby has a bad cough.

December 12, Friday — Clear and cold today. Meeting this morning by the lake. Ezra Mackey died from the consumption. Mrs. Hardman (the mother) will not be with us for long. We are bad off for food. If we had enough, we could endure here till spring. Tried hunting, no game but a couple of squirrels.

December 14, Sunday — Very cold, but not snowing. The McClain baby died last night. Krueger the German read from the Bible. Mrs. Hardman is failing. My teamster, Milt Ramsey, is making snowshoes. He and young Georgie McClain are leaving at dawn tomorrow to try to reach Sutter's fort. May God be with them.

December 24, Wednesday — It is without joy that we await the Christmas day. The Gibbs boy is the fourth of our party to die at the lake. One of the oxen was uncovered by Noah Tyler, frozen in the snow. The creature had been gaunt when we came here. Its meat will not last long.

January 2, Friday — Snowing again, not hard. No sign of snowshoe party or rescuers. I am sure they never made it to Sutter's. Ada Krueger died. Ate our children's dog, as there is nothing else. Everyone is starving. George Stillwell said we should think about eating the flesh of our dead. We heard stories at Fort Bridger of mountain men doing it. God in heaven help us if this is our only hope! So far I have forbidden it.

January 4, Sunday — Jordy Fry said he saw a figure through the trees in the direction of the pass. Tyler thought he saw it too. Maybe our Salvation is near.

* * *

Patches of snow dotted Fallen Leaf Meadow. Despite the cold, the winter camp of the Washo people stood far enough down the mountainside, and they were comfortable in their lodges. The fishing and gathering time was far off, when they would climb to the high water, the great Ta-ho lake, center of their world. For now, though, they had enough food.

Tall Runner, wearing three layers of rabbitskin blankets, hurried across the meadow to his lodge, where Red Fawn waited. He knew he'd made her angry for going off so many times lately. Perhaps he would tell her what he'd found in the mountains. In any case, the recent trek had been rewarding. Two plump hares were slung over his shoulder. Red Fawn would be pleased.

Strong Bow, the *tebayu*, knew about the white men's camp on the North Lake. It was Tall Runner's duty to inform him of anyone trespassing on Washo land. Strong Bow felt indifferent toward these white devils, these *mushege*, who had recently begun crossing their mountain world. But he continued to send Tall Runner back to watch them. Everything would be all right, Strong Bow believed, as long as the *mushege* left with the spring thaw.

A few village *suku* barked at Tall Runner as he neared the uneven rows of cone-shaped lodges. Smoke from many fires twisted upward above them. It pleased him to think of warming himself by one, with Red Fawn pressed alongside him.

The shaman sat in the sweat lodge. Tall Runner knew this even from afar. The steam that escaped from the small hole in the peak danced wildly, agitated by the *gumsuc*, the dream-thoughts of the medicine man, now wrapped in the stifling heat.

Red Fawn was grinding dried piñon nuts into meal on a flat stone when she saw Tall Runner. She stood with great effort, for at sixteen she was full with their first child. The old woman that helped her accepted the hares from Tall Runner.

"You were gone so long," Red Fawn said.

"Only three days," the man replied. "Are you well?"

She patted the roundness under her robe. "We are. Your son is strong. He kicks with the legs of a jackrabbit!"

Tall Runner smiled and gestured toward the lodge. "Come inside."

"Not now. Strong Bow stopped by earlier. He wants to see you. You must go." She touched his hand. "Later, my husband."

The *tebayu's* lodge stood at the other end of the camp, close to a stream that ran across Fallen Leaf Meadow. Strong Bow's old wife and young wife knelt by the frozen rivulet, looking for pockets where schools of minnows had been trapped by the ice.

"Uncle, I am back," Tall Runner called at the narrow entrance.

The tribal leader of the Washo band emerged from the lodge. Tall Runner took a step back. In his fifties, Strong Bow had always been an imposing figure, and remained so, even though Tall Runner stood a head above him.

"What news from the North Lake?" the *tebayu* asked in his blunt way.

"There are five death markers in the snow," Tall Runner replied. "They did much arguing before, but now seem too weak for that. They do not fish and are poor hunters. There is little food in the camp."

"Those who left have not yet returned?"

Tall Runner shook his head. "I met one of our western brothers. He said that only one of them made it, but was nearly dead when other *mushege* found him in the foothills. This happened a few days ago."

"He will send others back," the *tebayu* said.

Tall Runner shrugged. "It may be too late."

Strong Bow kept silent for a long time. Tall Runner knew his uncle well, and realized the troubled look on Strong Bow's face was from more than his report. Finally the *tebayu* said, "I dreamed."

Tall Runner nodded. "What was the dream, Uncle?"

"I moved with the wind, high above the snow, and saw the North Lake. The *mushege* were outside, holding up their arms, trying to speak to me, but without sounds. I looked down at them, turned my back, and went on."

The *tebayu* paused for a moment, shuddering. "I was traveling toward the great Ta-ho lake when the sounds finally came to me. It was like our women wailing over the dead. I ran on the clouds, and it grew fainter.

"Then, from Ta-ho, I heard the cry of Water Baby — "

"No!" Tall Runner exclaimed.

"It beckoned me. I turned in another direction, but could not control which way I went. Water Baby pulled me down from the wind, close to the snow. Then the wailing began again. It tried to pull me back, but Water Baby was stronger. I saw his shadow and knew that, in a moment, I would see him."

"That is when the dream ended," Tall Runner said hopefully.

Strong Bow nodded. "The shaman sits in the sweat lodge to learn its meaning. But from what you told me, I fear that I already know."

Tall Runner, though puzzled, knew better than to question his uncle. "What would you have me do?"

"Go to your woman, for now." His piercing eyes found Tall Runner's. "You may be returning to the North Lake sooner than you think."

The short winter day ended abruptly for Tall Runner. To his chagrin, he'd slept away most of it. He hadn't planned that; he wanted to lie with Red Fawn, tell her about what he saw in the mountains, listen to her talk about their baby. But their lodge was warm, his belly full from the rabbits.

Red Fawn still slept. In the way of their people she continued to work hard, despite her condition. Too hard, Tall Runner often thought but never said. As he slipped gently from her arms, he looked at the smile on her smooth child's face. It pleased him that Red Fawn was his.

Tall Runner stepped outside. The night air was crisp, but not as biting as it would be when the wind started. Although a few small fires burned, the light was too meager for him to see much beyond the lodges that flanked his own. As he stared into the darkness, a small boy appeared.

"Hurry, Tall Runner," the boy said. "Strong Bow wants you. The shaman has come out of the smoke!"

The boy turned and jogged back through the village. Tall Runner stayed close with long strides. Others watched them pass, aware that something significant was happening, a rarity during the snow time.

The boy completed his important task by leading Tall Runner to the opening of the *tebayu's* lodge. Inside, the shaman sat cross-legged on a thick pile of rabbit furs. Though not an old man he was respected, even feared. His was the power of Great Bear, the spirit being held in high esteem all through the mountain world of the Washo.

Strong Bow and two elders also sat inside the lodge. They looked at Tall Runner impatiently, not because he was late, but because they were anxious to hear what the medicine man had to say. As he joined the circle in the place indicated by the *tebayu*, Tall Runner suddenly became aware of his own importance, however brief it might be. He nodded solemnly at the others.

The shaman spoke immediately, his voice filled with emotion. "I waited for Great Bear by the bay of Ta-ho. It seemed to be the hunting season, for there was no snow anywhere. He came and told me to climb upon his back. We started for the North Lake. On the way we saw *mushege* riding in their wagons to the California land beyond the foothills. Then they were gone, and as we came to the North Lake the snow again covered the earth."

"What was their camp like?" Strong Bow asked.

The shaman closed and opened his eyes as he rolled a shell necklace around in his hand. He did this with the sacred fetish the entire time he spoke.

"Three lodges," he said, "together near the shore, and a fourth, apart, all covered with hides and branches. Thin strings of smoke rise from them."

Strong Bow looked at Tall Runner, who nodded. He'd never described the camp to anyone but the *tebayu*. This impressed him.

"None of the white devils were to be seen at first," the shaman continued. "Great Bear carried me to a place in the snow where small flat trees grew. There were many of them." He held up five fingers. "This, more than three times."

Tall Runner was confused. "Five. There were only five death markers," he said. The others glared at him. Strong Bow made a gesture that warned him to hold his tongue. The medicine man went on.

"It was as I looked at the flat trees that Great Bear suddenly reared and threw me into the snow. I felt his anger. Rising, I wondered what I might have done to provoke him. With one paw he pointed at the cabin that stood alone. *Mushege* were coming from it; not walking, but dragging their bodies through the snow. Their faces were gray, lips cracked and bleeding, eyes sunk deep. Their feet were bare; toes were missing from the cold. As they pulled themselves along, they left trails of something dark in the snow. It hurt them to move, and they cried out the whole time. I became afraid when I realized they were crawling toward me.

"'Make them stop!' I called to Great Bear, but he stood silent." The shaman twisted the necklace furiously now. "I turned to run away, and I saw many more of them coming from the other lodges. Arms were raised, fingers pointed, faces angry. The closest was a bow's length away. I could not run or say another word. It was then that Great Bear spoke.

"'*You knew the* mushege *were here*,' he said. '*You could have saved them but you did nothing. Now they are all dead.*' 'I will help them!' I cried. '*It is too late,*' said Great Bear. 'No, they are still alive!' I told him as the fingers of the first crawling corpse reached for my ankle. From somewhere I heard the call of Water Baby and wished that I could go to him. 'The Washo can help them!' I insisted."

The shaman paused for a moment. Tall Runner could see how shaken the others were. *For one to wish he could go to Water Baby!* Tall Runner, also uneasy, dared not do or say a thing.

"I spoke those same words, over and over," the shaman said, his voice wavering. "Then I became aware that I was sitting in the smoke. Great Bear had let me go free of the dream. I knew that I was right, that there was still a chance for our people to appease the spirit beings. Do you understand, Strong Bow? Do you see the meaning of your own dream?"

The *tebayu* nodded solemnly. "We must help the *mushege* at the North Lake. They cannot die on Washo land without our trying to do something about it. Tall Runner, you must return!"

"I will start at daybreak," the young man said.

The elders leaned over and spoke quietly to Strong Bow. Finally the chief said, "You must leave tonight. You will bring them food and blankets, gather dry wood for their fires. We will do this until their own people come for them, or until the snow is melted."

Tall Runner looked at the medicine man, who nodded. It was a strange request, to journey into the high mountains at night. The Washo usually avoided it. The thought made Tall Runner uncomfortable, but he understood the importance of what had transpired since Strong Bow's dream. He dared not question his fate.

In his heart he wished he'd never set eyes on the *mushege* camp at the North Lake.

"I will send others with him — " the *tebayu* began.

"He must go alone," the shaman interrupted. "The next time, others will go. But Tall Runner must do this by himself. I . . . know it from the dream."

The elders were puzzled, but Strong Bow understood. So did Tall Runner. *Mushege* were not fond of Indians. With their thunder sticks they could kill many before they realized the Washo just wanted to help them. This way, only one need die.

"Go, then, Tall Runner," the *tebayu* said. "Tell Red Fawn you are leaving. All will be ready for you. Do not take too long."

Tall Runner returned to his lodge. Red Fawn still lay under the blankets but was awake when he slipped inside.

"You are going back to the mountains," she said, not needing to ask.

"It is important," he said.

"So important that you must leave at night?"

"Yes. Do not worry about me, Red Fawn. I will return soon."

"I will worry anyway, no matter what you tell me."

He shrugged. "I must go."

Red Fawn lifted the rabbitskin blankets. "Just for a little while," she said softly. "They cannot deny you that."

Strong Bow had sent a travois to Tall Runner's lodge. The supplies were being tied down as Tall Runner came out. There were plenty of blankets, but not as much food as Tall Runner thought there would be. Piñon nuts, the Washo staple, filled two baskets. There was some dried meat and the whole carcass of *mogop*, the fox, which had been caught that day. Despite his respect for the spirit beings, Strong Bow knew he had to look out for his own people in this season, not a good one for hunting, gathering, or much else.

"Stay close by the *mushege* for a day or two," Strong Bow instructed Tall Runner. "If you can hunt for anything, then all the better. Make them understand that you will be back."

"I will try," the young man said, but with doubt.

No ceremony preceded Tall Runner's departure. The travois slid easily across the frozen ground of Fallen Leaf Meadow. It would become harder on the mountainside, and in the deep snow farther up.

Tall Runner was not concerned about finding his way in the dark. All Washo boasted that they could travel anywhere in the mountains with eyes covered. Something else worried him, something that his people had come to know at their earliest time of understanding.

Their world was a terrifying place, especially at night, with many spirit beings wandering through it. Even the benevolent ones were given to whims of frenzy. There was Ang, the great bird creature, and Hanglwuiwui, the cyclopean, one-legged giant, both of whose favorite food was Washo flesh. There were the hairy wild people, who people always saw darting among the trees, and the fearsome Water Babies, who occupied *every* body of water, no matter how small. And there were many other things that horrified the Washo. Some of these they dared not even think about, at the risk of bringing down the worst kind of misfortune upon themselves.

So Tall Runner was apprehensive as he started up an old trail from Fallen Leaf Meadow. Even the sight of the half-moon, appearing from behind clouds for the first time in a few nights, brought him no comfort. Its pale light cast twisted shadows of hemlocks and foxtail pines on the snow, shadows that moved, Tall Runner swore, when he crossed them. At times he found himself giving them a wide berth.

When he finally thought about it, he realized the sight of the moon meant less chance of another storm hindering his journey. The most recent one had ended just before his last visit to the North Lake. But lulls of more than a few days were rare. Perhaps the spirit beings planned on helping this time, rather than leave it all to the Washo, which was usually their way.

It would be well after sunrise before Tall Runner came anywhere near the North Lake. The narrow pass through the mountains was choked with the snows of all the storms that had come since the end of the gathering season. The pass had stopped the *mushege* the first time; now it held them prisoners. Tall Runner would get through — he always did — though not as easily with the supplies.

The rueful cry of *kewe*, the coyote, followed him during the night. He had never cared much for the sound, but at least it was familiar, unlike others he had no desire to hear. At times of silence he realized he would anticipate the next howl from the unseen creatures.

Early in the morning, before sunrise, *kewe* fell silent. The white world became as a place of the dead. The travois slid along soundlessly; Tall Runner's snowshoes crunched the snow where it lay soft and deep. Though glad for the noise, he also feared it would rouse the spirits of the ancestors, who inhabited the land during the time when men feared to walk.

The trees surrounding him were different now — lodgepole and whitebark pines, mostly. Their shadows danced in the snow all around him, and he could avoid them no longer. He moved quickly, ignoring the fatigue as his pumping heart echoed in his head.

There! Beyond the trees! Something had run in and out of his vision between two heartbeats. A wild man! What else could it be?

Can't stop, he told himself. Must keep going or it will bring others! The wild men kill the Washo, cut out their hearts . . .

Two mule deer stood upwind of Tall Runner, rooting for shrubs under the snow, and were not aware of his approach. He could see their silhouettes against the backdrop of white hills. Immediately the wild men were forgotten as he reached for his bow.

But he did nothing, for *memdewe*, the mule deer, was *his* spirit being. It was the deer that made him the swiftest of his people. To kill it would be to destroy part of himself. Leaving all this meat frustrated him, but that was the way.

"Go on, off with you," he muttered, and the pair bolted in terror.

For a while the valleys and slopes were less ominous to Tall Runner, and he put many miles behind him. At daybreak he reached a summit from which he could gaze at the distant northwest corner of the great Ta-ho lake. In other seasons all the Washo bands camped along its shoreline. Now it stood desolate. Usually he stopped to gaze at its jewel-blue splendor, but more important things were at hand. He started down another valley, and the lake fell from view.

The sun shone strongly and made the snow blinding. Though cold, the biting wind of recent days had diminished. Still, Tall Runner wished he had more blankets with which to cover himself. He looked wistfully at the pile tied on the travois, decided against it, and tried to shrug off some of the chill.

Only the tops of two towering peaks indicated the presence of a pass, now buried under tons of snow. Most of it had fallen from the sky, but the rest came from avalanches on the tenuous mountainsides. With each step the young man nervously scanned the slopes for any new activity that could threaten his passage.

"You are lucky, *patalni*," he said to an eagle riding wind currents high overhead. "The earthbound problems of man have no meaning to you. For you the way is ever open."

Unlike the *mushege*, who waited for death in the shadow of the pass, Tall Runner would open the way for himself, as he'd done all the times before. Not over the summit; he would turn away from that. The travois must be left where he stood, for now both hands must be free. His way to the North Lake was not without risk.

With the supplies tied on his back, Tall Runner climbed up to the rim of a steep bank. He slid down to a partially concealed base, actually falling the last six feet or so and jarring himself. Above, sheer cliffs rose thousands of feet, eventually tapering to form Arrow Point, one of their sacred places. There, known only to the Washo, was the start of the way to the North Lake.

An upheaval in the mountains centuries past had forced a crack in the rock facing. A crack hard to see, even harder to squeeze through. Tall Runner knew that for the first twenty yards or so the supplies would have to be carried along piecemeal. It meant undoing the pack and making several trips. But it was the only way.

The narrow passage turned sharply twice and in one place appeared to dead-end. There, Tall Runner pulled himself up nearly four feet of smooth, sloping rock until he could again see the rift cutting into the mountainside. Here he left the first load. Not until all the things for the *mushege* were there did he pull himself through. It took him four trips and more than an hour of time.

Fatigue began to affect him. But beyond this passage the North Lake was not far. And the rest of the way was easy, except for one place near the end of the rift, where for a couple of yards the crack yawned deeply and plunged into blackness below the mountains. The path along it, an arrow's length wide, seemed to be sufficient, unless you were the one traversing it. But the spirit beings walked with Tall Runner that late morning, and soon he could see the glint of sunlight off the ice covering the North Lake.

Something caught Tall Runner's attention before he left the base of Arrow Point. Even more than with the opening of the rift on the far side, none but the most skilled in the ways of the mountains would have noticed what he did. He knew it would do him no good right then, but he put it in his memory. Another time, he would be back.

Once again the snow was deep. Tall Runner refastened his snowshoes and wished he still had the travois. He could make another if he wanted, but why bother? The *mushege* camp was close, the way mostly downhill. He would be there soon.

Excerpt from John Thorburn's diary:

> *January 5, Monday — Very cold, but the sun is up. Our luck has turned slightly for the better. A Digger Indian came into camp at noontime. He brought food and blankets, which we have divided. He is gone right now, but I think he's coming back. The news is not all good, however, for an illness of some kind seems to be affecting many of our people. We have bigger fires going, and the extra food will help. Still, I am growing concerned.*

The first thing Tall Runner did when he came down the last hill was count the death markers in the snow.

The same five as before. At least no more had died, as in the shaman's dream. Perhaps none would now.

They had been watching him from the moment he appeared through the trees. First, one had called an alert; now most of the men awaited him at the bottom. Some held thunder sticks, but Tall Runner believed they would not use them. He had already made a peace sign, had held out the food and blankets for the *mushege* to see.

Not many Washo had come face to face with the white devils before. The excitement offset Tall Runner's uneasiness as he reached the bottom of the hill. Some of the *mushege* took a step backward. He laid the food and blankets on the snow then backed away as the *mushege* looked over the gifts.

"Has anyone let Mr. Thorburn know?" Louis Gibbs asked.

"Don't worry about him," Edward Stillwell said. "He'll be here soon enough."

Women and children, who had stayed back from the savage, the likes of which had worried them on their journey from the Great Plains on, were called forward. There was no outburst of emotion, only relief on their drawn faces. A few nodded at Tall Runner; some managed to smile.

Tall Runner recognized all of them, having watched for so long from the trees. He had grown fond of one yellow-haired boy, whose actions never reflected the hopelessness of his people. Often Tall Runner had watched Simon Parkhill search for wood in the snow or look for fish along the edge of the lake, his small black dog following closely. Even now, with the dog an inadequate meal of a few nights past, eleven-year-old Simon still walked more vigorously than the others.

"Boy, you get back here!" William Parkhill called, noticing where his son had gone. But too late, for Simon stood in front of Tall Runner, smiling up at him. He held out a hand; the Indian understood and took it.

"Hey, thanks a lot," the boy said, and rejoined his father.

People from the cabin on the creek were plodding through the snow now. Tall Runner watched them with interest because the silver *tebayu* walked among them. That was what he called the man who was obviously the leader of the *mushege*.

John Thorburn of Pennsylvania — successful businessman, would-be writer and historian, now pioneer — was a strong and dignified presence. Even the ordeal in the mountains, for which he wrongfully bore so much guilt, had not diminished that. His thirty-eight-year-old wife Nancy, sixteen years younger than he, stood just as straight as she kept pace with his long strides.

Trailing after them and the McClain family was a man who caught Tall Runner's attention. The Indian had never seen this one before. Yet that was impossible, for he had spent days at a time watching the camp. He had seen them individually, and together when they gathered for meetings or to bury one of their dead. Had the stranger been confined until now? Had he just arrived at the North Lake? The former seemed more likely, although Tall Runner found either possibility hard to accept.

The gaunt, stooped man wore a long dark coat and a wide-brimmed black hat. Half his face was covered by a gray scarf. He fixed his small dark eyes on Tall Runner, while the others looked down, paying more attention to the precarious footing. Tall Runner felt a growing concern within him.

The others parted to let John Thorburn through. Louis Gibbs spoke to him as he pointed at the Indian. Thorburn looked at the supplies then started toward Tall Runner. Some of his people followed, and for a moment Tall Runner lost sight of the stranger.

"My name's Thorburn," the big man said. "I don't know if you can understand me, but we're grateful for this. Why don't you come sit by a fire?"

The silver *tebayu* made elaborate hand signals as he spoke. The words sounded garbled to Tall Runner, but he sensed the gratitude of the whites. This pleased him, not so much for them but because the shaman's Great Bear and the other spirit beings would not be so angry now with the Washo.

Then the stranger reappeared and stepped forward, stopping at Thorburn's side. His disturbing gaze remained on Tall Runner, who shrank back a few steps.

"Here's the start of it, like I told you," the stranger said to Thorburn without looking at him.

"Coincidence," Thorburn said. "He would have come. There've been times some of my people swore they saw Indians watching us."

"You don't believe that," the stranger said in a mocking tone. "Your whole pathetic band is a few days away from death. Without food, and with the worst storm now on its way — "

"You're only guessing!" Thorburn snapped. "How can you know that?"

The stranger shrugged and started toward Tall Runner. The Indian backed farther away, until a tree blocked him. As his eyes bore into Tall Runner, the stranger pulled down his scarf. He resembled the other white men, with dark stubble across a thin, angular face. But Tall Runner knew something else lay underneath. The stranger motioned him forward; the young Washo obeyed.

"Go and get it, bring it back here," the stranger said in words Tall Runner understood. "You know what I mean."

"I know." He was not surprised that this one spoke his tongue.

"You can talk to him!" Thorburn exclaimed. "Will you tell him what I tried to before?"

The stranger glanced at Thorburn and nodded, then looked back at Tall Runner. "Do it quickly, and don't even think of not coming back."

Tall Runner turned and left. Thorburn watched him go then asked, "You told him?"

"Of course." The stranger again wrapped his face in the scarf.

The trek back went quickly. Tall Runner's footprints from the morning lay untouched. He tried not to think about what had happened but concentrated on what must be done.

At the base of Arrow Point, the keen-eyed Washo went right to the place he had noticed earlier. Around one side of a jutting boulder, where brush lay thickly, was a low but wide opening. Studying the spoor confirmed that he had found the den of *taba*, the grizzly, who slept his winter sleep. There might be more than one; Tall Runner would find that out first.

The deep cave twisted a few times. On the last sharp turn he nearly bumped into a slumbering mound of coarse fur. The tunnel ended a few yards farther along. This creature was the only one there.

Tall Runner backed slowly out of the cave. Near the entrance he began to shout; he unslung his bow and rapped it repeatedly on the walls and floor. He raised a terrible clamor, continuing it even when he stood outside again. He paused once, listened, and knew it had worked. With a last barrage of noise he climbed up onto the nearby boulder and waited, an arrow nocked in his bowstring.

Taba emerged, groggy and confused after being roused from its deep slumber. That became Tall Runner's advantage. Still, the formidable creature was enraged over the intrusion. It swiveled its head from side to side, looking for an enemy to maul. It did not see Tall Runner until he had loosed his arrow, the flint head lodging deeply in the creature's neck.

Bellowing in rage and pain, *taba* tried to raise itself up on its hind legs, but toppled backward instead. Tall Runner shot another arrow into its underbelly, then nocked a third, waiting. Mortally wounded, the creature roared a last warning that this matter would be settled in another place, then was still.

Here was meat for the *mushege*. Tall Runner would rather return with the prize to his people, but this time it was not to be.

Still, he had killed a bear. That was something that must be known to the tribe. Drawing his knife, he crept cautiously to the great carcass and prodded it with his bow. There was a slight reflexive shudder, then nothing. Satisfied, he cut off one of the front claws, drained it of blood, and put it inside a pouch. The silver *tebayu's* people would not care, nor — he hoped — would the other.

The heavy carcass could not be carried back to the North Lake, yet there were enough pine branches to fashion another travois. In a while Tall Runner departed again for the camp.

Partly fatigue, and partly the thought of what awaited him there, made the trip longer for Tall Runner. Daylight was fading when he again saw the thin smoke from the cabins. Only a few *mushege* wandered outside. The stranger was not among them, Tall Runner noticed on his way down the last slope. This time he dragged his burden to within five yards of the nearest cabin.

The *mushege* hurried to summon the others. In a couple of minutes those from the nearby cabins had gathered around the carcass and the silver *tebayu* was on his way.

"Move away, Washo. You're finished for now, but don't leave."

The stranger's voice startled Tall Runner. He stood behind the Indian, and close. Usually no one could take him off guard like that. He decided it must be the fatigue.

Walking past Tall Runner, close enough for the young brave to feel a thousand flint needles prick his flesh, the stranger intercepted John Thorburn. They met face-to-face, Thorburn glaring at the smaller figure. Yet something in Thorburn's expression hinted at defeat.

"Say it, then," he snapped.

"This was done, like I told you it would be," the stranger said. "Your time runs out tonight. Agree, and it will be over. Refuse, and the spring thaw will uncover a graveyard."

He walked off, not looking back. Thorburn watched him go then approached Tall Runner. This time he wasn't smiling.

"If only I could make you understand," he said, frustrated. *"Damn, what are we doing!"* Noticing that Tall Runner was startled, he added in a softer voice, "Please, come and get warm."

He pointed at a cabin and gestured the Indian forward. Tall Runner understood but shook his head, indicating a spot nearby, where the hillside and a couple of broad Jeffrey pines formed a natural shelter. Leaving Thorburn, he walked toward it, stopping to dig up brush from under the snow. When he had a substantial pile, he fabricated a windbreak for protection. Soon he huddled in front of it. By that time the sun was nearly down and the *mushege*, having apportioned the bear, had gone back to their cabins.

As darkness fell around the camp on the North Lake, Tall Runner ate his next to last strip of meat and a handful of piñon nuts, washing them down with clean snow. Just finishing, he noticed a figure coming toward him. He stiffened. Under the blankets his fingers tightened around a knife, although he knew how foolish that was. Soon the figure stood over him.

"Hi," Simon Parkhill said. "It's cold out here. I thought maybe you could use this. No one will miss it."

The boy held out one of the blankets Tall Runner had brought. Tall Runner stared at Simon, then took the blanket and nodded. Simon smiled and hurried off.

"Gotta go," he called back, waving. "They'll wonder where I am."

It was a mild night compared to others at that time of year. The young Indian, comfortable now, closed his eyes and thought of Red Fawn. He was with her in the meadow when the creeks ran full from melting snow, and at the piñon nut harvest, and at the great Ta-ho lake, with the other Washo bands. It would be that way after the snows, only next time they would have another with them. The idea pleased Tall Runner.

But he would not let his thoughts turn into dreams. As tired as he felt, he denied himself the comfort of sleep. Perhaps later, when the camp was settled. Occasionally people moved between the cabins, though, and Tall Runner sensed an unrest he could not explain. There was something disturbing about the night.

The moon rose in a clear sky. Its pale light cast eerie, dancing shadows of pine boughs on the snow. Now hours past dusk, the *mushege* remained active. None came close to Tall Runner's windbreak, but their conversations grew louder.

Looking toward the creek cabin, he saw a glow in the sky. A large bonfire had been started, and it summoned the people. They traversed the distance in small groups, probably by family. Another one of their councils, Tall Runner thought.

When all of them reached the silver *tebayu's* cabin, there was much talk. It was not loud, and it came to Tall Runner as an intermittent murmur. He watched, curious. It suddenly occurred to him that this seemed a strange time to hold a council.

It was nothing that concerned him, the young Washo told himself. He looked away from the cabin and pulled the blankets tightly around his body, for it had grown even colder. Must sleep, he thought. Must let the dreams have their way. But still he fought against it. If he were farther away from the North Lake, where he could not hear the *mushege* or see their fire, then maybe . . .

The meeting continued for an hour. Despite how hard he tried to ignore them, the intensifying voices pierced Tall Runner's defenses. So much anger there; so much. Why? What was happening? Was it because of . . .

The stranger. He had not gone with the *mushege* from the nearer cabins. Tall Runner had assumed he was already there, awaiting them. Not so. Without looking he knew the dark one lurked close by. His hunter's instincts told him, as well as the crawling of his flesh. If there was any consolation, it was that his faculties had not yet gone dormant from the terrible fatigue.

Tall Runner turned slowly. The stranger was not as close as he had imagined, a vague shadow standing in front of some trees thirty yards away. Tall Runner had no doubt the small eyes watched him across the snow. And while his fear screamed at him, he could not get up and flee.

The stranger started for the silver *tebayu's* cabin. Tall Runner's gaze followed him as he moved like a wraith. Soon he was lost in the fire's glow among the people of the camp. For the first time in a while the North Lake fell silent.

Tall Runner tried to watch the activity by the creek cabin. The silence grew as unnerving as the loud voices had been. They must be saying something, he thought. If he could be closer . . .

Soon the curiosity overcame the fear. Shedding all but one of the blankets, Tall Runner moved quickly to the nearest trees. Enough cover stood between himself and the *mushege*. Instinctively he used it, until he was more than halfway to them. Only then did he consider that the silver *tebayu* and his people would not care that he approached, while the stranger would *know* he was coming, even if he crawled through a tunnel below the earth.

Tall Runner stepped out into the open, ninety yards from the cabin. Why go there? he wondered. He could not understand what they were saying. Nor did he know how close he would come to them before he stopped. He walked slowly to prolong that decision.

The snow directly in front of Tall Runner lay smooth, unbroken. That the white people's footprints went off in wide arcs on either side of him, as though they had deliberately avoided the direct route, went unnoticed by the Washo. A single sound rose from where the *mushege* gathered, halting Tall Runner in mid-stride. It came from a woman's throat, he believed, but was catlike, a pitiful mewling that hinted at pain and fear. It was low and grew gradually, affecting Tall Runner as the proximity of the stranger had earlier.

Closer now, fifty yards from the cabin. Tall Runner suddenly wondered why the *mushege* had not walked straight across the snow. The mewling cry slowed him. He tried to find the source of the suffering but the blinding flames denied him.

Why did they go around?

Then, in his path, there was . . . something. *In* the snow or *on* the snow, he couldn't tell. There were three of whatever they were.

Holes dug through to the earth.

He stood frozen, watching them, which was how he knew they moved.

Stains. Some kind of spreading stains . . .

. . .each the size of a man's hand, but they were growing, moving farther apart.

Shadows.

But shadows of *what?* Were they cast by flames, or moonlight? Tall Runner looked up reluctantly, afraid of what he might see. But he saw nothing, even though he turned everywhere, and this made him more afraid.

The spots of darkness on the snow had grown three times their earlier size but for now seemed to have stopped moving. The cry from the meeting place trailed off into silence.

Then the shadows grew more rapidly than before as they stretched toward the *mushege.* It was as if the sun had fallen behind a triad of towering monoliths. A new sound was born at its full intensity, a sound of the wind howling fiercely through rockbound canyons. But at the North Lake he heard only the *sound,* felt no wind at all. Tall Runner tried to cover his ears but could hardly raise his arms.

The shadows stretched halfway to the cabin. The cry began again, and there were others, as loud and as full of fear. *They are watching*, Tall Runner thought. *They can see what is coming.*

Windsound ripped through his brain. *Please*, memdewe, *don't make me see this. Don't make me a part of what is happening.*

Tall Runner willed his body to turn away. The shadows touched the edge of the meeting place, but he saw nothing else. He covered his ears yet could not run, for his legs shook.

The whites knew the shadows now. Their screams and wails were like those in Strong Bow's dream. Tall Runner also screamed, mostly in fear, but partly in a hopeless attempt to deny the windsound and the shrieking death from the meeting place.

Turn around, Washo. Turn and see what casts the shadows in the snow.

He lowered his hands. It was senseless not to. There was something nearby, at his back — reaching for him, wanting him, willing him to turn. He fell forward, hands clutching at the snow, trying to grab hold of something, crushing the snow, feeling it seep through his fingers.

Look, Washo, look at them . . .

The cries of the *mushege* rose above the windsound, striking him like the back of a giant hand, driving him face down in the snow. His eyes squeezed tightly shut, for he was afraid that *it* would make him turn. His body knew pain as he dragged himself toward the lakeshore. Soon he reached the windbreak, where instinctively he gathered up his blankets and other possessions.

The thing eased its hold on Tall Runner. Able to stand now, he staggered toward the slope that would take him away from the North Lake. He opened his eyes, fighting not to look back. The windsound again dominated as the cries of the *mushege* grew faint.

But this changed halfway up. One loud, terrible scream was followed by more, probably from the throats of all the *mushege* — those still able to scream. This time Tall Runner nearly glanced over his shoulder. But he surmounted the need and again covered his ears as he struggled for the summit.

Turn around, Washo, turn and see . . .

He made it to the top without understanding how he had done so. Falling, he began to crawl again then pulled himself up. The pain of his first step warned him that he had twisted an ankle. *No time for this now.* He dragged the leg through the snow, still forcing himself not to look back.

Turn, Washo . . .

In a few yards the hill sloped down. He fell on purpose and began to roll, disregarding the scrape on his arm from a protruding clump of brush halfway down. He could no longer see the North Lake; nor would he look upon it till many hunting seasons had passed, for it would be shunned as taboo by the Washo people. Even so, Tall Runner could not escape the screams of the *mushege*, which never ceased but after a while faded into the night breeze beyond the snow-covered hills.

* * *

He had no memory of when the darkness ended and morning came. Even when he could think about it, Tall Runner didn't know how he came to be at Fallen Leaf Meadow the next day. He must have squeezed through the rift in the mountain below Arrow Point, a dangerous passage at night. But the young Washo remembered nothing until he saw the worried face of Red Fawn, who stood in front of a crowd of their people, between Strong Bow and the shaman.

"What is it, my husband?" she asked, holding out a hand but hesitant to touch him. "Why do you sit here like this?"

He sat just outside the camp, his legs spread. The bear's claw, taken from the pouch, lay beside him. His clothes were torn, with stains of dried blood from his cuts. He looked around from face to face, confused. Then he remembered, and his body shook. Someone handed Red Fawn a blanket. She put it around him, but it did not help.

Strong Bow knelt and caught Tall Runner's darting gaze. "Stop this!" the chief ordered. "Tell me what happened at the North Lake!"

Tall Runner stopped shaking. He looked into Strong Bow's eyes, and the rest of the people closed around him.

"The *mushege* have seen the shadows in the snow," he said and began trembling again.

Excerpt from John Thorburn's diary:

> *January 7, Wednesday — We rejoice this morning, but also grieve. Some men from Sutter's made it through the pass. We are going off the*

mountain and will soon be in California. But we are leaving sixteen of our people at the lake, because of the terrible illness that befell us so near the end. Mary Ann Parkhill was the last to die, at dawn. We buried her alongside William and their two children. Everyone else seems as well as can be expected. We said nothing of the epidemic to the rescue party, lest they turn and leave us here. I think everything will be all right, once we are away from this place.

CHAPTER TWO

November 28, 1991 — Thanksgiving

The clock read 8:07.

Damn digital clock, Paul Fleming thought. They used to make round clocks with numbers spaced apart, and hands that moved. A lot of the clocks ticked. Looking at them you thought of time in descriptive terms: *almost* seven, a *little after* four, *half past* noon. And the round ones weren't on your VCR or microwave oven, your pen or pocket calculator.

Now time was *precisely* 11:32, or 5:49, or 2:12.

Or 8:07. You seemed to notice it more when you were alone.

Paul figured it could be worse. Some of them read 8:07:42, then :43, :44 . . . This one wasn't so explicit. Just the hour and minute, just . . . 8:08.

Alone was the big damn half-empty Laguna Hills condo he'd taken after they'd sold the house. He had moved out first, even though Jeannie had started the whole divorce business. That had bothered him, thinking what it might mean to Jason and Bree. But they understood pretty well, though only ten and eight years old. They had been included all along and knew that Dad wasn't leaving . . . that no one was leaving *them*.

Alone was listening to children playing on the grounds below and knowing that none of them were Jason and Bree. It was looking at their latest artwork, held up by magnets on the refrigerator. It was talking to them on the phone every few nights, then hanging up and wondering why you couldn't help with that week's spelling words, or play zip-the-lip and try not to crack up, or read a couple chapters from *Charlie and the Chocolate Factory*. It was driving to John Wayne Airport to put them back on a plane to San Francisco every third Sunday evening, trying not to think about how long till the next time.

Alone was Paul Fleming's new state of being, achieved in his thirty-sixth year of life and — ironically — coming right after the success for which he had worked so hard. He accepted it now, because he knew that Jeannie had done the right thing. More, as hard as it was to admit, it was what he too had needed.

Jason and Bree were with the right parent. As much as he loved his kids, he could not deny that truth. All the times he hadn't been there for them — or Jeannie — working meaningless but necessary jobs, writing his stories, his pieces of dreams that never seemed to fit together, until finally they did.

But by then, Jeannie was gone.

Pushed away first, slowly, steadily, over years. Then pulled by a growing consciousness of who and what she was, of her changing needs. That had become the legacy of their earlier life together, a time when they depended so much on each other, and a time of a deep love that had been so good.

The old dream was real now. Three successful novels, one made into a blockbuster movie; a lucrative contract for more books. Everything that he had wanted.

So why hadn't he written a word in eight months? Or jotted down one workable storyline? Or even just polish some old material that would probably sell now?

He had played a mind game with himself: *Writing is the great catharsis, the consummate purge of emotions. This experience will draw the best from the deepness of my soul. And it will help take my mind off what I'm going through.*

What bullshit.

Writer's block was an affliction that log-jammed writers at a word, a sentence, a chapter. Paul's logjam had become his career. And the worst part: he couldn't seem to give a damn.

Gary Marks gave a damn. Paul's excitable, cadaverous agent — he looked as if his last meal had been many months ago — let him know as often as he could how he gave a damn. He'd stood by Paul when nothing sold, then surfed the Fleming wave. Now he feared the wave would break.

Empathy, Gary's first phase — a short one — had been right after Jeannie and Paul had split up. Paul hadn't shared his troubles with anyone until then.

"Paul, I'm really sorry, I know how tough it is. Christ knows I've been there! Listen, take some time off, fly to Vegas, drive down to Mexico. Don't worry about Ann, she understands. Been through a couple herself. After you get back we'll give her your new outline. That'll keep her people happy."

Phase two, castigation. "What is this, Paul? Two months and nothing? Tell me you're bullshitting. Tell me you've been working on something and keeping it to yourself. It's all that racquetball, that bicycling up and down the coast. How the hell much of it can you do? Get your ass off the bike seat, Paul, and down behind the desk. What the hell do I say to Ann this time?"

Finally, guilt, the longest phase. "Paul, this is bleeding me, it really is. You don't survive in this business on what you did before. I can't go out and find another Paul Fleming just like that! Ann's getting pressured too. She told me."

That's what bothered Paul the most. He felt indebted to Gary Marks and Ann McGill, his editor, who had stuck her neck out for him. He would do anything for them.

But he couldn't write a damned word.

Gary Marks had come up with something that he thought might be a solution. He had discussed it with Paul. No, he had *told* Paul what he was doing. Paul had agreed; he had to. But he knew it would be a waste of time.

The phone rang . . . at 8:10. Paul hoped to hear Jason's express "Hidad," or Bree's excited "It's *me*, Daddy!" But it was Gary Marks, as always skipping a formal greeting and getting to the point.

"I got it arranged, Paul. Jesus, you wouldn't believe what a bitch it was!"

"What do you mean?"

"Getting you in! Your name didn't mean shit. But I managed. Paul, you've got four weeks at the Thorburn colony."

"When?"

"You'll go up day after tomorrow. It's like we talked about. You'll be done in time to pick up the kids at the start of Christmas vacation. *Four weeks* at the most significant artists' and writers' colony in the West!" Gary's excitement poured through the phone. "Nothing to do but work. That's *work*, Paul, like in 'gimme something new.'"

Paul shrugged. "I hope you're right."

"Of course I'm right!" his agent exclaimed. "You'll see, Paul, things will change for you at the Thorburn colony. Oh, by the way, happy Thanksgiving."

"Right."

Saturday, November 30

"Stillwell? Yeah, mebbe twenty or so miles."

"Thanks."

"You're goin' to the art colony, I betcha."

"That's right. How'd you know?"

"Kin always tell, easy."

The attendant at Huey's Gas & Market in Tahoe City was over fifty and thin. Paul Fleming thought he resembled a rubber-faced actor on television who did lots of commercials and now made movies; the "Hey Vern guy," Jason called him. This one had on an Oakland A's cap, and he practically stuck his face against the windshield as he cleaned it. He worked hard to scrape off hundreds of miles' worth of bugs and road grime from the glass.

"Not many other reasons for goin' to Stillwell," the man continued. "No skiin' there. Some huntin' and fishin', but the season's 'bout over. Besides, you *look* like you'd be headin' for the art colony."

Paul wondered what he *looked* like but didn't bother to ask. The Hey Vern guy finished cleaning and pumping then came around to collect.

"Is there much snow up that way?" Paul asked. "I mean, I won't need chains or anything, will I?"

"Nah. Snowed some last week, no big deal. They keep the main roads pretty clean. Can't say what it'll be like comin' back down, though, if you're stayin' a while. December kin bring some nasty storms."

Wishing more than ever that Gary Marks hadn't made him do this, Paul guided his Cutlass Supreme SL back onto Highway 89. Twenty miles, the Hey Vern guy had said. At least he didn't have far to go.

Stillwell, California, was the mailing address of the Thorburn colony, and the nearest town. Not a big place; one map didn't even show it. Why *Stillwell?* Paul wondered. The information brochure they had sent him mentioned Thorburn Lake, Thorburn Pass, Thorburn Summit, and numerous other monuments to a man familiar to many as a writer, historian, and patron of the arts. So who or what was Stillwell?

December kin bring some nasty storms. Why couldn't it have been May? Paul, a born and bred southern Californian, didn't care much for snow. Drive up to the four-thousand-foot level, let the kids toboggan down a hill, throw a few snowballs, head back down, and walk on the beach. Jeannie had once talked him into a ski trip at Mammoth. For years he had been trying to forget that weekend.

But it didn't matter, he supposed. He was going to the Thorburn colony to *write;* to try to re-tap the flow of creativity that had once been impossible to turn off. Just Paul and his imagination, alone in a small room somewhere in the high Sierras. *Spartan accommodations*, the brochure said. *No TV, no phone. A place to work, and to know that you won't be interrupted from that work for any reason.*

Maybe there was something to it. On the drive up he had actually tried to work up a new storyline. He'd thought of something, although it was vague. But it could be pursued, because, after all, he was going to have the time and the *spartan accommodations* to shoot for it. The point was, it had a place in his mind again. Not the kids, not the end of his life with Jeannie, not the uncertainty of his future. Paul Fleming was thinking about *work*. Maybe just *going* to the Thorburn colony was a catalyst. Whatever, he had a positive feeling about it.

Highway 89 paralleled the Truckee River on its way north, passing the Olympian-ringed road to Squaw Valley. Until now he had been driving along the western shore of Lake Tahoe. The beaches along the jewel of the Sierras had been mostly empty, except for an occasional hardy local jogging alone or walking a dog. Tourists were filling up the surrounding ski areas, as well as the casinos and nightclubs on the Nevada side. Paul had almost detoured to the north shore for a couple hours of blackjack, a passion of his. But he figured there would be plenty of time to come down during his four weeks at the colony. No one was going to expect him to work *all* the time, seven days a week. This wasn't the Beverly Hilton, but it wasn't San Quentin either.

At the old picture-postcard town of Truckee the highway briefly joined Interstate 80. Paul could have taken

80 all the way from Sacramento but had chosen the slower route through the gold country. When the four weeks were done, the interstate would hardly be fast enough to get him to the Bay Area — to Jason and Bree.

Plenty of daylight remained when he saw the first turnoff for Stillwell, at Indian Creek Road. He had planned well, not wanting to drive unknown back roads at night. Low mounds of snow lined both sides. Although the sun had been shining brightly all day, only a few filtered rays reached the ground through the dense, overhanging branches of the surrounding pines.

Other than a single van, the narrow road belonged to Paul for three miles. He would have missed the last turnoff had it not been for a small sign nailed to a tree. *Thorburn Lake*, it read, with an arrow pointing to the right. As slow as he drove, Paul went ten yards past the sign before hitting the brakes and rolling back.

The narrow asphalt road was badly rutted. Some potholes were deep enough to cause damage for a careless driver. Paul never went faster than ten miles an hour. The road remained in disrepair for its entire length and was by far the longest two and a half miles he had ever driven.

Finally the road, which had been climbing gradually, emerged from the trees, revealing — impressively — Thorburn Lake. He'd read it was extremely deep in places, as most high mountain lakes were, its water like blue crystal. Paul admired its majestic stillness as much as its awesome beauty. Steep bluffs comprised part of its shoreline, although most of the frontage was high alpine woods. The lake covered more than a thousand acres, with many small inlets. Paul understood how someone could become inspired there.

The road sloped down then crossed a one-lane steel truss bridge over Aspen Creek, which flowed strongly ten feet below. Straight ahead, the town of Stillwell was nestled between pine-covered hills. Paul passed a city limits sign that had no population total on it.

Stillwell, California, looked even smaller than Paul had imagined. Washo Street, which the road had become, ran three blocks long through downtown. But it was wider and better paved. It ended at the lakeshore.

The information brochure was specific about dinner being served promptly at six-thirty. But that was over two hours away, and Paul was hungry. He'd had breakfast early, nothing since then. He pulled into the first angled parking slot on his right. Only two other vehicles — dusty pickup trucks — were parked on the block.

Without the paved road and the one flashing traffic light at Alpine Street, Paul might have thought he'd stepped back a hundred years in time. Stillwell's buildings were the once proud works of stonemasons and bricklayers. Wooden signs, weathered but readable, denoted either a historical landmark or a current enterprise: NUGGET BAR; STILLWELL GAZETTE; KEATS & MORRIS, CIVIL ENGINEERS AND SURVEYORS; FRY MERCANTILE; MULE DEER CAFE. Down Placer Street two buildings were linked by an overhead conservatory. There was a whitewashed schoolhouse surrounded by a picket fence, and a boarded-up barn topped by a dovecote.

The windows of the Mule Deer Cafe, farther up the street, were so thick with grime that Paul doubted it had been open for decades. But the smell of food had to be coming from somewhere. As he watched, the door swung open. A burly, middle-aged man stepped out into the growing cold of the day. The Mule Deer Cafe was open for business.

Pausing near the curb, the man spat noisily into the street. He lit a cigarette, glanced sourly at Paul then started for his pickup, parked beyond the Cutlass. His gaze remained on Paul as he passed.

"Afternoon," Paul said.

The man slowed and touched the brim of his Stetson. "'Lo," he said.

"How's the food at that place?"

The man spat again. "Depends. How strong's your stomach?"

He climbed into the cab of his pickup and worked at turning over the engine. So, Paul thought, to heed the restaurant critic's review, or not? He glanced at the Mule Deer Cafe and decided he wasn't *that* hungry. Just a bag of chips or a Hershey bar to make it to dinner.

Fry Mercantile looked as if it would have almost anything. The windows were not dirty. Inside, a rack crammed with bags of Laura Scudder snack foods was flanked by one containing assorted hardware items and another with household cleansers. An eclectic display.

Paul glanced at the pickup again. The man rolled down his window, spat a final time, and backed out of the spot. He pulled away so slowly, Paul wondered if he had a problem with his truck. By the time the man reached S. Lakeshore Drive, at the end of Washo Street, Paul had already gone into the store.

A disconcerting cowbell on the door nearly caused Paul to start a chain reaction of toppling snow shovels. These were stacked upright and rather precariously just inside. Carefully circumventing them, he went to the Laura Scudder rack and unclipped a bag of corn chips. That and a candy bar, he decided, should be enough.

Candy was often found near the checkout counter. He didn't see any, but he did notice the woman working there — about twenty-five, of medium height, thin. Blond hair hung limply to her shoulders. She looked pale; a faded yellow blouse and no makeup enhanced this anemic image. Her expression remained blank as she watched Paul approach. She had green eyes, he noticed, and he was thankful she had done nothing to diminish their appeal.

"Hi," he said.

"Is there something I can help you find?" she asked in a low, dull voice.

"Yes, where are you hiding the candy?"

"Hiding? I'm not hiding anything. Oh, candy!" This was louder, with feeling. "A heart-shaped box of candy for a lady. And some flowers too. How romantic!"

She closed her eyes and for a moment went somewhere else. Strange, Paul thought. Still, he felt guilty about intruding on her journey.

"I was just looking for a candy bar," he said.

She returned from the other world, raised a limp finger. "Two aisles over, halfway down on the left."

As he followed her directions, he realized that she walked a step behind him. Too close, it seemed. He would have passed the display had she not pointed frantically.

"There!" she exclaimed. "That's what you wanted, wasn't it?"

"Yes." He grabbed a milk chocolate Big Block, no nuts. "How much do I owe you?"

"My name's Jenny Fry," she said, holding out a hand.

Paul shook it, surprised by her firm grip. "Nice to meet you. I'm Paul Fleming."

She nodded vaguely. "Paul Fleming. We have some of your books for sale on the rack over there. I read one of them. It was about the Third World plan to kidnap both first ladies at the superpower summit conference. Found the plot implausible, but was impressed with the depth of characterization, especially the non-condescending strength and intensity of the female lead. You're staying at the colony, of course."

Paul was speechless. He didn't know what to make of Jenny Fry. In the front of the store the clanging of the bell heralded another customer. Jenny continued to stare at him.

"Uh, no . . . yes, I will be," he finally responded. "I just got to town." He grabbed two more Big Blocks.

"A dollar-fifteen," Jenny said.

"I'm sorry?"

"I was going to tell you that the chips and candy are a dollar-fifteen. But now you've taken more." She seemed flustered. "Give me a minute."

"Look, here's three dollars," he said. "That should cover it."

"No, no," she replied, taking the bills. "It's only two-something, I know — Walter? Oh Walter, come and meet Paul Fleming."

She addressed a small, jaunty man of about sixty, wrapped — almost comically — in an oversized tweed coat. Waving to Jenny, he smiled at Paul and stuck his hand out.

"I thought it might be you when I saw that Olds outside," he said. "Only vehicle in town I wouldn't have recognized. I'm Walter McClain."

Paul shook his hand. "You wrote the letter that came with the brochure. Then you're the director of the Thorburn colony?"

"*Associate* director," McClain said. "Been that for thirty years. Harriet Thorburn's the director. She's run the colony for almost half a century now."

"That's incredible."

"Well past eighty, Harriet is," McClain continued. "You'll see her every night at dinner. Not so much at breakfast anymore. Sleeps later these days. Still does some writing, like all her family. She's John Thorburn's great-great-granddaughter."

"Two dollars and twenty-five cents!" Jenny exclaimed. "Wait here, I'll bring you the change."

She hurried off to the counter. Paul shrugged as he watched her go, then immediately regretted doing it. Walter McClain smiled.

"Our Jenny is a . . . unique girl," he said. "Been burdened with some pretty sickly parents for a long time. Mother died a year ago, the father's still hanging on. Would you believe she's only been away from Stillwell three or four times in her life?"

Paul believed it and didn't respond. Jenny Fry returned and handed him six dimes. He pocketed the coins, saying nothing about the discrepancy.

"I'll see you again, Paul," she said. "Come by sometime and we'll talk about books. I read a lot. Anyone can tell you where the Frys live. Walter, was there something you wanted?"

McClain held up a box of finishing nails. "Already got it. Put it on the tab, Jen, okay? Good girl."

The two men went outside. McClain's Bronco stood alongside the Cutlass. More cars than before were parked on Washo Street; a line of three others caravanned up from the lake.

"This is Stillwell's rush hour," McClain said, laughing. "The *official* day at the colony ends at four. Dinner's not till six-thirty. Some of the residents come into town for one thing or another, mostly . . ."

He pointed across the street half a block down, where five vehicles were parked tightly in front of the Nugget Bar. A Coors sign crackled on and off in the window to the left of the saloon's double doors.

"The favorite watering hole," Paul said.

"The *only* one," McClain replied. "Listen, I would've been giving you the grand tour when we got to the colony anyway. Why don't I ride up with you and start now? I'll get a lift back to town later."

"Sure, fine."

Directly across the street, a vintage Volkswagen was parked in front of the Mountain Apothecary Shoppe. The bug had once been painted a bright purple, probably a ninety-nine-dollar special. Now the color had faded, peeled in places, with rust spots that had spread over larger areas. The tires were mismatched and needed aligning. Lambskin seat covers — or imitations — hid what likely was a devastated interior.

The owner of this vehicle emerged from the drugstore. Bright costume jewelry, excessive makeup, and blond-red hair cut in a short punkish style made her look like a rock band groupie. Contrasting her car, she wore an expensive-looking fur coat that swept around her ankles. She tossed a small bag on the front passenger seat, slammed the door in apparent disgust, and started across Washo Street. The heels of her white fringed boots clicked loudly on the asphalt. As she neared, Paul upped his estimate of her age from twenty to thirty.

"Believe it or not," Walter McClain muttered, "*that* is one of the most talented sculptors to do residency at Thorburn in years."

Before Paul could respond, the woman hopped the curb and faced them. "Hi, who're you?" she said bluntly to Paul.

"This is Paul Fleming," McClain interjected, which annoyed Paul. "I mentioned him at dinner last night. Paul, meet Sherri Jordan."

"Hello," he said. "That's a great coat."

She nodded. "You didn't bring any rubbers, did you?"

McClain groaned. "Jesus."

"What?" Paul asked.

"Rubbers. Condoms, for shit's sake!" She shrugged, holding up her hands. "This town! That *drugstore's* been out of 'em for a week. The biddy in there keeps saying, 'They're due in, they're due in!' Doesn't even like to talk about 'em. You got any, Paul?"

He smiled. "Sorry, I don't."

"My luck." She glanced at Fry Mercantile. "Maybe I'll check with the space cadet in there. Might have some hidden behind other stuff she forgot about ten years ago. See you at dinner."

She hurried off before Paul could respond. He grinned as he tried to imagine the conversation between Sherri and Jenny Fry. Seeing Walter McClain's exasperated look, he shielded his amusement.

"I suppose some people would find *Ms.* Jordan delightful," McClain said, shaking his head. "Speaking for the staff, I'm glad she's leaving us the day after next. Shall we go?"

With his passenger still grumbling about the eccentricities of Sherri Jordan, Paul drove to the end of Washo Street. A weathered sign on a telephone pole read COLONY, and under it, THORBURN LAKE MARINA, with arrows pointing in appropriate directions. He turned left onto S. Lakeshore Drive, and within a hundred yards the road was rutted again. There seemed to be more patches of snow.

"How far is it to the colony?" Paul asked, aware that he was interrupting Walter McClain's muttered complaints about Sherri Jordan.

"About a mile-and-a-half, on the west end of the lake. See where the trees are dense?"

"Where they come down to the water?"

McClain smiled. "That's an illusion, but they're not too far from the edge. Most of the grounds, and all the facilities, are within that forest. By the way, I'd like to formally welcome you here. I don't think I've done that yet."

"Thanks."

"I know some things about you. Had a couple of nice chats with your agent, Mr. — Parks?"

"Gary Marks. What did he tell you?"

"That you were having some . . . ah, trouble, that a change of scenery might do you good. That's what Thorburn is for, Paul. Creative people like yourself are often victimized by the constraints of everyday life. Here, the artist has only one thing to do: work. The outside world doesn't exist, *especially* from eight to four. We provide this wonderful setting; we feed you, give you a workplace, and take care of it. We make certain that *nothing* interrupts you. There's no television in your room, and no phone."

Paul smiled at McClain's words. The man had either written the information brochure or read it a few times too many.

"Mr. Marks probably told you," McClain continued, "that there's a nominal fee for your stay at Thorburn, because of who you are. You're a rarity, actually. Most of our residents haven't had their first big breakthrough yet. For them there's no fee at all. There's even some grant money available. That is often the only way they would be able to break away from their mundane but necessary jobs for a month and not have to worry about surviving. We nurture their talents by providing them this freedom. And it works, Paul, it really does! Successful careers might never have been started had it not been for a residency at Thorburn!"

Paul felt the man's enthusiasm. "But why do you do it? I mean, how is something like this supported?"

"Look out, there's a nasty one!" McClain warned, indicating a pothole. "To answer your question, we do it because it's what John Thorburn wanted. The colony, and all that it has done to encourage creative ability, is his legacy."

"I've heard of John Thorburn the writer," Paul said, "but what was the whole story on him?"

McClain glanced at him admonishingly. "You didn't read the biography in the brochure?"

Paul kept his eyes straight ahead. "I . . . guess I missed that part."

"John Thorburn was a great man," McClain said, reciting obviously familiar words. "He lived most of his life in Philadelphia, where he had a lucrative career as a merchant and investor. He did some writing then, but nothing of note.

"In 1845, deciding he had done all there was to do back home, he and his family headed west. *Trails of Promise — The Way to California*, his diary of that journey, is one of the finest works on the subject."

"I remember reading some of it back in college."

"For a number of reasons," McClain continued, "they were delayed in reaching the Sierras. By the time they got here, late in the fall, the snows had started. The pass was blocked. They were forced to stay and build shelters to try to survive the winter. Many of them didn't."

"That sounds like the Donner party."

"The Donner incident happened a year later, down by Truckee. It became more . . . notorious, not just because of the courage of the people, but because some of them ate their dead. Also, the Thorburn party was half the size of the Donner train."

"How did the survivors make it?" Paul asked.

"In December John Thorburn sent a couple of able-bodied men out to find a way through the pass and down to Sutter's fort. One died in the mountains. The other made it. He was a sixteen-year-old boy, Georgie McClain."

"McClain?"

The man nodded. "My great-great-uncle. They found him, nearly dead, in the foothills. He told his rescuers about those still trapped up at the lake. Eventually he was taken to Sutter's, but they couldn't save him.

"Sutter sent a rescue party, but a blizzard drove them back. Another group tried a week later; same result. Then, in January, some mountain men were able to make it through. At Thorburn Lake they found sixteen graves — that's the cemetery there, by the hill — but many people still alive. Seems that an Indian had shown up a couple of days earlier. He brought them food and blankets. If not for him there's no telling how many more bodies the rescuers might have found.

"So after Thorburn and his people were taken off the mountain, some of them came back here and settled."

Walter McClain turned and stared at the road. He was silent for a moment, then said, "It took a while, but all the survivors from that terrible winter returned to the lake."

Paul glanced at him. "*All* of them?"

McClain nodded. "Every one."

"Why? What was it that brought them back?"

McClain shrugged. "No one really knows for sure. With all the writing he did afterward, John Thorburn hardly mentioned returning to the mountains. Different stories were handed down, of course. But I have my own theory."

"What's that?"

"First of all, you should understand something about the survivors. The Stillwell brothers and their families had been poor dirt farmers. Same with the Hardmans. Jordy Fry was a peddler, Noah Tyler a teamster and his wife a cook, both in Thorburn's employ. Patrick McClain was a rancher. He started out the journey better off than the others but lost all his cattle and had his cash box stolen. Aside from John Thorburn, these were not people of means.

"What I think happened, Paul, is that while they were stranded at the lake, they found gold in these creeks. Maybe just traces, but enough to tell them it was here. Remember, this was 1846. Just two years later Marshall's discovery would bring half the damn world to California. The Stillwells were back that summer; then the Tylers. Before the first snow they were all here, except John Thorburn. I believe it was gold that brought them back. Not the mother lode, nothing big, but more than any of them had ever seen before."

"It makes sense," Paul said. "But if they found gold and had money for a new start in California, why stay here?"

McClain pointed ahead. "Take the right there. That's the colony road."

Paul turned, and they were immediately engulfed by lodgepole pines. The Cutlass bounced over the rutted path; Paul slowed even more.

"As far as why they stayed," McClain continued, "that might've been John Thorburn's doing. He showed up in the spring of 1847. Stillwell wasn't much more than the homes the families lived in. Good homes, though, since they'd already spent a comfortable winter in them. Learned their lesson the hard way. He told the others that for the past year he'd been sending word back east about this particular route across the Sierras to California. It hadn't been used much till then. The Thorburn party had tried it on the advice of a mountain man at Fort Bridger. It was a good, time-saving route. Thorburn believed it would become important.

"He was a prophet, as well as a good businessman. Later that summer wagon trains began heading for Thorburn Pass through Stillwell on their way to California. They found a place where they could buy food, drink, lodgings, anything they needed. All of the original settlers prospered, especially when the gold seekers came."

"But that still doesn't explain why Thorburn returned," Paul said. "He didn't need the money."

"Maybe it was the challenge of making a place as isolated as this significant," McClain replied. "That might have brought him back. Or maybe it was because this *civilized* man hated civilization. On the other hand he loved the Sierras, like John Muir — whom he once entertained. He built Big House and lived in it till the day he died. Had guests all the time, mostly artists and writers, whose company he enjoyed. It was toward the end that he came up with the idea for the colony. Left a huge endowment to make sure it was carried out. John Thorburn belonged here, and he accomplished exactly what he wanted."

Paul nodded. "I'll say."

"Over there, Paul, that's Big House!"

The day had turned grayer. Paul could barely make out the main building through the trees, a quarter-mile away. A ten-foot-high wrought-iron fence on three sides enclosed the colony grounds. Thorburn Lake's rugged western shore was the other boundary. The dirt road passed through a wide gate.

"I've rambled on, haven't I?" McClain asked. "Didn't mean to bore you."

"You didn't. It's an interesting story."

"About the colony: we have fifteen rooms in Big House that are used by residents, and twenty guest cabins. You'll be staying in one of the cabins. A real nice location; sits on a creek. It's warm, comfortable, plenty of hot water. The bed is soft. There's a desk also. Not much else. I can get you a typewriter."

"Thanks. I brought my own."

"Any other supplies you need — typing paper, pencils, things like that — are available to you. As far as the rules for artists-in-residence at the Thorburn colony . . ."

Walter McClain was a storeroom of information, Paul thought, but his administrator's way of speaking grated on his nerves. Paul endured it as he continued to concentrate on the road, which had become smoother.

"Breakfast is available until seven forty-five," McClain went on. "After that you're out of luck, unless you've made friends with our chef or have change for the vending machines. The formal work day begins at eight and ends at four. Our non-fraternization rule is strictly enforced during these hours. No one, not staff, not other residents, disturbs you, or vice versa. You understand that, Paul?"

"What if I get a phone call, from my agent or someone?"

"Unless it's an emergency, a message will be taken. If it's in the morning it will be brought to you with lunch, which is left by your door at noon. Otherwise, messages will be in your mail slot in the day room.

"As I think I mentioned before, dinner is at six-thirty. Harriet Thorburn wants everyone to be prompt. After dinner your time is your own. There are things to do in Big House. And there always seems to be an informal party in progress. Of course, you may want to get back to whatever it is you're working on. . . ."

Paul tuned out Walter McClain's voice as they approached Big House. The trees thinned as the road first dipped, then curved and topped a rise to some open acreage, where John Thorburn's magnificent home stood.

"Good Lord," Paul exclaimed.

John Thorburn had seen the Greek Revival style that dominated architecture in the East during the early nineteenth century. Big House — an appropriate name —

reflected his fondness for that style. The perfectly symmetrical mansion, three stories tall, was fabricated primarily of burned brick and redwood. Twin stone chimneys rose above either end of the gambrel roof. The impressive centerpiece of Big House was a gleaming portico that rose the full three stories on six Doric columns. Beneath the portico, a massive oak double door stood flanked by carved wooden friezes, the relief figures representing pioneer families, gold prospectors, and the animals and conveyances that brought them west.

A broad lawn fronted the entire width of Big House, eventually sloping down to Thorburn Lake. During other months of the year Paul guessed that they kept it well manicured and brilliantly green. Now the earth was frozen, the lawn brown and dusted with snow. A circular gravel driveway curved around two towering, denuded oaks. No vehicles were parked anywhere along the drive.

The road had become the driveway without offering an option. Stones crunched under the tires, although the way was better than before. Hardly able to take his eyes off Big House, Paul drove to within thirty yards of the portico. Only then did he become aware of Walter McClain's excited voice.

"Here, Paul, stop here!" the man exclaimed. "Back up a little. Didn't you hear me?"

"What is it?"

McClain pointed to another gravel path on the right, running along the side of the building. "Turn here," he said. "The main parking area is in back. Actually, it's the *only* parking area. There are footpaths to all the cabins."

Paul guided the Cutlass off the circular driveway. "You mean I *walk* between Big House and the cabin?"

"That's right."

"Even in the snow?"

"The footpaths are kept fairly clean most of the time." McClain laughed. "Don't worry, Paul, you won't be stranded out there."

"That's good to know," he said dryly.

Behind the mansion — strategically concealed from view in front — stood six wood and stone outbuildings, among them a smokehouse and a stable. Some looked old enough to have been erected prior to Big House itself. Between them and the rear of the mansion was the parking area, a broad asphalt rectangle, cracked in many places. Once there had been lines painted, but they had long since faded away. The area offered plenty of room for vehicles, however, regardless of how their owners chose to park them. More than twenty were scattered about, some covered by tarpaulins, most near a back entrance to Big House. That made sense to Paul, who eased the Cutlass between a Hyundai and a covered sports car shaped like a Karmann Ghia.

"Are we going right to the cabin?" he asked McClain.

"Not yet. Well stop back for your things. Let's go inside first and sign you in."

The service entrance opened into a long narrow corridor, which led past the kitchen. The aromas were good, reminding Paul of how hungry he was. The snacks he had bought at Fry Mercantile remained in the car. With McClain in tow he had not eaten any. Nor would he now, dinner being so close. The hallway took a turn and passed between rows of coat racks before ending at a wide door. McClain reached for the knob, paused for dramatic effect then opened it with a flourish, like pulling a drape to reveal a masterpiece.

"Welcome to Big House," he said, ushering Paul through.

They were inside an octagonal-shaped main central hall. From this side the door was framed with bottle-glass panels. The oiled hardwood floor gleamed. A magnificent crystal chandelier, hanging halfway from the beamed twenty-foot ceiling, lit the hall brightly.

There were a few freestanding columns topped by classic sculptures, and artwork in ornate frames hung on velvet-covered walls. The centerpiece: a huge portrait of a wagon train struggling along through an unrelenting assault of snow, people buried up to their waists, horses lying on their sides, defeated. The faces of the pioneers had not merely been painted, but imbued with anguish, as if the artist had known firsthand what they experienced. A single unmarked headstone rose from the snow in the foreground. Even from the distance at which Paul viewed the work, he found it unnerving, yet fascinating.

McClain guided him to a door near the foot of a graceful, carpeted colonial stairway that led to the upper floors of Big House. Paul continued to be mesmerized by the painting. Passing closely, he noticed a signature in the lower right corner. The letters were wavy, but easy to read: N. THORBURN.

"It was done by John Thorburn's wife, Nancy," McClain said, seeing Paul's interest.

"Incredible. I'd like to see more of her work."

"Most of Nancy Thorburn's early work was lost on the trail. And after this, she never did another one."

The colony's associate director started off briskly. Stunned, Paul glanced at the painting a final time and followed. McClain gestured up the stairway.

"This is used by Harriet Thorburn and some of the staff. That's all. You're not staying in Big House, but should you have reason to visit another guest you'll use the stairwell in back. I'll show you where it is."

Next came the day room. McClain called it that, but it was a misnomer, since for the most part it stood empty during the formal work hours. The comfortable room had mortared stone walls and a thick brown shag carpet. A fire crackled in a large brick fireplace, the mantel of which was lined with bronze western statues. There was an antique billiards table near the door, a newer pool table toward the opposite wall. Two men who Paul assumed were residents sat on a sofa, one of a few overstuffed pieces of furniture, watching a newscast on a big-screen television. Each held a drink; a mahogany wet bar stood against the same wall as the TV. Newspapers and magazines lay scattered on coffee tables.

"It gets quite . . . ah, energetic in here after dinner," McClain said, smiling. He looked at his watch. "Speaking of dinner, we'd better get you settled before then. We'll go through the library; there's another way out. You can see the rest later."

The message slots, like those seen behind almost any hotel front desk, were near the door. A map of the colony grounds hung on the wall next to them. McClain pointed to one slot, which already had Paul's name on label tape. He also indicated a thick, leather-bound book, the only item on a narrow wooden stand.

"Our guest register," he said, handing Paul a pen. "Please sign."

The book, quite old, had pages like parchment. Paul wondered what names from the past it contained. He signed where McClain indicated.

"Congratulations, Paul," the associate director said, "you're officially a resident of the Thorburn colony for the next four weeks!"

He led Paul across the main hall again, to the library. *Largest private collection west of the Rockies*, the brochure had said. Paul believed it. The number of volumes was staggering.

"There isn't much you won't find here," McClain said with pride. "And there are more in some smaller rooms. Magazines and newspapers are on microfiche. Jane Tyler's our chief librarian, and she has an assistant."

A lone resident, deeply involved in her work well past the four o'clock hour, sat at one end of a long table with a pile of books. She never looked up as the men passed. They exited in back through a plain-looking door, which Paul mistakenly thought led into a closet.

Once again they walked down a long corridor, which looked the same as the first, although Paul believed they hadn't come this way before. He knew one thing: given the opportunity, he could become hopelessly lost in Big House.

"Here's the stairwell I mentioned," McClain said, indicating a door on the right. "It goes up to the residents' rooms, which are on the second floor."

They arrived quickly at the service door, where they'd started. More cars were in the parking area than before, and others pulled in as the last gray-blue streaks of light faded beyond the western peaks. Riding along the hazardous lakefront road in the dark was probably not favored by anyone.

Paul took a garment bag and his briefcase from the car and locked it. He opened the trunk, which held one large suitcase, a shoulder tote, and his typewriter.

"I've seen cars arrive pulling U-Hauls," McClain said, "loaded with enough things for the owner to start a lifetime residency. Others come without much more than a toothbrush, as if we're supposed to clothe them too. You look to be packed just right."

Paul smiled. "You may not think that when you lift the big suitcase."

McClain picked up the typewriter and the tote. "That's why I'm not going to! Follow me."

They crossed the parking area to a path that ran between the smokehouse and a small, boxlike building. A few residents waved and called greetings to McClain. Paul did not see Sherri Jordan or her purple beetle anywhere. A vision of the woman desperately going from door to door trying to borrow a condom made him smile.

"There are six paths like this," the associate director explained, "three or four cabins on each one. The numbers don't make much sense. That's because three of the paths were cut later on. I figured you needed *extra* inspiration, so yours is number eleven. It sits right on the edge of Leanna Creek."

"That's a nice name," Paul said.

"John and Nancy Thorburn's daughter, Leanna was. Took ill suddenly in San Francisco and died before they came back up here."

The forest quickly engulfed the footpath. Pines hugged the twisting trail so tightly that in places Paul had to squeeze through with the large suitcase held in front of him. The way was well lit by lamps that shone down from the low branches of trees, each about fifteen feet apart on alternating sides. There were few traces of snow on or near the path.

A faint murmuring sound grew more distinct as they walked farther. Paul soon knew it to be the unmistakable sound of water rushing along a tributary. Before long the trail paralleled the clear, icy Leanna Creek, beautiful but unimposing. From the roar, Paul had expected something bigger.

The creek curved away from the trail as the first cabin appeared. No. 13, about the size of Sears' biggest storage shed, sat along the tributary, partly hidden by trees. Pungent smoke wafted from a narrow stone chimney on the side. A small storm window overlooked the path.

Struck by the idyllic beauty of the setting, Paul slowed down. Looking at No. 13, he noticed a sliver of light in the previously dark window. Someone peered out between the blinds. The crack closed abruptly, the watcher probably embarrassed about being caught. Paul stared at the window for a few seconds more then followed McClain.

"Number eleven is the farthest out on this path," the man was saying, "about, oh, a hundred and fifty yards from Big House. That's as the crow flies . . . but then, the crow doesn't fly along this path, does he?" He smiled at his own joke. "So it's, ah, a little farther. But actually, number eleven is hardly the most remote cabin at the Thorburn colony. There are some even farther away. We reserve them for composers, singers . . . the music makers, you know. They're usually pleased with the isolation."

No. 12 appeared. No smoke, no lights there. Paul put the suitcase down and switched hands. It had gotten heavier.

"I almost gave you this cabin," McClain said. "It was vacated yesterday. But there was a problem with the plumbing and we haven't gotten around to fixing it yet. Anyway, number eleven is nicer."

A minute later Paul thought about leaving the bag on the trail and coming back for it another time. But finally No. 11 loomed ahead. The path, which had narrowed to almost nothing, passed within a yard of the front step, while the rear of the cabin touched the rim of the creek's sloping bank. Branches of Jeffrey pines brushed the roof. Paul was pleased.

McClain took out the key. "You'll love it in the daylight. The lake's not too far from here. You can see a little of it through the trees. It's the spot where the Thorburn party — most of them — built their cabins that winter."

"Really?"

"But the Thorburn/McClain cabin," he continued, "wasn't all that far from here. Just up Leanna Creek, Paul, that's where my ancestors spent their first months in the Sierras."

Paul nodded. "Interesting."

McClain seemed absorbed by his recollection as he unlocked the door. Looking around, Paul suddenly realized he felt cold. Being dressed warmly and having been afoot for a while carrying his things, he hadn't noticed it before. Perhaps because the darkness was now total . . .

Dragging his suitcase, Paul followed Walter McClain into No. 11.

CHAPTER THREE

"So, Paul, what do you think? Almost as fancy as the Hyatt Lake Tahoe."

The associate director smiled as he switched on the light, bathing the room in a soft fluorescent glow. Actually, Paul thought, the light fixture might have been the most impressive thing there. He looked over the interior of No. 11, not time-consuming, considering its size and paucity of appointments.

"It's fine, really," he told McClain.

A narrow, tubular brass bed, an old high chest of drawers, a wood and steel desk with a swivel chair, and a lamp on a nightstand comprised the furniture A worn but serviceable rug depicting embroidered thunderbirds in bright colors covered a portion of the wood floor. The wallpaper, torn or curled in places, was a nondescript solid color, sort of beige, but darker. No curtains hung on either of the two full-sized windows, only rust-colored blinds that had not been fitted well and covered more than was necessary. The single wall ornament hung above the mantel of a small brick fireplace: a print of Olaf Wieghorst's *Apache Renegade* in a weathered wood frame. Paul liked Wieghorst's work.

There *was* a bathroom — proportionately small, but nevertheless it did exist. Paul wouldn't admit it to anyone, but he'd had doubts. Once he had read that the writers' quarters in Yaddo, the renowned colony in upstate New York, were originally built without toilets. It seemed that writers and artists were otherworldly beings who didn't have the need to perform bodily functions as the lower order of human creatures did. A Zappa song about yellow snow had been stuck in his head.

McClain sat on the bed. "Soft, like I told you." He indicated a floor grid in one corner. "The vent from the furnace. If you're not used to that kind, you'll figure out quickly not to step on it barefoot. There's the thermostat. I had it turned up earlier so you wouldn't walk into an icebox."

"It's comfortable," Paul said, but he still felt cold. He glanced at the Wieghorst again. "I'm glad to be here, Mr. McClain. This might be what I need."

The man smiled as he stood. "Call me Walter, please." He looked at his watch. "I have to go. Almost dinner. You want to walk with me?"

"I'd like five or ten minutes, then I'll be over. Thanks for the tour."

McClain walked to the door. "Don't be much later," he said fussily. "Harriet Thorburn likes to start things on time. Oh, here's your key, although you really don't need to lock things up here."

He put the key on the desk, then left. Paul stood alone in his aptly described *spartan accommodations*. A claustrophobic writer wouldn't stand a chance here, he thought. But he hadn't been lying to McClain. He felt positive about getting back to work.

At six-fifteen — a *quarter past* six, on his old Baby Ben travel alarm with the round face — having only managed to unpack a couple of things and set up his typewriter on the desk, Paul put his down jacket and gloves back on. He had finally gotten warm and wasn't excited about another bracing walk in the chilled night air. But Big House — and food — awaited. He locked the door and started for the Thorburn mansion.

The crisp mountain air felt surprisingly good, probably because it was so still, no wind knifing it into his flesh. Even with the frequency of lights along the path, his vision was limited. Yet he could feel the quiet majesty of the alpine woods that surrounded him. He looked forward to seeing it on display with the next dawn.

As he passed No. 12 it occurred to him that, without the luggage in tow, he had made it there quickly. Maybe Walter McClain was right about it being no big deal getting to and from Big House. But this was mild weather, no challenge yet. *December kin bring some nasty storms*, the man had said, and December would be here tomorrow.

Farther down the path, Paul caught the smell of smoke from the fireplace in No. 13. He could make out the silhouette of the cabin just ahead. A brief sliver of light appeared; the front door had opened and closed. Now he was nearer and could see someone stepping off the porch. The figure wore a gray warm-up suit with the hood up. Paul couldn't tell whether it was a man or woman.

The person saw him; Paul had no doubt of that. He waved and walked more quickly. In response the other turned, jogged rapidly along the path, and was swallowed by the trees.

"O-kay," he murmured, and slowed.

Leanna Creek, just off the path on his left, could not be ignored. Kneeling at the bank, he thrust a hand into the cold water — incredibly cold. Sooner or later, Paul figured, its flow would be clogged by ice.

The trail now snaked between the pines; the creek veered off and was soon a distant sound. Paul remembered this part, where the trees pressed in against the footpath: a narrow passage, with strewn brush and leaves covering possible obstacles on the ground. The jogger must have known the way well to have passed through so quickly.

One of the lights had gone out. For a short distance Paul could barely see a thing. He stumbled once over a rock wedged in the ground, caught himself, and went on. The path curved sharply ahead. He could see a faint glow from the next light.

He heard a sound and froze, listened. Rushing water, as in Leanna Creek. But the tributary was too far away. Still, that was what it sounded like . . . No, different now. A continuous sound, as of something coarse slowly brushing against . . . what? Not from one direction or another, but everywhere around him.

"Someone there?" he called, turning in a circle.

It stopped, the ensuing stillness almost as unnerving as what had come before it. Paul waited a few moments then started off, shaking his head.

Just an animal of some kind, he told himself. Get used to it, boy. These are the outer limits of civilization. What happens when squirrels start walking on the roof?

The footpath squeezed between a few more trees, then ended abruptly at the edge of the parking area. Paul hadn't realized he'd been that close. A few residents were just pulling in, Sherri Jordan among them. She parked the Volkswagen near the last outbuilding, as far away from Big House as she could get. Paul angled across the asphalt to meet her.

"Hello again," he said.

She had been preoccupied but then recognized him. "Hi . . . Paul, right? You settled in now? Had Walter's informative tour and everything?"

He nodded. "Did you find what you were looking for in town?"

Sherri tossed up her hands. "Not a single one! I don't think they *know* what a rubber is here. Amazing they don't have ten thousand kids swarming around!"

He grinned. "Are you on your way to dinner?"

"Where else? Come on, walk with me."

Someone had just opened the service door. The aromas of the kitchen teased Paul's senses across the distance.

"Smells good," he said.

"The food's not half bad, I gotta admit," Sherri replied. "Chef's a weird guy. Arthur Tyler. Old Lady Thorburn's always saying, 'If you enjoyed the dinner, please make sure you let Arthur know.'" She mimicked a shrill voice. "'Tell Arthur how good the apple pie was and he may give you extra ice cream the next time.' I swear to God!"

They reached the door. The warmth of the corridor felt good. Sherri peeled off her coat as they walked. She looked stylish in an oversized black and white cardigan sweater with rugby stripes and a pair of black knit pants that hugged her trim hips and legs.

"Anyway," she went on, "it's not the food that's the problem, it's the company. You wouldn't believe some of these people! David Van Ness is one of the biggest assholes you'll ever meet. And there's this composer, Allan Kroll? The man *wakes up* drunk in the morning, I'm not kidding! I don't know why they let him stay."

Given time, Paul might have heard the biographies of every artist-in-residence. But they were at the end of the corridor, where they hung up their coats. Once inside the main central hall they joined others on their way to the dining room. Most, it appeared, had been in the day room, unless there was somewhere else they could have poured drinks.

While Sherri called out greetings, Paul stared across the hall at Nancy Thorburn's painting. The piercing eyes of one dominant figure, a woman, followed him along the hardwood floor. He wanted to spend more time studying the work, but he couldn't now. A spirited din meant they'd reached the dining room. Reluctantly, he turned away from the painting.

The room, well lit by two wagon-wheel chandeliers, was as large and impressive as everything else Paul had seen in the mansion. Four long tables, each covered by a frilled linen tablecloth, stood on ornate wooden pedestals. Two sideboards were a century apart in their construction. An ample fire crackled in a large stone fireplace. Indian artifacts lined the mantel: a black stone pipe bowl in the shape of a nondescript animal, and a bird mask with a movable beak. More pieces hung on the oak-paneled walls: twined bags, ceremonial shields, colorful blankets, as well as western art, including a number of Albert Bierstadt's magnificent portraits of Lake Tahoe.

"That's the queen's throne, in case you couldn't tell," Sherri said above the noise, indicating a high-backed maple Brewster chair at the head of the last table on their right. Most of the other seats at the table were already filled.

"Do they all try to sit by Harriet Thorburn?" Paul asked.

"Actually, I don't think anyone would if they had a choice. Seating is — you ready for this? — assigned! See the little name cards?"

Paul noticed them now, blue rectangles of heavy construction paper, each folded in an inverted V. Names had been carefully written in cursive letters with a red marker pen.

"It changes every night," Sherri continued. "You never know where you're sitting. But sooner or later you'll be at Harriet Thorburn's table. Come on, let's find you."

The PAUL FLEMING card sat on the fourth table. Sherri discovered it. The place on one side was not set, the other was, for Thea Douglas.

Sherri frowned, shook her head. "That won't do at all." She picked up the card and palmed it. "Wait here."

Other residents took their places. Moving quickly, Sherri found her card on the second table and made the switch. No one appeared to notice, or care.

"That's better," she said, placing it on the table.

A man in a dark blue turtleneck sweater sat down across from Sherri. He looked to be in his mid- or late twenties; handsome, with thick blond hair and wide, curious blue eyes. He appeared ashen, as if ill. A curled lip left him with a transfixed sneer.

"You're Paul Fleming, aren't you?" he said, extending a hand across the wide table.

"That's right." The man's handshake was weak, his hand withdrawn an instant too quickly.

"Heard you were coming. I'd like to talk to you sometime. I'm curious about how a writer, if one can call himself that, justifies the creation of commercially lucrative but intellectually meaningless crap." He turned to another man, who had just arrived. "Robert, how're you doing?"

Paul stared at him and shook his head. He felt Sherri Jordan's hand on his arm. "*That* is David Van Ness."

"You were right," Paul said.

"I'll save you from his bullshit. Anyway, he's gay and has the hots for Robert Kingsley there. Maybe he'll forget about you during dinner."

For the first time Paul noticed a woman at the far end of the table. She must have sat down while Van Ness was talking. What caught his attention was her gray warm-up suit. Unless there were others similarly dressed, this had to be the person from No. 13. The hood was down, revealing reddish brown hair tied in a ponytail. Her round face was attractive in a natural sort of way, cheeks ruddy from the jog to Big House. Paul guessed her age in her thirties. Her expression seemed vacant; she stared at the place setting in front of her. Then she looked up and he nodded. She quickly averted her eyes.

He noticed something odd: none of the last two places on either side had been set for dinner. The woman at the end of the table sat isolated.

Sherri noticed his interest. "Forget *that*," she said. "Believe me, Paul."

"Who is she?"

"I'll tell you what I know — "

A grandfather clock in one corner struck the half hour. As if on cue, the room quieted. The double doors opened; Walter McClain entered with Harriet Thorburn holding onto one arm. The woman was small and incredibly thin, almost emaciated, her face a hodgepodge of sharp angles, her wispy gray hair pulled tightly in a severe bun. She walked with a dignified, almost regal bearing. Her clothing appeared old and elegant, a white satin dress with black lace flounces and a silk shawl thrown loosely over her shoulders. She glanced around the room once then kept her eyes straight ahead as McClain led her to the table. No one spoke during the procession.

When Harriet Thorburn was in her place, McClain went to his own, on her right. He waved benignly at the room, smiled, and said, "Good evening, everyone. I hope you all had a productive day. There are a few things I wanted to mention."

"He *always* does this," Sherri told Paul.

"First of all — "

Harriet Thorburn's hand went up, silencing McClain. She had been looking around and now seemed agitated. "The seating arrangement has been altered," she exclaimed in a shrill voice. Sherri's impersonation had been perfect, Paul thought.

"What's wrong?" McClain asked.

She looked around again. People fidgeted in their chairs. Finally she announced, "Miss Douglas and Miss Jordan, would you kindly exchange places? Thank you."

"Oh, shit, do you believe this?" Sherri muttered. "See you later, Paul."

She picked up her card and left. Thea Douglas, a fiftyish mannequin of designer clothes and too much makeup, made sure she passed Sherri on the way.

"Nice move, *dear*," the woman hissed.

Sherri stuck out her tongue behind Thea. There was an undercurrent of laughter, quickly silenced by Harriet Thorburn's icy glare. Thea Douglas sat down hard beside Paul.

Satisfied that everyone was in place, McClain began again. "First I'd like to welcome a new resident, Paul Fleming. Paul, show yourself."

Paul half stood to acknowledge some applause and a few greetings. Glancing down the table, he noticed the woman in the warm-up suit staring off to the side.

"The next matter," McClain went on, "is the generous amount of scotch that someone poured into the Chinese fan palm in the day room. We can only hope the plant will survive." Again, muffled laughter that threatened to erupt, but didn't. "If such a prank is repeated, I will close the bar for a day!"

Paul couldn't believe what he'd seen or heard so far. It was like summer camp for adults.

"And finally," said the associate director, "there's an item that Ms. Thorburn would like to share with you."

The old woman cracked a brittle smile. "One of our residents has had a breakthrough. The gallery exhibiting Robert Kingsley's work in Portland reported selling one to a knowledgeable patron for a fair sum of money. Congratulations, Mr. Kingsley."

David Van Ness waxed boisterous in his praise, but otherwise the response was polite and low-key. Paul understood. Creative people, even those caught up in the camaraderie that a place like the Thorburn colony could produce, were sometimes envious of the success of their peers. Prior to his own breakthrough Paul had stayed away from writers' workshops and conferences, book trade shows, any situation where his own envy could erupt. He had even avoided reading interviews with other authors. Nothing to be proud of, he knew, but it was a fact.

"Congratulations," he said across the table. Kingsley smiled and nodded.

"That's it," McClain said. "Enjoy your dinner."

A door from the kitchen swung open. Two men and two women, all Mexican and similarly dressed in white, wheeled out serving carts. They worked efficiently; within minutes everyone had a bowl of soup and a salad in front of them.

"I'm Thea Douglas," Paul's new neighbor said, "but you probably knew that from our embarrassing little scene. Nice to meet you, Paul."

"Same here."

"Sherri the juvenile always goes for the new ones right off. Watch out for her."

"I will. Thanks for the warning."

People began talking. This was what Paul had dreaded most about being there. He'd always been a loner, seldom socialized. It was one of the things that stood between him and Jeannie, who enjoyed the company of others. He had sworn to himself it would change, but he hadn't begun to make the effort prior to his arrival at the Thorburn colony. So with no choice, this seemed a good place to start.

"What kind of work do you do?" he asked Thea Douglas.

She smiled theatrically over a forkful of lettuce. "By vocation I'm a fashion designer. But that's not why I'm at Thorburn, is it? I'm a writer too. Oh, not like you. I write plays. One of them, *Idle Fortunes*, was commissioned by the North Shore Rep in San Diego and produced there earlier this year. It received wonderful reviews — for the most part. I'll show them to you sometime."

"That's great," he said. "So you're working on a new play now?"

"Well, what else is there to do here? Yes, I am, and it's coming along quite well. Even wrote a part in it — a small one — for myself. I do some acting too."

How come I knew that? Paul thought.

Thea glanced at the next table. "Oh, look, Allan's d.u.i. again."

"D.u.i.?"

"Dining under the influence. How disgusting. It's hard to believe, Paul, but that creature has produced some of the most significant concert music of the twentieth century. That was years ago, of course."

Paul assumed she was talking about Allan Kroll, whom Sherri had mentioned. He was a smallish, middle-aged man, dressed in an out-of-style tan suit with no tie. Leaning precariously on one elbow, he was bent halfway over the table. He tried to lift a spoonful of soup to his mouth, unsuccessfully. Those around him ignored the scene, probably because they'd gotten used to it.

Thea shrugged. "He tries, give him credit. But sometimes he doesn't even make it through dinner. He's a good drunk, though — if there's such a thing. He's not loud; you hardly know he's around."

"Can't someone help him?" Paul asked.

"The staff takes care of Allan. They even drive him here from his cabin in a golf cart. He's a project of Harriet Thorburn's — a losing one, if you ask me. She always liked his music. Allan's up here so much that he's practically a permanent resident."

As Thea continued to talk, Paul again glanced at the end of the table. The woman there ate but did not communicate with anyone or even look around. It appeared as if she were being punished, like an unruly child. Thea Douglas might know her story, he thought, but he decided against asking her.

There were some unusual people at Thorburn, he mused, and he'd met only a handful so far. Was that how *he* seemed to others? Was that why the Hey Vern guy *kin always tell, easy*, who were on their way to the artists' and writers' colony?

As the servers brought out the main course — an excellent pot roast — Walter McClain came over and sat down in the empty chair next to Paul. "Well, how's everything going?" he asked.

"Fine, thanks," Paul replied.

"Walter," Thea said, "you really ought to do something about Allan. The poor man's going to hurt himself."

"Everything's under control, Thea," McClain said in his peevish voice, then added to Paul, "Harriet Thorburn would like to meet you after dinner. Please be sure you stop over."

"I will."

McClain left. Thea Douglas fell quiet as she concentrated on her meal. David Van Ness remained engrossed in Robert Kingsley. Please, let it stay that way, Paul thought.

Then, Harriet Thorburn began to speak. The low murmur from the tables subsided.

"I was telling you last night what it was like in the forties, when Elliot Waterman and Maxwell Fryar and

Anya Trowbridge and others used to stay at the colony. Oh, it was different then, especially at dinner, when the women would come in their finest dresses, the men in suits and ties, tuxedos!" She looked around. "Not like now, not like now."

"She tells some good stories," Thea whispered to Paul, "but you have to wade through a lot of crap. Myself, I think she's senile."

"Maxwell Fryar hated women, thought they were insufferable," the old woman continued. "Hardly anyone outside of the colony knew that, though. So he had this reputation as one of the world's great womanizers, for which he was both revered and despised. He never contradicted it, and it preceded him wherever he went and helped him sell a lot more novels than he would have otherwise."

The residents laughed. Harriet Thorburn smiled with her reminiscences, was silent for a few moments then went on. "Elliot Waterman had a memory like a steel trap. He saw something once and it became a watercolor in his mind, every detail! His Haitian period? Two of those were painted right here, at Thorburn, in the middle of winter! And his Sinai sketches? And those wonderful Brazilian works? Yes, at the colony!

"Anya Trowbridge was considered the greatest historian of her time. Her books on World War I, the Depression, and pre-Hitler Europe are still among the definitive works on those subjects. As a great scholar she was considered a stern, self-effacing individual, and actually she was — everywhere but at the colony. Here, Anya let her hair down and was like a small child released from captivity. Other guests loved her, and the staff did also, although we couldn't let on and risk a total breakdown of authority. She was one of my favorites.

"You all know the statue of the Egyptian goddess in the central hall? Once, Anya dressed it in a diaper.

She even managed to stain the diaper brown! I was the one who found it first. Another time she brought up a store mannequin's arm hidden in a suitcase."

"Oh, don't tell that story!" Walter McClain pleaded.

"No one saw her carry it down to the lake late one afternoon. She had fixed it so that it stuck straight up from a flat piece of wood. After throwing it into the lake she stood at the edge and screamed for help, saying that someone was drowning. Young Walter McClain, a teenager at the time, ran down to the lake and jumped in. Everyone laughed when he saved that wooden arm. Anya Trowbridge was laughing the hardest of all!"

The dining room broke up. McClain shook his head but smiled. He would probably not hear the end of it for days, Paul thought, and he agreed that Harriet Thorburn told a good story.

The reminiscences continued as dessert was brought out. Thea Douglas had been right: every so often the old woman would digress into something totally unrelated, the trouble with the trash pickup in Stillwell or the shameful advent of gambling along Lake Tahoe, among other ramblings. But even so, the stories of the Thorburn colony, from the perspective of one who had been part of its past, proved fascinating.

"She's been writing this stuff down forever," Thea told Paul. "You'd think she would have it published already. There must be ten thousand pages!"

Paul was savoring a piece of German chocolate cake and had only taken a couple of forkfuls when he again glanced at the woman in the gray warm-up suit. She was nearly finished with hers, eating so quickly that her face was near the plate as she shoveled the pieces in. He didn't remember her doing that with dinner. He watched, curious, as she ate the last of it, dabbed at her mouth with a napkin, and got up. Apparently she was going to leave. But Harriet Thorburn continued to talk as the colony's nightly ritual continued. A confrontation seemed imminent.

The woman walked soundlessly in her L.A. Gear, passing behind Paul's chair but not looking at him, or anyone. Without question, McClain saw her. Still, nothing was said, and she reached the door, opened it, and slipped out. Everyone's attention returned to the first table.

Harriet Thorburn went on for ten more minutes, rambling often. Finally she was done. Paul sensed relief around him.

"Well, I've said quite enough for one night," she announced. "I hope the dinner was satisfactory. If it was, please make certain you let Arthur know, won't you?"

Sherri caught Paul's eye. She grinned. He shook his head and worked hard at hiding a smile.

"Yay, Arthur," one resident muttered.

People began to leave. Thea Douglas said to Paul, "You don't want to be late for your appointment. She may fall asleep before you get there. See you later."

"Okay."

Sherri waited for Paul by the second table. "You have to see the biddy, right?" she asked.

"Uh-huh. But I'd like to talk to you after."

"I'll wait in the day room. Or would you rather meet me at my place?"

He grinned. "See you in the day room."

Walter McClain, the dutiful servant, stood next to Harriet Thorburn's chair. "Ah, Paul, come here!" he exclaimed. "Ms. Thorburn, I'd like you to meet Paul Fleming."

The woman extended a thin hand. "Mr. Fleming, your reputation precedes you. When we knew you were coming, Walter went out and found copies of your books. I've even read *Summit of Fear* . . . a little of it, anyway. It's very good."

Paul nodded graciously. "Thanks. It's nice to meet you, Ms. Thorburn."

"But the book of yours that will hold a special place in our library," she continued, "will be the one that you begin here, at the colony!"

"I hope you're right."

"Mr. Fleming, I *know* I'm right! These wonderful mountains are therapeutic. If you can't find the muse here, then you are no writer!" Her voice had risen shrilly in excitement but now softened. "What happened, Mr. Fleming, to make you stop?"

He shrugged. "The divorce, I suppose. My wife and I split up earlier this year. It just became final, and — "

"There are children?"

"A boy and a girl. I see them once or twice a month, holidays, that sort of thing."

"Good luck to you, Mr. Fleming," she said, practically interrupting him. "Don't hesitate to tell Walter if there's anything you need." She looked at McClain. "I'll go upstairs now."

McClain helped the old woman up, nodded at Paul, and led her out. Paul walked behind them, thinking it would be rude to pass. Aside from them, the dining room was empty.

Before they exited, the kitchen door swung open. A man in a chef's hat and apron emerged, an immense figure, barrel-chested, six and a half feet tall. Something appeared wrong with his moon face: one eye drooped low and was nearly closed. His lips were thick, the lower one protruding in a fixed pout. Paul felt sure that, to some degree, the man was retarded.

"That's Arthur Tyler, our cook," McClain said.

Paul nodded, then circled around the table and approached the man. "That was a fantastic dinner tonight, Arthur," he said, offering his hand.

Arthur Tyler grinned a crooked grin of widely spaced teeth. "Tha-a-nks," he said in a deep, slow voice, engulfing Paul's hand as if it were that of a child. He then turned and went back into his domain.

Eight o'clock. Paul suddenly realized how tired he was. He'd been on the road since before dawn. No. 11 sounded like a haven to him. The last thing he needed was another roomful of people. But he'd asked Sherri Jordan to meet him because he was still curious about the woman in the warm-up suit.

By the time Paul crossed the central hall to the day room Walter McClain and Harriet Thorburn were part of the way up the stairs. It seemed like the rest might take forever. Wasn't there an elevator, he wondered, or some other means of getting the woman to her rooms? But she'd been doing this all her life and probably wouldn't have it any other way.

After the stillness that had prevailed at dinner, the noise level in the day room was deafening. One large group congregated around the bar. Others watched a Warriors-Sonics basketball game or played pool or billiards. Some were paired off in what might have been more intimate conversations.

Paul expected to find Sherri Jordan surrounded by people. But she sat alone, waiting for him on a worn but comfortable settee near the fireplace. She saw him, stood, and waved. He made his way through the crowd, some of whom offered a few complimentary words about his success. It took him a minute to get there.

"Hey, you're a popular guy," she said. "Come and sit. How did it go with Harriet Thorburn?"

"Fine. We didn't speak long."

"Really? God, not with me. She practically pumped me for my whole life story! Anyway, you said you wanted to talk."

"You'd started to tell me about that woman at our table, the one sitting by herself. I was curious."

"*That's* what you wanted to talk about?"

He grinned. "We can talk about other things."

"I hope so," she said in mock indignation. "Actually, there's not a lot to tell. Her name is Gail Farringer. Of all the weirdos up here, she's at the head of the class. She paints — I think. No one's ever seen her work, except maybe Walter. She doesn't talk to *anyone*; eats alone. You saw. At breakfast, which is buffet, she takes what she wants and goes off somewhere with it. You talk to her, you're asking for trouble. I know. I tried it once."

"That's it?"

"That's it. Can't imagine how she got here. She must be good at something or they wouldn't have let her in. We all got our problems, right, Paul? But that girl's got a few more."

He shook his head. "Sad. Okay, tell me about Sherri Jordan. Walter McClain praises your talents."

She smiled. "That's the *only* thing about me Walter praises. Yeah, but I guess he's the closest thing to a friend I got up here. Talks to me whenever I need it."

"What kind of work do you do?"

"I work in clay. Animals. Wildlife, not poodles or parakeets. People like it, I guess. I make money."

"Where is it shown?"

"San Francisco, mostly. But there are a few pieces here and there."

"Is San Francisco home?"

"Sometimes."

"Sometimes?"

"I've got a place there. But I . . . travel a lot. It's just something I do."

"No man in your life?"

She shrugged and stared at the ceiling for a moment. "Lots of men in my life — one night at a time. Maybe two. Can't even remember names after a while."

She turned and they looked into each other's eyes. Behind the façade of wild hair and garish jewelry, Paul saw a different woman from the one he had first met in downtown Stillwell. A vulnerable person, hiding past, maybe present hurts behind an outrageous lifestyle. She seemed to sense his perceptiveness and wanted to talk.

"What about family?" he asked.

There, that was the question! She looked away. For a moment Paul thought she might cry. She gazed at him again then lifted her eyes.

Another resident stood over them: a young man, still with acne, dressed in patched jeans and a Dickies shirt.

"Sherri baby, voilà!" he exclaimed. "Or up here maybe I should say, 'Eureka, I found it!'"

He held up a small blue square of foil. Paul knew what it was.

"Hey, all right!" Sherri was punkish hair and jewelry again. "But Richard, I'm sort of busy — "

"It's okay," Paul said. "I still have to unpack."

Reality seemed too much, he thought. She needed this escape. He wasn't going to stop her.

"You sure?"

"I'm sure."

"Will you come over and look at my work tomorrow?"

"Yeah."

She smiled. "Thanks, Paul. See ya."

They hurried off. She glanced back at Paul. Her smile had left her. Richard took her hand and led her through the maze of the day room. Paul watched them leave.

He couldn't stay by the fire any longer; its warmth would put him to sleep. He started for the door, thankful not to be accosted, and spotted a message in his mail slot. One of the staff had printed it in thick letters:

Hi, remember me? Hope your trip was wonderful. Did you find inspiration already? Looking forward to hearing from you REAL SOON. Gary

Paul smiled as he tucked the note into his shirt pocket. Sooner or later he'd have an outline for his agent — assuming everything went well. That would make him happy.

Retrieving his coat, Paul left Big House. As he crossed the parking area, he realized it had grown colder. His thin southern California blood wasn't ready for this. A wind blew from the northeast, which made it worse. The moon, a thin crescent, drifted in and out of passing clouds. Turning up his collar, he walked briskly to the footpath.

He remembered the spot where earlier he had heard the sound. The light worked now. He stopped there, listened, but heard nothing.

He also paused in front of No. 13 for a moment. It was too cold to stand in one place for long. Gail Farringer, whatever her problems, had one good idea. He started jogging and quickly passed the empty No. 12. But he was tired, and the altitude was over sixty-five hundred feet. Panting, he walked the rest of the way to his cabin.

Still a few yards from the door, it began to snow.

"Swell," he said, and went inside.

Unpacking, other than immediate necessities, would wait till morning. Paul climbed into bed within ten minutes. He slept a dark, dreamless sleep his first night at the Thorburn colony.

Even the squirrels on the roof didn't bother him.

CHAPTER FOUR

Sunday, December 1

The sound that awakened Paul the next morning was not the familiar soft ring of his Baby Ben, which had been set for six-fifteen. This came from outside twenty minutes earlier, loud and harsh. Groggy, he staggered to the window and peered out.

A snowplow — a riding mower anyway, with a narrow blade in front.

An inch or so of snow had fallen overnight. Plowing didn't seem worth the effort, although it was good to know they kept on top of things. The plow, misfiring badly, pushed the snow from all but a couple inches of the path on both sides. After clearing the way to No. 11's front step, the driver turned it around and started back the other way.

Before it fell quiet, Paul had climbed back into bed. The extra sleep helped. He took his usual "instant" shower — Jeannie had called it that — and was dressed and ready in thirty minutes.

For the first time, Paul had a look outside the place where he would live and work for nearly a month.

Lodgepole and Jeffrey pines, their branches sagging under newly fallen snow, sheltered the cabin and path. Beyond them, white-capped peaks thrust high in the clear morning air, barely piercing the undersides of a few low clouds. Leanna Creek purled busily toward the lake. And everywhere the plow hadn't touched, a dusting of white lay over the floor of the forest. Yes, Gary, he thought, inspiration may be arriving on schedule.

Then he heard the sound again.

The one from last night, only this time near his cabin. Not the rushing water; that was the creek for sure. The scraping, the long, continuous . . .

There was a wind, not strong, but enough to make the tops of the thin, towering lodgepole pines sway like tules. They grew close together, these ubiquitous Sierra trees.

So close that they rubbed against one another.

Paul smiled and started for breakfast.

The plow had done a good job. Hardly any snow remained on the path all the way to the parking area. He noticed that some of the cars were missing. Maybe it was okay to go into town for breakfast. Where, at the Mule Deer Cafe? Whatever Arthur Tyler cooked up would be fine.

Paul loved breakfast. When he was writing, he usually skipped lunch. As he piled his plate high, he looked around. Less than half of the people who'd filled the room the previous night were scattered about, Gail Farringer not among them. No surprise, after what Sherri had told him.

But Sherri was there, at the third table with her young man. They were involved in an intense conversation. Paul sat by himself at the first table.

The food was as good as it looked. He noticed that hardly any other residents came into the dining room after him. It wasn't late, just past seven. Apparently this conclave of creative personae meant business in the morning. Paul had never been that way. The brain cells usually lay dormant until at least mid-morning, and the best work came at night.

Sherri and Richard weren't getting along. Their conversation grew loud, heated. The man finally rose and stormed out. Sherri might have followed but noticed Paul and joined him.

"What a jerk!" she exclaimed. "He's in love with me now, he says. I think it was the first time he ever got laid. Took him almost the whole time here to even talk to me. Anyway, he's leaving today, thank God! Hi, Paul, what do you know?"

Paul grinned. "Not much."

She glanced at her big yellow watch. "Can't stay now. Finishing up a piece today, then I have to pack and stuff. I'm outta here tomorrow. Walter's going to celebrate!"

"I doubt it."

"You still coming over tonight?"

"If you want me to."

"Sure. It's number sixteen. My car's parked near the start of that path. See ya."

"Bye."

Sherri turned and walked away. Then she stopped. Looking back, she said softly, "We'll talk, okay?"

He nodded. She hurried from the dining room, nearly colliding with Walter McClain, who shook his head as he watched her run across the central hall.

"That girl, I swear," he muttered, approaching Paul. "Well, today's day one for you, isn't it? How do you feel?"

"Anxious," Paul admitted, "but looking forward to it."

"Good, good. Well, I'm off. A million things to do. See you at dinner."

McClain went into the kitchen. Paul continued to work on his breakfast. Finally he accepted the fact that he was procrastinating. Anything to delay the start of a project. This wasn't new. Anxiety overwhelmed him before he put down the first word of any story he'd ever written. But until this year it had never been more than three or four weeks before sitting down again.

Now he was out of excuses, and almost out of food and coffee. No place to go, nothing else to do. It was time. He pushed the plate away and left the dining room.

As Paul crossed the parking area a red TransAm — not old, but dented in a few places — burst out of a parking space near the service entrance. Hearing the screech of tires, Paul turned. The car sped across the asphalt, leaving rubber, and nearly tipped onto its side as it made the turn around Big House.

"Idiot," Paul muttered as he reached the footpath.

A tranquil Sierra morning. In the aftermath of the previous night's teasing snowfall the sun shone, and the earlier breeze had gone. The glare off the broader patches of snow blinded Paul. He wouldn't forget his sunglasses next time.

Inside his cabin, he began preparations of a ritualistic nature. He lit a fire, something he did not do well, although the starter packets of fuel made it easier. Next he opened both blinds and raised them to the top. He straightened the Wieghorst, which didn't need it, pushed the typewriter over to the end of the desk, and in its place put a white legal pad and a five-millimeter mechanical pencil. He was ready.

In a time of word processors and laptop computers, WordPerfect and WordStar, Paul Fleming the dinosaur created by hand. He never professed to understand exactly why — some metaphysical thing, maybe: words flowing in an unbroken line from brain to hand, through the pencil and onto the paper.

But he remembered when it had started. Not many years ago, when he'd had to accept the reality of working at mundane jobs that paid money with regularity, his writing time became precious. A lull during a tedious night shift; a lunch hour on a park bench or in his car. No typewriter there, no computer, only the ever-present pad and pencil. Even when things changed for the better, that part of him did not. Later drafts went through his Macintosh; first drafts would always happen this way.

For more than an hour the paper remained blank. That idea he'd had yesterday on the way up: what was it? Why the hell hadn't he scribbled it down somewhere? But it soon came to him, as it usually did. One day later it sounded ridiculous, but a part of it was salvageable. He wrote it down.

Did you hear, Gary? I wrote something.

Another thought struck him. Ideas begat ideas that begat more ideas, a wonderfully biblical outpouring on to one, then two and three pages of his pad.

It was as if he had never been away.

When it read noon on the face of Baby Ben, he didn't know where the past three hours had gone. If not for the noise he wouldn't have looked up.

It came from outside, on the porch. This time he knew what it was. Someone had opened and closed a hinged wooden box that sat near his door.

Noon. Lunch. One of the staff had brought him lunch. He opened the door. A woman in a red coat hurried along the path. She turned when she heard the door, waved but said nothing.

Paul opened the box. A Styrofoam carryall held a ham sandwich, an apple, a bag of chips, and a Coke Classic. A note read: *Wasn't sure what you like to drink. Let us know.* It was signed *Nora Hardman.*

This was great! Paul thought. He actually had an appetite. But he wouldn't stop what he was doing. He threw another log on the fire, sat down at the desk, ate, and worked.

An hour later he decided to go to the library. He had written down more than enough; now he needed some background to decide where he was going with it. Even though he subscribed to over two dozen periodicals, of late they'd only been piling up unread. When you dwell inside yourself, the world passes you by and means nothing.

Paul hadn't realized it, but it had grown stifling in the cabin. He perspired, and his down jacket only made it worse. Even outside, where the sun shone and the temperature had risen above forty degrees, he felt no immediate relief. Still, he thought how fine it would be if the weather stayed like this for a while.

When he stepped off the porch, it changed.

A chill ran through him, feeling like a deliberate probing of his body. Apprehension gripped him — not the same as the morning, when he confronted the start of his work, but something more disturbing. He glanced around at the forest but saw only a jay and a couple of woodpeckers in the trees.

He took another step, and it grew stronger.

No. 11 was the last cabin on the footpath; Walter McClain had told him that. But the narrow trail continued on, veering away from the creek again twenty yards farther along. He followed it, not quite sure why. Ice spirits danced inside him, occasionally skimming the blood in his veins. Maybe that was what pulled him along, drawing him toward . . . something.

Paul's body trembled. His steps, though tentative, always went forward. The path snaked through denser trees for at least another hundred yards then passed between two ancient Jeffrey pines.

Just beyond them, it ended.

Leanna Creek had twisted back through a thicket of quaking aspen and rabbit bush, its bank now a couple of yards away. Across the tributary, which appeared wider there than anywhere else, Paul saw a clearing. Once, from this spot, Thorburn Lake must have been visible, a third of a mile or so to the east. But the forest, not ravaged by man, had grown dense in the past century or more.

Only this clearing remained.

Cold, so damn cold! Paul stood between the two sentinel pines, shivering, all his senses tuned to what surrounded him. Above the rushing of the creek he heard a shrill sound of wind passing through a narrow space. Distant, but clear. He glanced across the clearing, through the trees, then up at their boughs. Nothing stirred; not a breeze blew.

Still, he heard the sound of wind.

Paul turned and hurried away, denying whatever it was that had drawn him there. He ran, until a large jackrabbit raced across the path in front of him. Nearly stumbling, he swore loudly.

He stood in front of No. 11 again. The ice spirits had fled his body. There was no more windsound.

He shrugged. "It's a good sign, actually," he told a jay in a nearby tree. "I'm getting crazy, and that means I'm ready to write again."

Nodding, he started off slowly for Big House.

SHERIFF'S DEPARTMENT, STILLWELL, CA was what it said on the green and white squad car parked near the back of the mansion. No one sat in it. But as Paul started down the corridor, two burly men wearing Stetsons came toward him. One looked about fifty, the other half that. He noted a vague resemblance between them. Scowling, they barely acknowledged Paul's nod as they brushed past him.

"Have a nice day, guys," Paul muttered as he went into the main central hall.

The door to the day room was open. Paul noticed Walter McClain standing near the fireplace and he went in. McClain saw him and waved.

"Had some trouble?" Paul asked.

The man looked at his watch. "You know, I'm really not supposed to talk to you."

"You're not, I talked to you first."

"Trouble? Oh, you saw the sheriff. That's Roy Stillwell. Deputy's his nephew, Carl."

"What happened?"

"One of our residents was in an accident. He drove too fast, spun out, and ran into a tree just the other side of the Aspen Creek bridge. Took out a rail on the bridge too. Lucky he didn't go into the water."

"Was it a red TransAm?"

This surprised McClain. "How'd you know?"

"Educated guess."

"Richard Sadler is the boy's name. Today was his last day, and he was on the way home. Talented; writes some fine music. But headstrong."

"Was he badly hurt?"

"Broken wrist, some cuts and bruises, slight concussion. They took him to the hospital in Truckee. He'll be okay. I'll go see him in the morning. They shut the bridge down as a precaution till they get that rail fixed."

"Isn't there another way down?"

"Not for anything on wheels."

Paul shook his head. "Sorry I asked."

"It happens once in a while," McClain said. "They'll have it fixed before long. Anyway, right now I'm trying to think of a way to tell his parents without alarming them too much. Then I have to let Ms. Thorburn know. Oh, she won't like this!"

McClain excused himself and left. Paul followed him into the central hall and went on to the library. Three other residents were there, at different tables. He recognized Thea Douglas and vaguely remembered the faces of the other man and woman from dinner. Thea ignored him; the man half nodded. They took the Rule seriously, Paul thought. No problem.

Jane Tyler, the librarian, was a plain-looking, austere woman. Although Paul doubted she was any older than he, in her presence he felt like a schoolboy suspected of mischief. But she knew her domain and helped him find everything he needed. In a few minutes he sat alone at another table, engulfed by stacks of books and periodicals.

Paul enjoyed researching his projects. He knew some writers found it tedious, an undesirable but necessary vocational exercise. Before his life had changed, he hadn't been able to get enough of reading about places he'd never seen, facts he scarcely had been aware of. Sometimes the creativity itself would be neglected as he became lost in a *National Geographic* from forty years ago or Volume 5 of the *World Book Encyclopedia*.

But he didn't plan on that today. He worked for two hours, getting done what he wanted. Leaving everything on the table — Jane Tyler had told him to do that — he headed back to the cabin to type up his notes.

The man and woman had similar elongated faces with dark round mouths but otherwise nondescript features. They had run hard and were still in the foreground, yet could not put any distance between themselves and the Pursuers. The twisted night things mocked them silently, rising mist-like in changing ripples of colors so vague as to be disturbing. Tendrils of fiber (or maybe flesh; hard to tell) snaked out of the mist, reaching for them with coarse, misshapen hands that were disproportionately large. This was what the man and woman feared most.

Something reared up in front of them. Long and silent, weaving like a deadly snake, it was a nightmare come alive. Not one of the Pursuers. Oh, no, they could stay ahead of the Pursuers throughout time. This thing floated down toward them, slowly but nearing steadily. Closer, until they could see a crimson slash at one end that might have been a mouth, although it had nothing remotely shaped like a head. They couldn't turn or scream.

The black thing thrust itself at the man and woman.

Gail Farringer put her brush down and stepped back to have a better look at the work. She wasn't satisfied with it. She never was. A bit more red there . . . and there. Better. Leave it alone now. Been at it too long, since early morning. What time was it? Almost the end of the work day! How had that happened? She'd forgotten to stop for lunch — again. It was still out there. She could eat some of it, save the rest. Wouldn't be the first time. But dinner wasn't far off, and dinner was always good.

Why did the old woman make her go there every night? Gail peered out between the blinds. Someone walked along the footpath. It was *him*. She narrowed the crack to almost nothing, because he would look there when he passed No. 13. He always did, and it was the same now. But when he moved farther up the path she opened the blinds more and watched him until he was gone.

She retrieved her lunch from the box on the porch and hurried back inside.

Unreal! Paul thought. He'd never imagined it would happen so fast.

At six o'clock he was halfway through typing his notes. He liked what he'd come up with, three sound, commercial storylines. Tomorrow he'd choose the best one, or meld them together. It was a hell of a start. He'd thought it would take him a couple of weeks to get a working outline to Gary Marks, but at this rate he would have it ready to go in a couple of days. And if they had a fax machine at the colony, his agent would get it that much quicker.

Time to break for dinner. No reason to be late. He could finish the notes later. But what about Sherri Jordan? Okay, he'd do the notes tomorrow. He was much farther ahead than he could have imagined.

Sunset brought the night chill, but nothing like what he had felt earlier. He made it to Big House quickly and realized how familiar the path already felt.

The dining room buzzed with Thorburn's artists-in-residence. Looking around, Paul knew that at least one was missing: Sherri. He remembered seeing her purple Volkswagen outside.

His place card was on the third table. He sat between Michael Whitney, a cellist-composer, and Kathy Parrish, a journalist who had come to the colony to begin a work of political nonfiction. Allan Kroll, in his rumpled tan suit, sat at the same table, farther down. He seemed alert; he even smiled and talked to the woman next to him.

All the residents were in a different place than the night before — except Gail Farringer. Isolated, preoccupied with her thoughts, she awaited dinner for reasons that clearly had something to do with survival. The staff must have made these concessions for her, Paul thought, and he wondered why they couldn't have just let her avoid the obviously unwanted exposure to others.

Gail Farringer mystified him and he felt sorry for her.

The grand procession began exactly at six-thirty. Again. Walter McClain made a couple of mundane announcements. As he talked, Paul realized Sherri Jordan was still absent.

As the servers began pushing around their carts, Sherri burst into the room. She grinned sheepishly then moved quickly to a vacant place at the first table, under the cold glare of McClain.

Michael Whitney was a pleasant, soft-spoken man. He and Paul quickly discovered they shared a number of interests. Kathy Parrish, confident and strong-willed, had worked hard to achieve her success. Some tension arose between her and Paul at first, but afterward Paul found that he enjoyed her company.

Harriet Thorburn resumed her reminiscences. She regressed a decade from the post-World War II era she'd been talking about the previous night. This time she seemed to have trouble and rambled more.

Dessert was apple pie and ice cream. Paul's server gave him a piece nearly twice the size of the others at his table with two scoops of ice cream.

"From Ar-toor," she told Paul in a heavy accent. "He say you have it."

"Tell him thanks," Paul said, wondering how he was going to eat it all. But he did.

Gail Farringer left early again. This time, Paul swore she had been looking at him as she walked to the door. Or did he imagine it?

Harriet Thorburn had finished. Residents began to drift out of the dining room. Paul said good night to Michael and Kathy, declining an invitation to join them for a drink in the day room.

Sherri met him at the door. "Whoa, wasn't that a great entrance? Were they pissed! Well, they can't do anything to me now. You coming over?"

"Right away," he said. "I need to do something in the library."

"Perfect. There are a few last things to pack. See ya."

Paul had forgotten to look something up earlier, and it had been driving him crazy all evening. He thought his books might still be on the table, but the efficient Jane Tyler had long since put them back. It took him several minutes to find what he wanted. He started making notes then realized he was becoming engrossed. Leaving the book on the table, he started out.

A freestanding bookshelf near the librarian's desk caught his attention. He'd noticed it earlier but hadn't stopped to look. These were the works of John Thorburn. Not an extensive body, but still impressive. There were multiple copies of everything, the greatest number being *Trails of Promise — The Way to California*. Hardbound volumes a century old stood next to copies of the trade paperback edition Paul remembered from college and even smaller, more inexpensive versions that were distributed in grade schools. Even knowing he might not get a chance to look at it, Paul pulled out one of the trade copies and stuck it under his arm.

He stepped out into the main central hall, empty for the moment, and stopped in front of Nancy Thorburn's painting. The tormented eyes of the snowbound pioneers cried out to him, pleading for help he could not give them. So real, this work; so real that he could almost hear the whistling of the wind as it piled snow before their wagons and froze their spent bodies.

So *real* . . .

Two residents emerged laughing from the day room, and the feeling passed. Paul retrieved his coat and hurried outside.

The path to Sherri's cabin looked the same as his. No. 16 was the second one. Despite the cold, the door was open. Paul went in, closed it behind him.

Sherri sat on the bed. Paul knew that — again — she had dropped the façade. She began talking at once, as if afraid that if she waited any longer, it might come harder, or not at all. He sat in a chair across from her.

"Home was once Pennsylvania." She spoke in another woman's voice too. "I ran away when I was fourteen. My mother was horrible; my father, when he was around, was worse. A year before I split, my older sister committed suicide. If I had stayed any longer I would've done the same thing."

"Jesus, I'm sorry," Paul said.

"I wound up in L.A. Where else, right? Five years on the Strip. It could've been worse. Pimp was okay to me, as pimps went. Plenty of action, drugs." She tucked her knees up to her chin and reflected for a moment.

"It was the drugs that really screwed me up. There are a couple of years I can hardly remember. I don't know how I lived through them; I'm not sure I gave a shit. Probably wouldn't have made it if it wasn't for that." She pointed across the room.

Paul had been so intent on Sherri since coming in that he hadn't looked around her cabin. Behind him, against the wall, stood an old but serviceable electric kiln with a front-loading door. Next to it was a long narrow workbench. Three of her pieces sat there: a snowshoe hare, an osprey with a fish held in its claws, and a ring-tailed cat. Had he seen them out of place, he would have sworn they were alive. The cat's eyes gleamed; the fish hawk waxed triumphant over the capture of its prey. Sherri had painted the hare's winter coat with uncanny detail.

"Those are fantastic!" he said. "Walter was right."

"I always liked animals, from when I was a girl," Sherri continued. "At one of those drug rehab places I got to molding things out of clay, you know, to have something to do. Christ, you'd think it was nursery school! But I liked it, and somebody told me I was good. So I took art classes and got better at it, and that's that. I couldn't change a lot else about me, but at least I've laid off the drugs for a long time."

Paul had become absorbed by the pieces and didn't realize Sherri had stopped talking. When he looked at her again she was standing, arms crossed, staring blindly at one corner of the room.

"Did you ever try to sell your work in Laguna Beach?" he asked.

She shook her head. "Not yet. Maybe someday."

"I know some people; I could introduce you. If you came down after the first of the year, I'd be back for sure. We could go to dinner or something."

She looked at him; light reflected from the moistness in her eyes. Her expression appeared hard. When she spoke he could hear the confusion in her voice.

"Why, Paul? Why would you do it? You're a class act, and in case you didn't notice, I ain't. You gonna want *this* parading around on your arm? Come on, get real! What's the motivation, be kind to a fellow artist or something?"

"In the first place," he said patiently, "your work is fabulous. I think it would benefit both you and the galleries that represented you. Second, I wouldn't have asked you if I didn't want to, okay?"

She sat down again. Staring at him, she ran her long fingers through the blond-red shock of hair. Then she turned away.

"I . . . gotta be alone right now," she said, her voice husky. "Can't remember when that happened last. Please. We'll talk at breakfast."

He nodded reluctantly and went to the door. "I know how hard it was to share that," he told her, "but I'm glad you did."

He'd opened the door when she said, "Paul?"

"Yeah?"

"Thanks."

She stretched out on the bed and buried her face in the pillow. Paul closed the door gently and went out into the night.

A clinging fog had crept across the Thorburn colony. From the edge of the outbuildings Paul could barely see the nearest cars. For a moment he thought about returning to Big House and joining the other residents. Then he found his path and started for the cabin.

It was colder than it had been that morning. As he passed No. 12 the fog closed more tightly, smothering him. A few times he swatted at it, momentarily freeing individual vaporous wraiths, which always re-formed to adhere again to their unwilling captive.

As he neared the cabin, he felt it again.

That same disturbing chill as before. Maybe stronger. He shivered inside his heavy down jacket.

"Fleming, you're losing it," he muttered to himself. "Hyperactive imagination, a cross writers have to bear. It's cold out. *Damn* cold for your wimpy southern California blood. But that's it! Nothing mysterious, supernatural, or metaphysical. Move your ass, get it in front of a fire — and stop this shit!"

He ran then, even though the fog was so thick he could hardly see the path. No. 11 was close; he knew that. The ice spirits wove a web inside him, encircling his bones, dragging him toward what he knew to be the core of this . . .

The clearing.

Turn around, something in his head screamed. *Go and see McClain, ask him for a room in Big House. Or another cabin, away from here. Now.*

He reached the porch. Fog swirled thickly between himself and the door. He shook uncontrollably. It took him a few moments to find the key, longer to fit it into the hole.

The warmth inside took him.

He left his jacket on until three good-sized logs blazed in the fireplace. Even then he removed it slowly. The furnace, turned up high, worked hard. To others, No. 11 would have felt like a baker's oven.

He had planned on working. After a while, when he was warm enough, he sat down at the desk and added the evening's notes to the others. He immersed himself in the pages, and for the moment nothing existed beyond the four walls of his *spartan accommodations.*

An hour later he got up, stretched, and looked out the front window. The fog had rolled back and the footpath was visible. Snow fell. The small flakes floated down gently, not diverted by wind. Watching the snow, Paul felt curiously at ease.

Now the cabin was too warm. He lowered the thermostat and gathered up his notes. When it was cooler, he took the notes into bed, working until his mind began digressing into realms that had nothing to do with reality — always a sign the time to quit had arrived. He read John Thorburn's diary for a couple of minutes but never made it past the preface.

Monday, December 2

He was the Cloudwalker but now soared with the wind. Although long past sunset, he could see everything clearly on the ground far below. Snow carpeted the meadows and the forest. No snow fell now; the untouched surface offered the moon's light back to him.

Never had he felt freer.

Closer to the ground now, just over the treetops, which sped by so quickly they were almost a blur. He saw the lake and dipped low so he could skim its surface then soared again, high above the clouds. Even the eagle himself would be envious, he thought.

Then, from somewhere, a sound reached him. Vague, but he listened then nodded when he knew it to be the crying of a baby. No, it was . . . a cat, that was it! The sound a cat made that people often mistook for a child.

A cat, but not quite . . .

It disturbed Cloudwalker, and he fled faster, until he was away from it. Mostly away. He should have soared higher but instead found himself close to the ground, where the trees were dense and he could not go as quickly. Even darker here, the moon's glow denied by the snow-laden branches.

Then he was following a light.

At first he thought it came from the direction of the sound. But the sound neither grew nor diminished, whichever way he ran.

The light appeared far off through the trees, an uncertain flickering that nonetheless indicated where he had to go.

He rose again. Not to earlier heights, but more than halfway to the tops of the pines. Closer to the light now, he knew it was a blaze that burned, not by accident. Focused on it, he was unaware that the distant sound had faded into silence.

A big fire burned in a clearing. Small dark figures stood around it. The fire looked real. So did the trees, a nearby creek, everything else. There was, however, something about those figures that made them look out of place, as if the forest floor wasn't what it seemed but instead an artist's unfinished canvas. Against that background someone had painted a company of matchstick people, their "heads" the right size, but the faces featureless.

Cloudwalker continued to soar with the wind, but only across the clearing and back, then around its perimeter. The matchstick people clustered together, all except one, who stood taller than the rest.

They began to move strangely, their stick bodies twisting grotesquely in a mockery of a dance as they surrounded the tall one. Against his will Cloudwalker swooped down, passing over their heads. Even that close he could only distinguish the vaguest of features on their narrow faces. But the tall one's mouth was clearly different from the others.

It seemed to be crying out.

Cloudwalker was aloft again when the holes in the snow opened. Three of them, small but growing. The movements of the matchstick people grew more animated. Even the tall one gyrated wildly, though unlike the others it never moved from its place. Cloudwalker felt uneasy hovering there, looking down at the black spots, but found himself too curious about what was going to happen to leave.

The holes widened, and as they did he was flung through the air. He tumbled out of control, certain he would crash. Still, he tried to see what went on below yet saw nothing he could understand. The snow had darkened, even though the moon hung above him with nothing in its way. There! He saw the edge of a shadow as it fell over the clearing. No, more than one. But how, from where?

The sound of wind came from below, deafening. But not the wind that blew Cloudwalker from one end of the clearing to the other, buffeting his rag-doll body. It was like a hand he couldn't see but knew existed, toying with him, flicking him like a mote of dust, maybe preparing to squeeze out his life when it tired of the game. Yet in his terror he could think of only one thing: deny the roaring wind, make it stop, and this won't be happening. So even falling earthward he covered his ears.

It didn't help.

The matchstick figures had been touched by the shadows and now twirled furiously. He saw the dancing circle tighten around the tall one, then he heard . . .

A scream.

He should not have heard a scream, or anything, above the windsound. It came from the tall one; he knew that. The tormentors were closer, their twig-arms reaching, undulating as the snow darkened . . .

The scream was stilled as the tall one exploded.

Matchstick shards rained on the dancing figures then something liquid spotted the snow all around where the tall one had been. The dancers reveled in what was happening to them.

The explosion thrust Cloudwalker far up, but not high enough. While the stick-pieces fell to the snow, the dark droplets reached higher, staining his rabbit skins, searing his flesh. In pain, he realized that whatever cast the shadow was above him. Don't look up. Don't look.

But the dark liquid continued to fly up at him, threatening to burn out his eyes. He couldn't look down anymore. Turn away. Turn to the clouds.

Slowly he willed himself to roll over. . .

"Jesus!"

Paul's head throbbed. He sat in the swivel chair, which had been pulled out from the desk and turned around. Baby Ben's luminous face read four-thirty. He had no clue why he sat in the chair, or how long he had been there. His blankets were half off the bed. Maybe it had been a dream, but he couldn't remember a thing.

A few last embers glowed in the fireplace. He was awake enough to be aware of the cold. He put on another log, prodded it mechanically with the poker. Somehow it blazed up a minute later.

"Back to sleep," he mumbled, but instead walked to the front window. It had stopped snowing; the forest seemed tranquil. He stared up and down the footpath, nodded, and climbed back into bed.

He slept until the alarm called him at six o'clock.

The first thing Paul thought about was Sherri Jordan. He wrote down his phone number and address to give her at breakfast. The second thing he thought about was snow. He looked out the front window, wondering, didn't I just do this? Another inch or two covered the path.

He walked out the front door a few minutes before six-thirty. Remembering the previous night, he stepped off the porch warily. But he already knew that whatever had been there was gone — if anything *had* been there. It was cold, no denying that, but likely just the normal chill of a Sierra dawn in early December, nothing more.

The plow had already cleared the way to No. 11 then turned around. That made sense; no one used the rest of the path, which went nowhere and ended abruptly. But Paul chose to go that way, not sure why. It felt uncomfortable sinking into the snow in his Adidas. In some places, where the wind had piled the snow into drifts, he sank down above his ankles.

The clearing. How uneasy it had made him feel yesterday. Now he crossed Leanna Creek on stones and walked slowly along the other bank, not really certain why he had come or what he looked for. The virgin snow stretched all the way to the surrounding pines.

He stopped, gazed around, listened. Overhead a few clouds drifted lazily by. Below them an eagle sailed on wind currents. Somewhere nearby a squirrel scolded.

Shaking his head, Paul hurried back to the path and followed it to Big House.

Sherri's purple Volkswagen was not in the parking area. When he didn't see it in its usual isolated spot, Paul looked through the cluster of vehicles parked closer to the mansion. He saw no beetles at all, not under the tarps or the blankets of snow.

He wondered about that as he started his Cutlass. The car also had thin southern California blood and uttered a few groans of protest before its engine turned over. He let it run, thinking he should do this at least every other day. Better still, put in some antifreeze.

A rap on his window startled him. Michael Whitney, dressed in so many layers of clothing that he looked like a bear, smiled and waved a gloved hand. Paul rolled down the window, cracking a thin layer of ice.

"Are you driving to town?" the cellist asked.

"No way," Paul said. "Just trying to revive it. Have you been inside yet?"

"In and out. The muse is strong this morning. I'm on my way back to the cabin to start working. It's out toward the fence, about ninety miles from here. That's where they put us noisemakers." He winked. "O' maybe it's jes' dat dey puts us darkies in de back of de colony!"

Paul grinned. "Right. Listen, you didn't see Sherri Jordan around, did you?"

"The wild lady? Not since last night."

"What about Walter?"

"Not at breakfast, but he's usually here. Try his office."

"Where's that?"

"Two doors past the library. Hey, it's cold! I'll see you tonight."

Michael left. Paul turned off the engine and went inside. At six-fifty most of Thorburn's artists-in-residence were already there. He took a quick look inside the dining room then crossed the central hall.

Walter McClain's office, a modest cubicle, seemed hardly befitting his thirty-year tenure as associate director. It was cluttered, but in a comfortable way. There were many small sculptures around. One of them stood next to a stack of papers on an old metal desk, where McClain worked: an incredibly lifelike snowshoe hare. Sherri Jordan's work, probably the same one Paul had seen in her cabin.

"Good morning!" the older man exclaimed, standing. "What can I do for you?"

"I was looking for Sherri. Do you know if she went into town or something?"

"A couple of people asked about her this morning." McClain chuckled. "A purple car can be conspicuous by its absence! She's on her way back to San Francisco."

"She left?"

McClain nodded. "Her four weeks were up."

"When did she leave?"

"Real early. She stopped over to see me; knows I'm here before the roosters get up. The reason she stopped was to give this to the colony." He raised the sculpture. "Isn't it exquisite? I have to say, she was an exasperating person, but her talent is wonderful. To be honest, I hope she'll do another residency here someday. I told her so."

"I wonder why she left so early," Paul said.

"Asked her the same thing. She said she couldn't sleep, was anxious to get going." He put the piece down and looked at Paul. "Why did you want to know?"

"Thought I might see her at breakfast. She was a . . . unique person."

"Indeed. But with over thirty artists-in-residence here, I'd say we had quite a few unique people, yourself included!"

Paul laughed. "Thanks. I'll see you later."

McClain sat down with his pile of papers. Paul went back to the dining room, filled his plate with pancakes and bacon, left his coffee black, and chose a place away from anyone else.

It bothered him that Sherri had left without saying good-bye. He was glad she'd opened up to him. But in the end, apparently, she couldn't handle it and had run off, something that, by her own admission, she often did.

Paul looked at the piece of paper with his address and phone number, crumpled it, and left it in an ashtray.

Kathy Parrish joined him before he was done. They talked for a few minutes then Paul excused himself and went outside.

Crossing the asphalt, he glanced at the spot where Sherri's car had been. He'd thought for sure she would meet him this morning. But Sherri was Sherri, low self-esteem and all. Tonight she would be in bed with another post-adolescent and would continue to run around aimlessly while her wonderful art sold by accident, probably for much less than it was worth.

Paul shrugged and started back to his cabin. Halfway there, his mind was already filled with other matters of the day.

CHAPTER FIVE

Tomorrow. Gary Marks would have his outline *tomorrow*. Or at least it would be ready to go by then.

Paul's day had been exceptionally productive. Even before lunch was left on the porch, his abundance of notes had begun to make sense. By the middle of the afternoon he felt certain of his storyline, and he liked it. Even at his best it usually took longer.

Now, at three o'clock, he furiously scribbled the rough draft of the outline. He would type it up that night. By the next day he would be into the novel itself.

He had taken few breaks all day; his back felt stiff. He got up, stretched, and wandered over to the side window. The nearest pine was alive with squawking jays, most knocking snow to the ground as they flitted from one branch to another. But that wasn't what caught Paul's attention.

Gail Farringer walked along the footpath. She wore a heavy blue ski jacket over her warm-up suit, a brightly colored wool cap, and matching gloves. A sketchpad was tucked under one arm. Already past No. 11 when he saw her, she soon fell from sight because the snowy trail turned.

Paul went back to work. Ten minutes later he realized he was concentrating more on the enigmatic woman from No. 13 than on what lay in front of him. He put on his jacket and went outside.

Gail probably had some favorite places, he figured, beyond where he had explored in his brief time at the colony. He was curious and the sun felt good on his face. He retraced his steps of the morning.

She sat in the middle of the clearing on an old log, sketchpad open but hands folded. Sitting as still as the woods around her, she stared in the direction of Thorburn Lake.

Paul leaned against one of the sentinel pines. He had no intention of disturbing the woman. In the first place, interacting with a fellow resident was the Thorburn colony's major offense, a breach of the Rule. Second, he remembered Sherri's warning and had no desire for a confrontation. He would not remain there long . . .

For whatever reason — perhaps he had shifted a foot and crunched the snow — Gail suddenly turned. Seeing him, she stood, her sketchpad falling to the snow. Her startled look became annoyance. She glared at him as she knelt to retrieve the pad.

Paul felt like an idiot, a voyeur who had been caught in the act. He smiled weakly, held up a hand, and walked off. "Way to go, Fleming," he muttered. "Jesus!"

He hurried back to No. 11 and tried to finish the outline but got nowhere. The colony's official day still had more than a half hour to go. So what? he thought, since he was going to work that night anyway. He stretched out on the bed and opened John Thorburn's diary.

From where he lay, Paul could see a portion of the footpath out the front window. By four-thirty it occurred to him that he had glanced over there numerous times. Gail was either still in the clearing or had returned another way, which he doubted. Now nearly dusk, it would soon be getting colder. She would have to pass before long.

He took the diary and sat outside on the porch step. The book was open, although he hardly looked at it. This time he would say something to Gail Farringer, at least try to apologize for what had happened earlier. However she reacted, at least it would be off his conscience.

When she came down the path, he stood. She saw him, hesitated then continued on. He stayed on the porch. The trail was narrow and he didn't want it to seem as if he were accosting her.

"Hi," he said when she was closer. "Listen, about before, I wasn't — "

She stopped, her face red. "Leave me alone, please!" she snapped then hurried off.

"I'm doing great with the ladies today," he mumbled, and went back inside, slamming the door.

Harriet Thorburn seemed different that night, more animated, personable. She told wonderful stories of colony guests during the flower-child days of the sixties. She hardly rambled at all and seemed tolerant — more so than Walter McClain — when Paul arrived ten minutes late. He'd lost track of time and had been lucky to glance at the clock when he did, or dinner might have been whatever he could beg from Arthur Tyler's kitchen.

He had been seated at the third table again, between Allan Kroll and David Van Ness. The composer was drunk, worse than he'd been on Paul's first night.

Van Ness, an obnoxious man, did not have a good word to say about anyone when there was nothing in it for him. While Harriet Thorburn spoke, Paul was spared having to listen to him. But there were lulls when the tables were on their own. Paul's had his restraint tested severely.

"So we saw *Summit of Fear*, my friend Russell and me," Van Ness said. "It's not the kind of thing we usually see, but hell, everyone and their sister was talking about it, so we decided to check it out. Well, Russell thought it was a piece of shit. That's exactly what he said, 'Jesus, what a piece of shit!' Now that isn't how I felt. I like that actor, you know, the one with all the muscles who mumbles his lines. But it was *not* good, really."

"It wasn't meant to be *film-noir* or anything like that," Paul said patiently. *Lord, get me the hell out of here!* "A movie like *Summit of Fear* is supposed to entertain people and make money. It did both."

"Seems like it's prostituting oneself," Van Ness said, and shrugged. "But then I suppose prostitutes make good money."

Thea Douglas, who sat across the table from them, had been listening. "Paul, just because you're new doesn't mean you have to be polite, not to *him*. Here, read my lips: 'David, fuck off.' We all say it at one time or another."

"Love your makeup, Thea," Van Ness said. "Who does it, Sherwin Williams?"

Paul shook his head and tried to hold back a grin. Luckily, Harriet Thorburn began talking again.

It had been strangely calm in the clearing that day, Gail thought, back in her cabin after dinner. During her nearly three weeks at the colony, she had always been able to rekindle the motivation depleted by too many hours at the canvas without a break. An hour there, or less, stirred her in a dark way, prodded her with fear, sometimes made her want to run.

But for her kind of work it was appropriate stimulus.

That afternoon, however, she'd felt nothing there. The only disturbing moment was when *he* had been watching her. He hadn't meant anything by it; she knew that. Maybe she should have spoken to him. . .

No, she couldn't. Not ever, not to anyone.

Maybe she would never feel it again. No matter. She had regenerated the creative flow on her own and could do it anytime she wanted. So much pain to draw from; it was easy.

Just like now.

She had put the brush down for a minute to rest her eyes. She picked it up again.

Tuesday, December 3

Paul finished his work after midnight, then forgot to set his alarm — or maybe not — and didn't make it to Big House until eight-thirty. Half a dozen assorted delivery vehicles were parked near the service entrance. More than yesterday, which undoubtedly had something to do with the time.

Walter McClain showed him where the copy machine was but told him that they had no fax. "I suppose we'll come out of the dark ages someday," McClain said. "Why don't you go into town later and mail it? Dan Fry's the postmaster. He or Jenny can get it off for you, overnight if you need it."

Paul copied his outline then called his agent in Los Angeles. Gary *kvelled* — his word — to hear the news.

"*That* is great!" he exclaimed. "I'll call Ann right now. When will I see it?"

"I'm taking it to the post office this afternoon. Forget tomorrow, but you should have it there on Thursday."

"Are you hearing me okay, Paul?"

"Yeah, why?"

"Lousy connection or something. Jesus, sounds like you're in Uzbekistan! So, it's going good for you up there, huh?"

"Fine. I'm starting the book today."

"What?" Gary shouted.

"Never mind. I'll talk to you soon."

Paul hung up, thought about calling Jason and Bree, then remembered it was Tuesday and they were in school. Back outside again, into a gray morning, cold and windy with a threat of snow or rain. Instead of going back to his cabin, Paul walked around to the front of Big House. From the circular driveway he gazed across the shimmering expanse of Thorburn Lake, mist-enshrouded and less blue in the overcast. No cars drove along the colony road.

A man in dirty blue coveralls was polishing the wooden friezes beneath the portico. Paul wanted to have a closer look at the carved figures, which had been commissioned by John Thorburn over a century ago. The handyman, thin and stooped, stood on the second rung of a stepladder, his back to Paul. Not wanting to startle him, Paul crunched some gravel under his Adidas as he neared the first of the columns. The man turned, looked down.

"How's it going?" Paul said.

The handyman's face was gaunt, covered with stubble. He had black, oily hair, haphazardly combed. A scowl seemed natural to him.

His cold gaze made Paul uncomfortable, but Paul held it for a couple of seconds until the man, with a brusque nod, stepped down. He folded the ladder and pushed his way through the huge oak doors.

Shaking off the encounter, Paul studied the friezes. The people, horses, and wagons were finely detailed and well cared for, considering how many decades they had been exposed to the harsh Sierra winter. It was an impressive welcome for visitors to Big House — assuming anyone ever went in that way.

At midmorning Paul finally started working. Even knowing the story in his head, even having an outline, it was hard to put the first words down. A cartoon in a frame hung over his desk at home: Snoopy sitting cocksure with his typewriter on top of the doghouse, Linus reading what had just been written and saying, "Your new novel has a great beginning . . . Good luck with the second sentence!" That was Paul, and that was why it hung there.

But he did have a page done by the time lunch came. Starved, he threw the door open when he heard someone outside. Nora Hardman nearly fell off the porch.

"Sorry about that," he said. "Here, you don't even have to put it in the box."

The stocky, fortyish woman in the red coat handed him the carryall. She smiled but seemed reluctant to say anything.

"It's okay," Paul told her, "you can talk."

"Just followin' the rules, ya know," she said in a deep, friendly voice. "Uh, Arthur stuck in an extra piece of chocolate cake. An' I put in a Diet Coke, like you wanted."

"Thanks."

"Yeah. Gotta go now."

Nora started back, probably hoping she would not be censured for this offense. Paul went inside, consumed his lunch too quickly, and kept working.

By three-thirty he'd forgotten his earlier anxiety. Paul was satisfied with the quantity of work, pleased with how it read. He stopped, put a copy of the outline in an envelope, and carried it to the car in his briefcase to protect it from a light but cold rain.

Again the Cutlass groaned to life. He couldn't warm up the interior fast enough. Finally he set off for town. Even without McClain to navigate, he avoided most of the potholes on S. Lakeshore Drive. The rain slackened, and by the time he turned onto Washo Street it had stopped.

Jenny Fry was talking to some women when Paul walked into the store. She excused herself and met him in the first aisle. "Are you looking for candy again?" she asked. "It's not over here, you know."

"Hi, no, I just need to mail something." He held up the envelope.

"Go and see my mother, then." She thought for a moment. "No, she's dead. My father will help you."

Jenny went back to her customers. Paul followed a dry, racking cough to the checkstand. Dan Fry was a short jowly man with a thick head of pure white hair. He appeared as pale as his daughter and between spasms would dab at his mouth with a handkerchief. Paul noticed dark spots on the cloth.

"Help you?" Fry wheezed.

"I'd like this to go out in next-day delivery," Paul said.

"You just missed a pickup. Next one's early tomorrow morning. It goes to Truckee then they take it over to Reno. Won't get where you want till Thursday. That okay?"

"Yeah, it's fine."

He addressed the label as Fry, coughing again, slid the envelope into an express mailer.

"Anything else?" Fry asked, tossing it into a bin behind the counter.

"I can use some antifreeze."

"Don't have none. Try Dooley's Garage, up the street."

Paul paid for the postage and a newspaper and left Dan Fry in a bad fit of coughing. He walked past the Mule Deer Cafe and across Alpine Street to DOOLEY'S GARAGE, WAYNE DOOLEY, PROPRIETOR, with its one service bay and twin Texaco pumps that probably had been there when gasoline cost a quarter a gallon. The owner was a personable man, tall and thin, in his forties. His clothes and hands were covered with grease. Paul told him what he wanted.

"Sure, that's easy," Dooley said. "Want me to put it in for you?"

Paul glanced at his watch. "It's not necessary, but — "

"Hey, no problem. Won't take long. Go on, run your car in. Just finishing up one other thing."

"Thanks, I appreciate it."

He drove the Cutlass into the service bay. "You can wait inside if you want," Dooley said. "There's some magazines."

"I think I'll take a walk."

He bought a shredded beef taco at Salazar's, a four-table restaurant next door to the garage. Back at Alpine Street, where Stillwell's sole traffic light flashed endlessly, he turned right and began studying the façades of the old buildings. By wiping off layers of dirt from long-untended storefronts, he was able to read signs and look inside windows. One, a coffee shop, had its entire menu carved into the wooden door, prices included. However long these stores had been closed, it looked as if no one had bothered emptying them of either fixtures or furniture. Their value as antiques would probably be staggering. But that didn't seem to matter in Stillwell, a place that had been largely ignored by time.

On the other side of the street, next to the Tin Shop, stood Idlewood Livery. Its weathered sign above a stone front was easy to read. The only window was a small one on the front door. Paul rubbed some thick dirt off and peered inside. As with the other buildings, he found it difficult to see anything clearly, especially with the daylight beginning to fade. He could make out bales of hay both on racks and in bays along the base of one wall. The bales were probably so old they would crumble to dust if someone touched them. There were skeletons of a buckboard and what must have been an elaborate sleigh. Wood shavings still littered the floor.

And in the farthest corner was something he could barely see. It was in one of the stalls, mostly concealed by a tattered burlap cover.

Something purple.

He strained for a better look, but it didn't help. Even with more light there wasn't enough showing of whatever it was to matter. He tried the knob, but the heavy door was locked.

Purple. A crazy thought filled his head. No, there wouldn't be any reason for it. But whatever the thing was, it seemed out of place in the old stable. He decided to look for a way inside.

Jenny Fry appeared from an alley across the street. She was looking up at the fluffy white clouds and didn't notice him. He moved away from the door of Idlewood Livery. She saw him now and walked across the street.

"I'm sorry we couldn't talk before," she said. "You know how busy you can get sometimes."

"Yes, I know."

"What are you doing?"

"Sightseeing. My car's in the garage."

"Oh, let *me* show you around! Among other things I'm on the board of the Historical Society."

"Well, it'll be ready right away — "

"Our population is about three hundred and fifty people," she began, apparently not having heard him. "That's not impressive, is it? Would you believe there used to be over four thousand people in Stillwell? But that was a long time ago, before they shut down the logging camp and the Liberty Mill. You heard about the foreman saying the jobs are going and not coming back."

Paul looked at Jenny curiously. "What?"

"That's Bruce Springsteen, didn't you know?"

"Oh, right. Where do the people live?"

"Some up on Whiskey Hill. See?" She pointed west up Alpine. "That A-frame near the top is Walter McClain's home. Others live on Trout Lane, just down the street from here. Oh, and there are a few houses overlooking the west end of the lake."

They began walking as Jenny continued to talk. She seemed excited about leading the tour. And she knew her town, no question about it. But Paul hadn't planned on driving back to the colony in the dark. Fortunately, after ten minutes, they wound up back on Washo Street, where Dooley saw them and waved.

"Oh, I forgot," Jenny said. "Wayne closes early tonight. You'd better get your car. We can finish another time."

"Sure. Thanks."

Jenny left. Paul paid Dooley and drove up Washo Street. Rain fell again. He slowed at the flashing light, glanced down Alpine, thought about stopping then drove on.

A few days of isolation can do strange things, Paul decided. Returning to the colony, walking out to No. 11, he had the feeling of being cut off from the world in a way that was more than physical. He hadn't even noticed that he'd picked up the previous day's Sacramento *Bee*. While day-old news was still news to him, it hardly overcame the remoteness.

But he did that with a phone call to Jason and Bree, and a few minutes of Dan Rather, before dinner.

After dinner he sat in the day room, watching a Lakers-Pistons game. Eventually he got into a spirited conversation with Michael Whitney, Kathy Parrish, and two other residents over the boundaries of freedom of speech and the press, and the moral responsibilities of those who dealt in the written word. That led to a poker game that went on for hours.

Paul still felt uncomfortable with people; maybe he always would. But that night he needed them, and it was all right.

The rain had become light snow by the time he made his way back to the cabin. He felt tired. The walk shouldn't have had any effect on him. But with his mind on the book, he hadn't exercised at all. Arthur Tyler's great food wasn't helping either. Tomorrow, he told himself, he would get up earlier and jog a couple of miles. Or maybe a mile to begin with, at this altitude.

But in the morning half a foot of snow pressed against his door, with more on the way.

Wednesday, December 4

The storm had hit in the middle of the night. Snow fell in large flakes that were sometimes blown horizontally by gusts of wind. The plow did its work at dawn, but by the time Paul — dressed in almost every bit of winter gear he'd brought or borrowed — started for Big House the path had been covered again.

"Hell, this one is nothing," Thea Douglas said at breakfast.

Paul was dubious. "It's not?"

"The radio said it'll blow over by this afternoon. I did a residency here earlier this year, parts of January and

February. One storm lasted for almost a week! Power was out, phones, everything."

"Power?"

"They have generators. We all survived, but talk about *bor-ing*!"

Later, Paul spent an hour in the library then trudged back to No. 11 and worked all day. Nora Hardman brought him lunch shortly after noon. He couldn't believe they would make her deliver it in such bad weather.

"Heck, this snow ain't nothin'," she said.

He shrugged. "That's what I keep hearing."

"Besides, you folks hafta eat, don't you?"

"I think we could live without one meal."

She grinned. "You don't know a lotta these people."

"Why don't you stay a few minutes and get warm?"

"Uh-uh. Too much work. Thanks anyway, Mr. Fleming. You're one of the good ones."

The snow stopped falling in the middle of the afternoon, as predicted. But the temperature remained in the low twenties, with a wind chill factor of far less than that. Had there been a way of avoiding another trek to Big House, Paul would have. But that was part of the price for being there.

Incredibly, two new residents had arrived that day. Paul figured they must have thought themselves crazy as they came up from the interstate on those miserable roads. He sat at the first table that night, a few places from Harriet Thorburn, whose stories of past storms made this one seem like a picnic in July.

The book was coming along better than Paul could have imagined. By late afternoon that day he knew it had begun to consume him. In a way that was good, because, after all, he had traveled there to try to regain what he thought might be lost, and in that he'd succeeded beyond measure. Still, this obsession with his work had done so much to destroy his relationship with Jeannie. And if he was still like that, would it happen again with someone else —

assuming there would ever be another in his life? That was what scared him.

But for now he was on a roll and had no intention of slowing down. Refusing an invitation to party in the day room, he returned to his claustrophobic, snow-covered *spartan accommodations* and worked until the words made no sense.

The purple Volkswagen was parked in front of his cabin. He saw no snow on the footpath, or anywhere else. The door on the driver's side was open. Watching from his window he could see inside clearly.

Sherri Jordan, naked, stretched languorously on the front seat. Her long legs dangled outside the door. Returning his gaze, she ran her tongue across bright red lips. The nipples on her small breasts were hard, possibly from the cold. Her sculptor's fingers brushed provocatively along her thighs, at first circumventing the golden mound of hair, then working nearer in short, circular turns. He stood, realizing how much he wanted her, as her legs parted. . .

Darkness filled the car, as if someone had been hiding in the backseat and now rose over her. Paul could see nothing except a shadow. Sherri was pulled inside; the door slammed. She might have been screaming, but he couldn't hear a sound.

The car shook. Sherri thrashed wildly, but he only glimpsed her in the shadow that engulfed the interior. He continued to watch, unable to help.

Her head slammed against the window three times. Blood trickled down the glass. Her dead eyes stared at him, mouth agape. The car stopped shaking.

The shadow inside was gone.

Thursday, December 5

When he awakened with the alarm in the morning, Paul figured one of two things had happened: either no new snow had fallen, making it unnecessary for the plow to come at its usual ungodly time, or it was snowing right now and thirty inches lay on the ground.

His first guess proved correct.

It was still freezing, though. The thermometer at the service entrance of Big House registered 17°. Paul wished Gary Marks were standing there with him, sucking in the crisp mountain air. The man would probably turn brittle and crack into a thousand pieces.

Paul had been unable to let go of Idlewood Livery. All right, don't be stupid. At that moment Sherri Jordan was waking up next to some young stud and would have to think hard to recall his name. There was no reason for her car to be there. None. Lots of things in life were purple. And he might not have even seen *that* correctly, considering the light.

But he was determined to make sure.

He would drive into town after four. He wanted to pick some things up anyway. Not that he needed an excuse, but it helped.

It remained cold and threatening all day, but no new snow fell. Paul left right at four. A few other residents had the same idea.

S. Lakeshore Drive had been cleared but still required caution because of many slick spots. The potholes were filled with hard-packed snow and ice, temporarily nullifying their hazard.

This time Paul parked in front of Mountain Apothecary. He took a flashlight from the glove compartment and stuck it in his back pocket as he walked to the intersection. A few people walked on Washo Street, but Alpine was deserted. Still, he moved cautiously, until he stood at the door of Idlewood Livery. Wiping away more of the grime, he peered in.

The stall was empty. He saw the burlap cover draped over one of the side panels. It had been folded.

Maybe what he thought he'd seen was nothing at all.

But one thing he knew: someone *had* been inside Idlewood Livery in the past forty-eight hours.

Then he thought, so what? The building had owners. People stored things in them. There was no mystery, only his overactive imagination.

An alley ran along the side of Idlewood Livery. There had to be another door, he thought, probably larger. He decided to explore. First he shone the flashlight into a few dark corners but saw nothing. He put it back in his pocket and turned.

Someone stepped out of the alley. Paul froze. Sheriff Roy Stillwell walked down the street, his gaze on Paul. A yard away, the big man stopped.

"Need something?" he asked gruffly.

"Hi, no," Paul said. "I was just looking at these great old buildings."

"You like old buildings?"

"Sure. I may want to use them in a story sometime."

"You're from the colony, huh?"

"That's right."

Stillwell nodded and glanced at the door of the livery. Paul wondered if he noticed the clean spot. Then he looked past Paul, toward Washo Street. Carl Stillwell, the nephew, walked toward them.

Finally the sheriff forced a smile. "Not too many of you people wander our streets, 'specially when it's so damn cold. Just checking." He touched the brim of his hat. "You have a good night."

"Thanks, Sheriff, you too."

Paul turned and started for Washo. *Too fast,* he told himself. *Slow down.* He nodded at Carl Stillwell as they passed. The deputy joined his uncle, and they watched the "crazy damn writer" turn the corner.

Keep it up, asshole, Paul thought. *Why not come back tomorrow and try to get into Idlewood Livery? Then they can arrest you for breaking and entering, and you can see the inside of what is probably their very old jail.*

He went into Mountain Apothecary for toothpaste and razor blades then drove back to the colony, too fast. A spinout slowed him down.

At dinner Paul wished that *he* were isolated at the end of a table. Ten minutes after Harriet Thorburn dismissed the gathering, he was at work in his cabin.

She had been watching him at dinner and knew something was bothering him. Once, in another life, Gail Farringer had possessed an understanding of people so acute, others called it her "gift." She could see hurt, feel it, draw some of it into herself to relieve the burdened one and help begin the healing.

But that was a million years ago, when she had cared.

Usually he glanced at her while Harriet Thorburn shared her reminiscences. She knew it, even though he might not have been able to tell. But not that night. He had been preoccupied and seemed anxious to be out of there. When he passed her cabin he was running.

Still, it was none of her concern. . .

Maybe something that was part of who and what you are can never be lost. Maybe it only lays dormant, awaiting rebirth.

Friday, December 6

The next morning Paul awakened before the alarm. The night's sleep had been his best yet. Yesterday seemed like a bad joke. He put on warm-up pants and jogged past Big House to Thorburn Lake, then along a path that skirted the shoreline. A mile and a half, at least.

Among the delivery trucks at the service entrance was one that Paul hadn't seen before: GRAPEVINE HILL STATIONERS, TRUCKEE, CALIFORNIA was scrolled in black on a purple Dodge van.

Purple.

Paul smiled and went inside to fill himself with Arthur Tyler's pancakes.

The morning's work was productive. And if Paul needed more incentive, it came in the form of a message that Nora Hardman delivered with his lunch.

"Saw it in your box," the woman explained. "It got put there just before I left, so that was real good timing."

Loved it! Faxed it to Ann. She's excited too. Keep it up, boychik! *Gary.*

Paul taped the message on the wall above the desk and kept working.

Droplets of melting snow ran down the window by the time he stopped in the middle of the afternoon. The temperature soared to the high thirties and the sun had been out since early morning. It felt like a mild day to Paul, and he figured his blood must have already begun to thicken.

The dialogue in the scene he'd been writing sounded insipid. Time for a break. Normally when that happened he would jog or ride his bike and enact the scene as many times as he had to until the words sounded right. Today he would settle for a walk.

He followed the footpath to the sentinel pines, crossed Leanna Creek, and paralleled it until the tributary disappeared into the forest. Playing out the troublesome scene, he walked along the perimeter of the trees. A jay looked down and scolded him.

Fifteen minutes and a lot of pacing later, the scene began to come together. He had no pad or tape recorder; that wasn't how he worked. With nearly total recall, he could transpose it verbatim when he got around to it, which he expected to do in a few minutes.

But as he turned to cut across the clearing he saw Gail Farringer sitting on the log.

He had no idea how long she'd been there. The sketchpad sat on her lap; she was watching him, her expression blank, dispassionate, as usual.

How was he supposed to react? he wondered. He wasn't about to approach her. Maybe he'd just go back along the forest's edge. But what did *she* have in mind? She had seen him first. If she had wanted to avoid a confrontation she wouldn't have stayed there. On the other hand, maybe she was determined to work at her spot regardless of who came around.

This was stupid, he thought. Okay, he wouldn't go right up to her, but he wouldn't go out of the way to ignore her, either.

He was a third of the way across when his foot found a rock hidden under the snow. He stumbled, fell hard, the rock scraping his ankle. Nothing serious, but it hurt. Grinning, he got up.

Gail had half stood but sat again as he continued across the clearing. Despite how comical he must have looked, her expression remained unchanged. He angled toward the sentinel pines, passing within ten feet of her.

"Are you all right?" she asked.

He stopped and looked at her. "Fine. A little embarrassed, that's all."

"Don't be," she said, glancing at the log. "Will you sit down?"

He was surprised. "Uh, sure, if you want."

"I apologize for my rudeness the other day, if that's what's bothering you."

He sat next to her. She stiffened, then eased. "I deserved it for spying on you," he said.

"You weren't spying." She held out a hand. "I'm Gail Farringer."

He took the hand. Her grip was firm. "Paul Fleming."

"I guess we both knew that."

"I guess. Aren't you afraid of violating the Prime Directive?"

"The what?"

"The non-fraternization rule. Walter McClain has a thing about rules."

"I'd forgotten. Maybe we shouldn't talk, then."

"Not a chance! I'd been hoping to talk to you since the first night I was here."

She looked at him. "Why?"

He shrugged. "Maybe I . . . "

"Felt sorry for the weird lady who sits by herself?"

"I don't know. A little, I suppose."

"I . . . wanted to talk to you also."

"Yeah?"

Gail was trembling, not from the cold. Paul sensed how difficult this was for her. She rose suddenly and stared down at the snow.

"I have to go back now," she said.

"What is it?"

"I have to go!"

"When can we talk again?"

"Soon. I don't know . . . "

"What about dinner? I can arrange — "

She wheeled to face him, eyes wide. "No, never there!" she exclaimed. "So many people! Don't try to talk to me *there*!"

"Okay," he said.

She softened. "Please, Paul?"

He nodded. "Will you tell me when we can talk again?"

"Tomorrow. Here, this time."

She ran off, leaving her sketchpad, which Paul didn't notice until she was beyond the twin pines. As puzzling as the encounter had been, he was glad she had emerged, however briefly, from her private hell to speak to him. He wanted to see her again, learn about the demons that possessed her. But it would come slowly, and he had to accept that or risk driving her away.

Gail Farringer needed someone, needed *him*.

Maybe Paul Fleming was ready to need someone also.

CHAPTER SIX

At dinner, Walter McClain had an interesting proposition for Paul.

"A couple of the guest rooms in Big House will be available tomorrow," he said. "We're under thirty residents right now and that'll continue to drop until after the holidays. You're welcome to one of the rooms if you want to come in from the cold."

Paul thought about how nice it would be: meals downstairs, no treks through the snow or squirrels on the roof. Then he remembered how much he'd accomplished in his *spartan accommodations* and how he liked the crackling fire and the Wieghorst on the wall.

And he thought about Gail Farringer.

"Thanks, Walter, I'll stay where I am," he told the associate director.

Curiously, his dinner place was at table four, as close as anyone could get to Gail. This was a chance, he felt, to win her trust. He hardly looked at her.

Earlier, on his way to the mansion, he had dropped off the sketchpad. He'd been tempted to knock on the door but left it on the porch instead.

Satisfied with his day's work, Paul stayed in Big House after dinner. He stopped for a minute in front of Nancy Thorburn's disturbing vision on canvas. But this time, with the central hall full of residents, he couldn't feel the bitter chill of the blizzard or share the anguish of those trapped there forever. He went into the day room.

Before the evening was over he learned that David Van Ness would be leaving in the morning.

All in all it had been a gratifying day at the Thorburn colony.

Gail sat cross-legged on the floor, as far across the room as she could be from the half-finished work on the easel. She'd been back in her cabin for a couple of hours but still hadn't picked up a brush. Earlier, it had been easy. Now, the painting annoyed her. So did others scattered about the room. She chose instead to stare at the fireplace.

The sketchpad sat on her lap, a piece of charcoal on the floor next to her. It hadn't taken long to finish the picture of him.

But something was wrong with it.

The face was cold, a lot like so many others she had done on canvas. It wasn't the way *he* looked, not the face she had studied so closely that day. She wasn't capable of capturing that kind of emotion.

Not yet.

She tore out the sheet, crumpled it into a large ball and gave it to the fire.

How long had it been since she'd gotten any sleep? She couldn't remember. Two, three days. It all seemed the same. She could try tonight; but then, why bother?

She would fall asleep and the Dream would come.

It always came. There wasn't a time when it didn't. Still, how many more caffeine pills could she take? How much deprivation could her body stand?

Did it matter?

Maybe, now. She had to try.

But the Dream . . .

The . . . damned . . . Dream . . .

Gail stood. Her purse lay on the bed. She dug inside, finally extracting a small pillbox. She had to; she couldn't handle it yet.

Later.

She would challenge the Dream later.

Paul spent a pleasant evening sipping wine and discussing all things creative, mostly with Michael and Thea. Robert Kingsley joined them for an hour, while other residents drifted in and out of the circle.

At midnight the day room was nearly empty. After politely sidestepping a proposition from Thea, Paul left Big House and walked to his cabin. The temperature had fallen into the teens, but there was no wind and the crisp air felt refreshing. As he passed No. 13, Paul noticed the lights were still on. Thinking about it, he couldn't recall a time when the cabin had been dark.

He had assumed he would be asleep almost before getting his clothes off. Wine usually did that to him. The opposite was true. He lay there, wide awake, staring at the ceiling. Finally he picked up *Trails of Promise* and read John Thorburn's account of crossing the treacherous Great Basin. There, the wagon train lost considerable time in the race to beat the winter storms across the Sierras.

When he finally acknowledged how wide-awake he was, Paul put the diary aside and started working. He'd pay for it; no doubt of that. But until four-thirty, when he fell asleep with his head cradled in his arms on the desk, he was productive.

Saturday, December 7

It played on a wide-screen television this time. She had seen it on every size monitor, one as small as a Watchman. That wasn't what mattered. What played on them was always the same.

117

The images: so lifelike. Not thousands of high-resolution dots, but miniaturized real people and things in a box, people who could be touched and would keep on playing the scene even when she clicked off the remote. In the foreground the reporter, dressed casually in a khaki shirt, spoke into a microphone. His eyes, which should have been toward the camera, darted from side to side; his head moved as he tried to look behind him.

People were sprawled face down on the floor, their hands behind their backs, but not tied, although they might as well have been, because the people didn't move them. A head would bob up occasionally, but otherwise they lay still. There were more than the few that could be seen; she knew that.

Those who strode among them were similar in appearance, swarthy men and women of medium build, all dressed in tattered fatigues. Some wore service caps, but most were bareheaded. Bandoleers crisscrossed their chests; their weapons were old Soviet PPS-43 submachine guns, although one, the leader, also brandished a gleaming pearl-handled Colt .45.

She recognized the room they moved in; she'd been there before. Elegant tapestries, thick carpeting, fine leather couches. It didn't seem right. Why should *this* be the stage for some perverse drama?

The camera panned the room, revealing more of the hostages. In front of one tapestry lay a man and a boy — so alike, with fair skin and blond hair. The man had a small bald spot — the mark of his mortality, he called it. They were pressed together, the man wanting to cradle the boy but knowing his arms must stay where they were. One of their captors, a woman with long black hair, saw the man's head move, and just before the camera left them she pushed it down with the heel of her boot.

Again the reporter stood in the foreground of the diorama, the leader next to him, holding the revolver against the side of his head. The image wavered as the cameraman's legs shook. He'd done Vietnam and Nicaragua and places like that but always questioned to what limits the world's need to know would be extended.

"You, *quedar aquí!*" the leader said to the cameraman. "Don' go, no way! *Comprende?*"

The cameraman said something that she couldn't understand; the reporter kept up a stream of words into the microphone.

Until the leader pulled the trigger and blew out his brains.

The camera, blood spattered on the lens, jerked toward the ceiling for a moment then found the reporter again. Still falling, but already dead. The leader waved a warning finger into the camera then swept his arm around the room as if he were introducing the next act.

They opened fire everywhere, at close range. People screamed and pleaded, then died. The cameraman, covered with blood, panned the room. In a van a safe distance away the moments were being recorded for all time.

The camera held on the blond man and the blond boy, and she watched the bullets rip them apart and got to hear the boy cry out one last time.

For her.

Later, Paul would not remember waking briefly just after five. There was a sound, distant, carried by the wind. An animal's cry. Or maybe it had been the wind itself. He listened but didn't hear it again.

He fell back to sleep in a few seconds.

Gail was thinking about it. She thought about it a lot, all the different ways it could be done: painless, quick, dramatic. But in the end she was still around.

Still around for the next time the Dream would come.

It never did come twice in one night. Knowing that, she slept for another hour before it came time to go to Big House.

* * *

Paul wanted breakfast, he really did. But an hour and a half of sleep! Somehow he made it to Big House, aware that he looked as bad as he felt. Avoiding human contact, he ate quickly but drank only decaffeinated coffee.

He was back in the cabin before seven-thirty and slept until Nora Hardman brought lunch.

The next day was Sunday. The non-fraternization rule and other Thorburn laws were still valid for those choosing to work. But Paul had checked with McClain and knew that it was all right to get away from the colony for a day. It sounded great to him, a chance to do something else.

Like play blackjack.

Maybe North Lake Tahoe, or even Reno. He wasn't sure yet if he would do it. The book was going well and in the grip of creativity like this he felt cheated if he stopped working for even a short time.

In the middle of the afternoon the decision fell out of his hands. A storm from the northeast struck the region with sudden, devastating force. Snow piled up quickly as gusting winds drove it against the cabin. Paul questioned the structure's ability to withstand the assault. But then, it had been there for a long time.

What bothered him most was missing the rendezvous with Gail. He had been looking forward to it. Maybe he could go to her cabin. It wouldn't be an easy walk, but he'd have to do it later anyway if he wanted dinner. He might as well get used to it.

He'd been warned that "December kin bring some nasty storms," and December just did.

At three, while getting ready, someone knocked on his door. That being the last thing he expected, he nearly jumped. Snow flew into the cabin as he opened the door. Gail hurried in and together they forced the door shut.

"Where were *you* going?" she asked, peeling off layers of clothes.

"To your place," he replied.

"Are you crazy?"

"Yeah. Are you?" He took her coat.

"I suppose. You'd better hang it over your tub or there'll be a puddle when the snow melts."

"Sit down anywhere," he told her. "Not much choice."

"Can I move the rug in front of the fireplace?"

"Sure. I'll put some more logs on."

When the fire was going strongly, Paul sat down on the other end of the thunderbird rug. Gail looked around the room. For a few moments her gaze stayed on the Wieghorst painting. Then she pointed at the desk.

"Is that your new book?" she asked.

"Yes."

"How is it coming?"

"Real well. It's been good for me up here."

"I know what you mean."

Outside, the wind blew, whining through the trees, throwing another barrage of snow at the cabin.

"It's pretty bad out there," Paul said. "How'd you manage?"

"I grew up with winters like this. You get used to it, or you don't do anything."

"Where was that?"

She stared at the Wieghorst for a long moment. Paul was afraid he had asked the wrong thing.

Finally she said, "It's not easy for me to be sitting here talking to you. I think you know that."

"I do."

"Then don't ask me to talk about myself. I can't. Not yet. If that's not okay, then I'll have to leave."

"I don't want you to go," he told her. "What do you want to talk about?"

"Paul Fleming. Tell me about him."

He smiled. "It's not my favorite topic of conversation, but I am well versed in it."

He talked. She listened intently, occasionally asking a question. She was especially interested in the last couple of years. Paul found it easy talking to her and did not gloss over any of the more unpleasant details.

But Gail Farringer never smiled. Paul's stories of good times with Jeannie, anecdotes about Jason and Bree, did not change her, although she acknowledged each one with a nod.

When he finally grew tired of listening to himself, Paul stopped. He wished there were something he could offer Gail.

"I keep forgetting to pick up some stuff," he said. "Maybe with this kind of weather I'll remember. How about a Diet Coke and half a Hershey's Big Block? Best I can do."

"It's fine," she assured him. "I love chocolate."

"That's two things," he said, breaking the bar.

"What?"

"Two things I know about you, that you're from somewhere cold and you're a chocolate freak — like me."

They watched the fire and ate in silence, occasionally glancing at each other. Seeing her up close for this length of time, Paul decided she was more attractive than he'd first thought. He tried not to stare.

"It feels good in here," she said at last.

"You don't think it's too warm?"

"No, it's fine. Paul, I'd like to read one of your books sometime."

"There are a few in my trunk. I'll get one for you." He turned toward her. "Gail, I wanted — "

"I have to start back now," she interrupted, standing. "It sounds worse out there."

"Will you be all right?"

"Yes." She held out a hand. "Thanks for having me over."

"I want to see you again."

She nodded. "So do I."

"What about tonight?"

She got her coat, not answering. As she pulled on her boots, the light went off.

"You didn't answer my question," Paul said.

She looked at him. "No, Paul, not tonight."

"Then you tell me."

"Tomorrow. After dinner. Come to . . . my cabin. Please don't let anyone see you. Will you promise me that?"

"All right."

The light came back on. "Paul?"

"Yes?"

"You be careful going to Big House."

"I will."

She went out into the storm. Paul watched through the window but lost sight of her in seconds. He went back to his desk, thinking he'd resume work.

The light flashed off again.

"Swell," he muttered, sitting down on the thunderbird rug.

But it wouldn't have mattered, because even when the light came back on, all he could think about was Gail Farringer.

What was the enigma of her? He would find out. Soon.

Maybe tomorrow night.

Until dinner Paul decided to read more of John Thorburn's diary. He'd been anticipating this part, the account of the party's seven weeks in the Sierras. It was an unnerving story, made even more real by the sound of the wind and driving snow outside his cabin. And he knew what the scene looked like. All he had to do was conjure up an image of Nancy Thorburn's painting.

One of the entries puzzled him. On January 4 Thorburn wrote: *Jordy Fry said he saw a figure through the trees in the direction of the pass.* What confused Paul was that, as significant as such an event would be for a party that had been stranded so long, no other mention of it was made.

On the following day, January 5, Thorburn wrote: *A Digger Indian came into camp at noontime.* That must have been what they'd seen. But if that were true, why did the Indian, who proved to be their immediate salvation, wait until afternoon of the following day to come into camp?

Paul doubted that the two entries were related. Jordy Fry had probably seen an animal moving through the forest on the fourth, or maybe he'd seen nothing, considering the party's condition. The shadows of swaying branches could have been mistaken for a rescue party from Sutter's. But why hadn't John Thorburn, usually so thorough in his entries, made mention of the mistake? Maybe it was the disappointment of finding nothing there.

Another thing Paul found interesting was the "illness" first mentioned on January 5. Until that date, five people had died at the lake. By the time the rescue party arrived, only a couple of days later, eleven more had been buried. That didn't seem so improbable. In their weakened state some virulent strain of influenza could easily take its toll. But where had it come from? One or more of them must have been a carrier. Or maybe it was the Indian. Unlikely. It was usually the other way around: the Indian, who knows nothing of disease, meets the white man and is introduced to cholera, smallpox, and the like. With no immunities, half or more of his tribe is killed.

In any case, it seemed an irresponsible thing on Thorburn's part not to mention it to the rescue party. But then, Paul wondered what anyone, himself included, would have done under similar circumstances. Listening to the storm lash his cabin, he understood the reason for Thorburn's silence.

At six o'clock Paul set the diary aside to get ready for the trek to Big House. He figured he'd need the extra time.

He guessed right.

The worst of it was the wind. Without it, the snow might have been tolerable. But together they were a formidable barrier, especially in places where the trees were not as dense. There, Paul turned his body away and sliced sidelong through the blizzard. Only the close spacing of the tree lights kept him on the path, now obliterated by the soft powder.

Gail's cabin, more exposed than his own, also stood farther back from the path. He could barely make out the lights as he passed. Footprints in the snow indicated she had already left for Big House.

Worst of all was crossing the unsheltered parking area. A few token paths had been made by the snowplow, but they were already filling in. Paul couldn't identify his Cutlass among the white mounds.

When he hurried to the day room to thaw out in front of the fireplace, he saw that other residents had the same idea. Michael Whitney knelt in front of the screen like a supplicant at an altar.

"Hey, don't hog all the heat," Paul said, smiling weakly.

The cellist looked up. "I swear, if it's like this tomorrow I'll stay in the cabin and go hungry! Thank God I'm leaving Tuesday."

"Don't rub it in."

Contrasting the previous night, Paul sat at the end of Harriet Thorburn's table, as far away as possible from Gail. His immediate neighbors were Michael Whitney and Mary Sherman, a recent arrival. The genial, middle-aged woman from St. George, Utah was a teacher and historian. Paul enjoyed the company.

As if to apologize for the weather, Arthur Tyler outdid himself. His fried chicken was exceptional, the Black Forest cake after dinner the best Paul had ever tasted.

"I will definitely seek out the chef after this!" Michael exclaimed.

"Count me in," Paul said.

Later the cellist said, "So how do you figure it, Paul? Old hands like us are stuck out in the snow belt, while Mary here — who arrived yesterday, mind you — has a nice warm room in the manor!"

"That's obvious, isn't it, boys?" the woman said, laughing. "An old, chubby broad like me would probably die on the trail! Young studs like you, no problem."

Paul looked forward to talking with Mary Sherman again. His immediate plan, though, was to get back to work. Before facing the elements he and Michael went to the kitchen to heap praise on Arthur Tyler. Grinning, the massive descendant of John Thorburn's hired help put up both hands.

"Wait . . . hee-re," he said slowly, and was gone for a couple of minutes. He returned with two paper bags. "For la-ter, or . . ." He glanced around like a mischievous boy. "Or the mor-ning, case ya can't get . . . to breakfast!"

They took the heavy bags, thanked him, and left. Michael headed for the day room.

"You might find me asleep there in the morning," he said.

The plow was hard at work when Paul crossed the parking area. Snow continued to fall, but the wind had abated and made the brief walk less of an ordeal.

Gail watched for him.

She thought he would be going back to his cabin right after dinner to work on his book. That would be a while after her usual early departure. Even so, she had been to the window a few times already.

On the bed lay a second charcoal sketch. Better. Not good enough, though. Not real.

Not him.

He was coming. She could see the patch more clearly than before. As usual he glanced at No. 13 when he passed. He couldn't see her, not through the tiny slit. But he waved, because he knew.

For a moment she thought about hurrying to the door, calling him to come in. But she stayed at the window, watching, until she could no longer see him through the storm.

She gave the second sketch to the fire and began a new one.

At no other time since coming there was Paul more pleased to see the outline of No. 11. Taking off one glove, he hunted for his key. Earlier he had considered not locking the door; it didn't seem a night for looters. But he reconsidered because of the force of the storm against his cabin, since he had no desire to return to a snowdrift on the rug. He found the key as he reached the front step.

He felt it again.

The cold.

Not the engulfing cold that was the snow or the wind or the temperature on a December night in the high Sierras. Rather, the pervading chill he'd known during the first couple of days, the gelid fingers that had touched him inside. Weak, nothing like before.

But without question it was there.

Paul turned and looked around. The falling snow brought the forest alive. Glancing up, he felt disoriented. Sagging branches seemed to bend toward him, like warning fingers.

He was getting crazy again, he decided, and went inside.

It took him only a couple of minutes to turn the dying embers into an ample blaze. After this experience, he would find some use for the fireplace in his condo. There *had* to be one or two cold nights in Laguna Hills during the winter.

With clothes dripping all over the cabin, he returned to work in earnest for the first time since before Gail's visit. Satisfied with his output, he quit at twelve-thirty. He ate a ham and cheese sandwich from Arthur Tyler's bag — there were two sandwiches, another piece of Black Forest cake, and a bar of Ghirardelli milk chocolate; Arthur Tyler would be the death of him — and climbed into bed with *Trails of Promise*.

The brief remainder of John Thorburn's diary was anticlimactic, except for one thing. After reaching

Sacramento, most of the families went their separate ways. But Thorburn, in one of his briefest entries, reported the violent, accidental death of the youngest Hardman child. He was not specific.

John Thorburn's final entry was his proud proclamation of being a "new Californian."

Paul closed the book with an unsatisfied feeling.

Sunday, December 8

The snowplow worked through the night. Paul remembered coming half-awake a few times and listening to it, usually distant, once closer. Other than that, it remained still. The storm had ended. He figured they were getting a jump on the morning.

But at dawn the nor'easter had returned to its full fury. Paul stayed in his cabin all morning and worked well, in spite of the light flickering off and on. He finally moved the desk over to the side window.

At noon he heard someone on the front porch. Did *anything* deter the staff? This time he was determined Nora Hardman would stop in for a couple of minutes. He opened the door, leaning a shoulder against it.

"Bring it inside," he called. "Hurry!"

Someone in a dark hooded coat stepped into No. 11. Paul shut the door and looked up.

The handyman stood there, holding a carryall. He offered it to Paul as he peeled back the hood.

"Here's yer lunch," he said in a gruff voice.

Paul took it. "Thanks."

"What'd ya think, I was Nora?" the man asked.

"I guess so."

"She's workin' in the kitchen today. They sent me instead."

"Sorry you got stuck with it. You can stay and warm up if you want, Mr. . . ."

"Name's Landry; Joe Landry. Maybe for a minute or so."

"Go over by the fire."

Landry shook his head. "Right here's good enough."

Paul put his lunch on the desk and moved some papers around. Landry stood near the door, sullen, watching him.

"So, how long have you worked at the colony, Mr. Landry?" Paul finally asked, wishing the man was gone.

"Long time," he replied. "Mos' my life, I suppose."

"Do you like it here?"

"Somethin' to do, someplace to be." He pulled up the hood. "I gotta go."

Landry exited quickly, hardly letting in any of the storm. Paul watched through the window as he walked away. Despite the force of the wind, he moved easily. When he was gone from sight Paul resumed his work.

At one-thirty, with the storm easing, Paul trudged through the snow to Big House. A football game in the day room seemed a fair alternative to a missed afternoon in a casino. He had work to do in the library afterward, which would fill the time until dinner.

And when the ritual was done he would go to Gail Farringer's cabin. Admittedly, it was the one thing he anticipated above all else.

He joined other residents in front of the big screen. A 49ers-Falcons game became a rout for the Bay Area team by the third quarter, but the game between the Chargers and Seahawks remained in doubt until the final minute. A few wagers on the former gave Paul a profitable afternoon.

Robert Kingsley, the artist, lost five dollars to him. Paying him, he said good-naturedly, "An extra day here and already it's costing me!"

"What do you mean?" Paul asked.

"I was supposed to leave this morning." He gestured toward a window that overlooked part of the circular driveway in front of Big House. "Fat chance. Walter said they don't even bother clearing these roads until after a storm is over."

"You could be stuck here for days!"

"Walter thinks it'll end tomorrow, so I'm hoping for Tuesday morning. I can live with it."

"Hope that doesn't happen later this month," Paul said. "I'm cutting it fine, trying to get my kids right before Christmas."

Kingsley shrugged. "Good luck."

Jane Tyler oversaw a study hall crowd of one as Paul arrived. Mary Sherman sat at a corner table, enclosed in a fortress of thick leather-bound books. She waved Paul over.

"Quite a collection, I must say!" she exclaimed, gesturing around the room. "Nothing like it in St. George."

"Have you been at it long?" he asked.

"All blessed day. Didn't realize it was this close to dinner till you came in and I looked at my watch."

Jane Tyler shushed them with an admonishing finger. Mary suppressed a laugh, winked at Paul, and sank behind her literary bastion. Paul gathered what he needed and sat down at a nearby table.

By the time he was done, Mary had said good-bye and left. There was still half an hour until dinner. Paul thought about returning to the day room. Instead he wandered over to the section of John Thorburn's works and began thumbing through some of them. He read a sentence here, a page there, not sure what he was expecting to find. Nowhere did Thorburn make more than a passing reference to being stranded in the Sierras.

"Interested in our founder, are you, Mr. Fleming?"

Jane Tyler appeared from a narrow aisle between rows of tightly crammed shelves. Paul nodded and said, "I just finished reading his diary. Oh, I read it before, of course, in school."

"Of course."

"Maybe you can answer a question for me."

"About John Thorburn? Anything."

"It's something he wrote." Paul extracted a copy of *Trails of Promise*, found the January 4 entry, and read it aloud. "Do you have any idea what they saw?"

"Oh, that. Yes, certainly I know. After all, Noah Tyler saw it too." She paused.

"What was it?"

"The Indian. It was the Indian who brought them the food and helped them survive while they waited for the rescue party."

"But according to Thorburn he didn't show up until the next day."

"It *was* the Indian, Mr. Fleming. He came upon the cabins late in the afternoon. In those years his people had not seen many whites. He watched them and knew they were in trouble, but he was too frightened to help. So he returned to his village and told the chief, who sent him back the next day with supplies. That was what happened."

"But how come Thorburn made no mention of it?"

"It was that very evening when some of his people started showing symptoms of the illness. As leader he was preoccupied with their wellbeing, and his diary was secondary. He didn't write again until the following night."

It made sense, Paul thought. Sort of. In any case it seemed to put Jane Tyler on the defensive. Maybe it was time to be done with the matter.

"Well, thanks for enlightening me," he told her.

"Consider this, Mr. Fleming," she said, persisting. "Although John Thorburn's reputation for thoroughness is well warranted, I can tell you that many things on the journey from Missouri were not chronicled. Oh, I suppose they weren't that important. But if all the stories handed down to us were put on paper, *Trails of Promise* would have to be published in volumes."

"Thanks again," Paul said, sliding the diary back onto the shelf.

The librarian nodded curtly and returned to her work. Paul picked up his briefcase and started for the door. He knew she was watching him. Even as he went out into the central hall he could feel her gaze.

He wondered what button he had pushed in the prim, bookish Jane Tyler.

He looked at Nancy Thorburn's painting. Was he the only artist-in-residence so fascinated by it? People walked past and glanced at it, as they did with all the *objets d'art* in the hall's eclectic collection. To them it was just one more.

Despite its size he thought that by now he'd isolated each brush stroke on the canvas, every puff of frosty air, the cracks on the wagon wheels. Then he would discover something new.

Like now.

In the background on the far left, amid a hazy, almost surrealistic pine forest, stood a figure. Unmistakably a man; dark, but not a silhouette, because there were features. They were so minute as to be barely seen by the naked eye. Paul leaned closer, studying it.

"You want to borrow my specs or something?"

He jumped. Mary Sherman stood next to him, smiling.

"Jeez, I had no idea you were there!" he exclaimed.

"Sorry about that. Great painting, huh? I noticed it the first day."

I'm glad someone else appreciates it."

"Been watching you for a minute. The way you were looking at it reminds me of an old Rod Serling story."

"How's that?"

"It was about this Nazi-in-hiding. Seems that he's fascinated by a painting of a fisherman in a rowboat on a calm mountain lake. He stares at it endlessly, even wills himself into it a couple of times. When the Israelis finally catch up with him he decides that now he'll stay in it forever. He sneaks into the museum at night, not knowing the exhibits have been switched around. So instead of the fisherman he becomes a concentration camp victim consumed by flames for all eternity."

"I remember that," Paul said. He nodded toward the painting. "Can't say I'd like to be part of this one. Come on, I'll walk you to the dining room."

"I stopped in there before," she said. "Looks like it's you, me, and Michael again."

Paul shook his head. "That's impossible, it's never the same."

"Trust me, the little name cards are in the same place."

Mary was right. They were back at the first table. At six-thirty, instead of the grand procession, Walter McClain hurried in alone.

"Ms. Thorburn won't be joining us tonight," he said. "Oh, it's nothing to be alarmed about. A slight cold, that's all. She sends her regrets and hopes you all enjoy dinner."

Gail Farringer was not there. She had never been late, and only one time had Paul arrived before her. Perhaps, after the anticipation, tonight wasn't going to happen. He tried not to think about it.

During the first course he asked Mary, "So what were you up to with that formidable-looking stack in the library? Or is your new project a secret?"

"Not as much as yours!" she replied good-naturedly. "Actually I've been kicking around a few ideas. The one I like most is a study of the Mormons during the gold rush. You know, their involvement in it, their influence. They played a big part in the opening of the West and all, but you don't hear about them as much in the context of the forty-niners. Thought it might be interesting, and I've already come up with a few colorful characters."

"Sounds like a good idea to me," Michael said.

"Likewise," Paul agreed. "I take it you enjoy research?"

"Love it!"

"It involves a lot of detective work. Do you ever think of yourself as one?"

"Are you kidding? My heroine is Jessica Fletcher on *Murder, She Wrote.*"

Paul thought for a moment then said, "I have a proposition for you."

"Well, I'm old, chubby, and married, but what the heck!"

Michael nearly choked on his salad. Paul grinned then recited from memory John Thorburn's entry of January 4, 1846. He explained his curiosity over the events of those couple of days, as well as the unsatisfying explanation offered him by Jane Tyler. Mary was interested.

"Too many holes in that," she finally said. "Right off the bat, if it *was* an Indian, the only way they would have spotted him was if he wanted to be seen, which is doubtful. But even if it was, there's no way he could've gotten back to his village, gathered up supplies, and returned by noon the next day."

"Why not?"

"I'm sure the Indian was a Washo. This was their hunting ground then. The Washo made their camps — lots of little ones — mostly on the eastern slopes of the Sierras, the Nevada side, although there were some who stayed in California during the winter, on meadows down toward the foothills. Either way it was a long trek, especially at this elevation with all the storms that had hit. You said it was late afternoon when they supposedly saw him?"

"That's what she told me."

"Then the daylight was almost gone. That cinches it, because he wouldn't have traveled at night. He would've just camped nearby."

"How come?" Michael asked.

"Monsters. Creatures of darkness, whatever. The mountains swarmed with them, so the Washo believed. They hid behind the trees, lurked under the surface of every lake and stream. No, that fellow would have stayed put. Even his proximity to the white devils would have been preferable."

"So the question still remains, what did they see?" Paul mused. "And why did they pass that story down?"

"It's a mystery, that's for sure," Mary said.

"Why don't you ask Walter?" Michael suggested. "He seems to know everything. Or better yet, Harriet Thorburn?"

Paul shook his head. "We'll get the same story. I would bet on it."

"I agree," Mary said.

"Besides, talking about it really set that woman off. No, we need another approach. Mary — "

"I'm way ahead of you, dear boy. Do some research into the Thorburn party incident, some textbook sleuthing, if you will. Find out if any *funny business* went on up here."

Paul smiled. "I wouldn't get so melodramatic. But that's the idea. I'm aware that the ordeal of the Thorburn party was overshadowed in history by the Donners. Still, anything written on it would more than likely be here."

Mary rubbed her hands together. "This'll be fun. It may take me a couple of days, since I'm still doing my own work."

Paul nodded. "Sure, no problem."

"Well, I wish you two luck," Michael said. "Since I'm leaving Tuesday, I won't be around to hear the ending."

"It keeps snowing like this," Mary said, "you'll be around way past the ending!"

With the matriarch absent, Walter McClain dismissed the hall half an hour earlier than usual. Paul said good night to the others. He lingered until everyone was gone then stopped in the kitchen to heap more praise upon the appreciative Arthur Tyler. An even heavier bag became his reward.

Snow fell lightly as Paul hurried across the parking area. The thermometer outside the service entrance read 16°, but the wind had died down. Salt crunched under his boots as he quickened his pace. The plow had been busy, for the path was clear except for a dusting of the new powder.

He could feel his heart pumping as No. 13 loomed ahead, and he knew it was not from the exertion. Smoke curled from the chimney. Good, she was there.

Someone walked toward him on the footpath.

He had not yet turned off for the cabin. He slowed, waiting for whoever it was.

The handyman.

They both approached one of the tree lights. He knew it was Joe Landry even before he saw the man's face.

"Working late?" he asked.

The scowling man nodded. "Makin' sure it was clear all the way to your place. The other guy sometimes only does half a job if you don't watch him." He pointed at the bag. "Musta been real nice to Arthur, huh? That crazy bastard."

"Well, good night," Paul said, walking off.

Landry shrugged. "Yeah."

Ten yards up the path, Paul glanced over his shoulder. Landry stood there, watching him. Paul walked on until he could no longer see No. 13. Then he stopped and waited, the frozen night clawing at him.

Gail wanted it this way. She had asked him to be sure no one saw him going to her cabin. Before, he would have only done it for her. But when he'd seen the handyman, he'd known it was what he wanted too. He didn't know why. He only knew that, for them, it was the right way.

For now.

A minute later he started back slowly. Soon he could see down the footpath. It was empty. But he continued to look around until he stood in front of the cabin.

Turning, he strode to the door.

CHAPTER SEVEN

Sketch number five.

Gail stepped back to have a better look. Still not perfect, but it had always been hard to please herself. Maybe something about the turn of the mouth. . . Anyway, she hoped he would like it. She laid it face down on the desk.

He stood at the door now, tapping urgently. For a moment she hesitated, afraid. Not of him but of what she had to do, what she had never done before.

What she had never spoken of. To anyone.

She knew she could talk to Paul Fleming. And she had to do it, because the Dream would kill her if she didn't.

She opened the door to the frozen night. Paul looked behind him then hurried in.

"Hi," he said. "It's cold out there."

"I saw what you did with that man," she told him. "Thank you."

"You weren't — "

"— at dinner, no. I wasn't. There was something I had to do."

He held out the bag. "I brought you this. Right from the kitchen of Chef Tyler."

"That was nice of you. Take your coat off and warm up by the fire."

He looked around. "If it wasn't for your things I'd swear I was in my own cabin. The only obvious difference is that you've got the Remington."

"I like your Wieghorst better."

"Where is your work? I'm interested to see what you do."

"Another time, Paul." She was defensive. "Maybe I'll show you them . . . later. Look on the desk. I made that for you. It's not a big deal."

He turned over the page from her sketchpad. He and Jeannie once had their portraits done by a sidewalk artist in Sausalito, but nothing as good as this. In the brief time they had spent together, Gail had memorized his face: the birthmark by his left ear, the tiny cleft in his chin, the nearly invisible scar on his forehead from a childhood fall. She had captured him as he once had been, as he hoped to be again. This was how she perceived him. It was the only way she could. The charcoal image smiled — not broadly, but with warmth and humor that bordered on the mischievous.

Paul Fleming was looking at the inside of himself.

"I . . . it's excellent," he said, touched. "Thanks."

"We'll figure out some way to protect it when you go outside."

She sat down in front of the fireplace. He looked at the sketch one more time then joined her. They were silent, Gail's chin resting on her knees as she stared at the flames. Paul did not intrude on her thoughts.

Finally she said, "Minnesota."

"That's where you're from," he said.

She nodded. "I was born in St. Paul but grew up in Devon, about thirty miles north. It's an upscale little town. My husband was Lyle Farringer. We'd known each other since we were children. He was a big man in high school. Voted Most Likely to Succeed at Just About Everything. All the people said we were the perfect couple.

"We went to the University of Minnesota together and got married after graduation. Lyle went on to law school; I worked in an art supplies store. It wasn't like I was trying to support us. Lyle's parents were wealthy and had set us up quite nicely. The job was a part-time thing. Mostly I took art classes and worked on my paintings.

"Lyle's career had been programmed from day one. Within five years of passing the bar he became a junior partner in a prestigious Minneapolis law firm, compliments of his father. I opened a gallery, showed some of my own things, but mostly other artists' work. Really, I wasn't very good and I accepted it. We had a big house with all the trimmings, belonged to everything we were supposed to. The ultimate yuppie dream come true, I suppose.

"We had a son. His name was Todd." Gail paused, breathed deeply. "You couldn't tell his baby pictures apart from his father's. Lyle called Todd his clone. He loved him so much.

"Just before Todd's sixth birthday we took a vacation. We traveled a lot. Lyle was into photography, would take hundreds of pictures every trip. We went to Costa Nueva. It was my idea. I'd vacationed there with my parents as a girl and had wonderful memories of it. They wanted to go to Disney World, but I got my way." She shook her head. "Just *Disney World*, for God's sake. It's all they wanted."

"When . . . was this?" Paul asked hesitantly.

"Late summer, five years ago."

"Oh, Gail, no!"

She nodded. "So you know about Costa Nueva. Beautiful island paradise, one of the most popular resort places in the world since the turn of the century. Then a revolution, and for ten years the country was shut down. Another revolution, and the good guys are back in. Every television station is playing that commercial with the dancers and the catchy song. We were lucky to get reservations two months in advance. Lucky . . .

"We stayed at the Hotel Presidente. It was a new one and very luxurious. The first three days were wonderful: sightseeing, fishing, shopping. Todd loved the fishing. Lyle kept running out of film, he shot so many pictures of old stone fortresses, the wall around the harbor, the marketplace, even the inside and outside of the hotel. He finally told me what a great idea I'd had.

"Of course we heard reports of another revolution brewing. But it's an everyday thing in countries like that. The official word was that a handful of peasants armed with stones and pitchforks were causing trouble in some remote mountain province. There was no threat at all to Cartago, the capital city, where we were staying.

"On the fourth day I got up early. Todd was still asleep. Lyle was awake but too comfortable to move. I told him I was going over to the marketplace, about ten blocks from the hotel. He said he and Todd would meet me there in two hours, at a restaurant we liked. I looked forward to getting in some serious shopping.

"An hour later the noisy marketplace became silent as gunshots filled the air. Cartago fell into a panic. People screamed; everyone was running. I ran too, back to the hotel. Jeeploads of government troops passed me. I tried asking people what was happening. No one knew.

"Then I reached the hotel and saw that it was the center of whatever was going on. The troops had already cordoned it off. Two bodies were sprawled on the front steps by the main entrance. My heart sank when I saw that. I told people that my family was inside and again tried to get information. All I could learn was that someone had seized the hotel, that employees and guests were being held as . . . hostages!

"For an hour nothing happened. That feeling of utter helplessness is indescribable. Someone said that the terrorists — revolutionaries, they called themselves — were in touch with authorities by phone. But nobody seemed to know what was going on. At least there weren't any other gunshots during that time.

"The van from CBS News had gotten there right at the beginning. They were the only network with a correspondent on the island, and that was because Maury Levin was doing a feature on Costa Nueva's rejuvenated tourist industry. We had run into him at the pool once, and again at dinner. An interesting man, very intense. Now he was doing reports from the perimeter of the barricade. I spoke to him for a couple of seconds but found that he was as much in the dark as everyone else.

"Then an official told Levin that the terrorists were demanding a reporter and cameraman so they could voice their plight to the world. Levin accepted without hesitation; the cameraman was more reluctant but finally agreed. They went in, the reporter with his hands above his head, the cameraman holding his camera aloft. I walked to the van and in a couple of minutes saw what the whole world was seeing.

"The terrorists were holding the hostages — over a hundred — in the lobby. When the camera panned the room, all you could see was the backs of heads. I saw Lyle and Todd and tried to imagine what my child, so sheltered and safe all his life, could possibly be thinking just then. At least they were still alive.

"Maury Levin interviewed the leader, tried to find out what his organization was and what it wanted. The man's tirade, partly in terrible English, made no sense. '*Yanqui* ass-kisser!' he would call the government over and over, along with other revolutionary rhetoric.

"Later they found out that this gang of fourteen thugs — *fourteen* — was acting entirely on its own. None of the worst terrorist organizations in the world claimed affiliation with them.

"Finally their demands became tangible: safe passage to the airport, lots of money, a plane to fly them to Libya. They wanted an answer by eleven. For every minute beyond that time they would kill a hostage. The leader told this to

Maury Levin, who was translating it when the bastard gunned him down.

"No one knows why it started then. People in the remote van were screaming. I watched the monitor and saw them being butchered. For whatever reason, the camera froze on Lyle and Todd. My son looked up and cried *'Mommy!'*

"Then I watched them die."

Gail's body trembled; tears streaked her face. Paul wanted to hold her, but she stood up and backed away, then turned and stared at the floor.

He knew all about the Costa Nueva Massacre. He'd researched it and given thought to a story or screenplay about it, then decided to leave the tragedy alone. Other writers would doubtless exploit it, he figured. And they did, for it spawned a few books and a poorly done TV movie. Sixty-three hostages, more than half Americans, had been killed. Eight Costa Nueva soldiers had died in the ensuing raid, as well as all the terrorists.

"It was my idea, Paul," Gail said softly. "They wanted to go to Disney World."

"Gail, listen — "

"And it wasn't just them!" She turned. "I hadn't told Lyle yet because I wasn't sure. Afterward I found out that I was pregnant. I miscarried, of course."

Paul sighed. "No."

She grabbed tissues from a box on the mantel and wiped her face as she sat down again. "You don't have to listen to any more of this," she said. "I'll understand."

He started to put his hand on hers, hesitated, then did it when she gave no sign that she would resist. "I'll stay with you. And I don't mean for just now."

She nodded. Her mouth twitched, then she said, "There's a bottle of wine in the desk drawer. Do you mind?"

He poured them each a generous amount of three-year-old white Zinfandel. He needed it. Gail sipped hers slowly and stared at the fire, composing herself.

"The time right after is a blur," she continued. "I was sedated a lot, even during the funeral. People tried to be helpful, understanding. I wanted no part of it. They urged me to go to shrinks. I tried one, but that made it worse. Soon I had alienated my friends, then Lyle's family, finally my own. I had nobody. That was the way I wanted it.

"I left Minnesota a year after Costa Nueva, and I've lived in a hundred places since then. Two or three months at a time, that's it."

"Where are you now?"

"Woodland Hills."

"You're in the Valley?"

"Yes. I've been in California longer than anywhere else. It's a place where it's so easy to be anonymous. All I do is paint. There's plenty of money left over from my other life, so I don't have to work. I would never be able to if it meant being around people."

"Do you think you're ready to change that?" he asked. "Is that why you told me?"

"Maybe. I suppose. There are other reasons." She looked at him. "Paul?"

"Yes?"

"I don't want to talk anymore."

"Do you want me to leave?"

"I want you . . . to hold me. Just hold me."

He put his arms around her. She stiffened, then eased, and her head lolled on his chest. He held her for more than an hour, sometimes touching her hair with his lips. Once, she hugged him tightly. Another time she buried her face in his sweater and sobbed softly.

"I'll show you my paintings, if you want," she finally said.

Some were in the closet, others under the bed. She withdrew eight canvases and propped them up. Paul looked at them, stunned, trying to remember that this was the woman who had done the sketch of him.

The colors that dominated her paintings were red and gray, in all their shades. Her subjects were misshapen people, mostly elongated, as if they had been stretched on some medieval torture device. While many of them had features that were vague, the eyes were always precise: opened wide, staring ahead or glancing back, always in fear.

In fear of what pursued them, of what threatened them.

Dark formless things, mostly in the background. Twisted shapes that melded into one another until you couldn't tell if you looked at one or many. The gray hues blended together so skillfully it was impossible to see where the change was happening.

She had painted walls also, broad barriers of dripping mortar over which some of the formless things scrambled. And large buildings done in crimson with more of them in the windows and people reaching out with impossibly long arms.

Large buildings like hotels.

In one painting a clock floated amid the colors. The numbers on its face were precise; so were the tiny lines between them.

But the clock had no hands.

Gail Farringer painted nightmares. Although no expert, Paul knew her work was brilliant. And so disturbing.

So full of pain.

"Do you still want to see me, Paul?" she asked, not looking at him.

"Of course."

"Then I'll come to your cabin after dinner tomorrow — if that's all right with you."

"You know it is."

She leaned over and kissed him on the cheek. He wanted to take her in his arms but restrained himself. She backed away to the desk and picked up the sketch.

"I'll put this between the pages of my pad so it won't get damaged. Don't worry, I have another."

He went through the ritual of putting on his outer garments — they were still damp and felt cold — tucked the pad under his arm, and walked to the door. Before he opened it, Gail looked outside.

"It's clear," she said. "Good night, Paul. Thank you."

He hugged her. She first stood with her arms at her sides, then returned it. They separated, and Paul — still trying to comprehend this woman's anguish — went out into the night.

Gail didn't watch him from the window this time. She hurried to the bed and fell on it. Sobs racked her body until her chest hurt. She stopped only when no tears remained.

The paintings bothered her. She thought about stuffing them into the fireplace but changed her mind and put them in the closet. Hungry, she ate some of the food Paul had brought. After washing her face and brushing her teeth she peeled off her clothes, donned an old flannel nightgown, and climbed into bed.

The Dream would not come, and she would have a long night's sleep. It might never come again because of her courage.

And because of him.

Paul, preoccupied with images of Gail, gave no thought to what might be awaiting him at No. 11.

It was there again, still not nearly as strong as the first couple of times, but disturbing enough. This time it annoyed him, more than anything else. Nothing much beyond Gail's revelation could shock him that night.

"Bullshit," he said, and continued past his cabin through the light snowfall.

Toward the source.

To the last tree light, where the path veered away from the creek. Almost to the trees that formed the gateway to the clearing.

A dark figure emerged from the sentinel pines. Paul stopped. "Who's there," he called. "Landry, is that you?"

The handyman walked toward him. Paul took a few steps back.

"You ain't polite," the gruff voice said, "passin' someone who's wanted to see you all night."

He pointed past Paul, who spun around. Two yards away, Harriet Thorburn crawled through the snow. Or something that wore her clothes, for under a head of white stringy hair was a gray, leathery death's-head. Fleshless fingers reached for him.

The mouth of the death's-head snapped open, and it spoke. "I'm not feeling well tonight, Mr. Fleming, that's why I can't be at dinner."

Something dark gushed from the mouth, staining the snow. Paul could not move. The bony fingers curled around his ankle.

"Holy shit!"

This time Paul sat on the foot of the bed. He got up slowly and washed his face at the sink.

Baby Ben said it was ten minutes to four.

It had been so real. What was happening to him? Here he was, playing some small part in Gail Farringer's courageous quest to heal herself, and he had begun to have trouble separating nightmares from reality.

Though tired, he avoided the bed for a few minutes. The fire had nearly gone out. He rekindled it, watched it grow, then went back to sleep.

Monday, December 9

Neither the alarm nor the snowplow at his door could rouse him the next morning at six o'clock, and Paul only made it to breakfast just before they took the food away.

Around midmorning the lurking storm emerged from its cover. For the next hour it was worse than at any other time in the past few days. The electricity went out, and soon after that the backup power. Then, as the cabin grew colder, Paul realized the pilot light in the furnace had died.

He groaned. "Jesus."

He quickly stoked the fire and brought his work over to the rug, which he hadn't moved since Gail had put it there. Surprisingly he managed to continue working and did not even realize that the storm's fury had begun to subside.

Soon he heard a noise on the porch. One of the staff bringing lunch, he assumed, Joe Landry, probably. This time the man could leave it; he had no desire to see him.

A loud knock on the door startled him. "Mr. Fleming? It's me, Nora Hardman."

Paul let the woman in. "You're being bold today," he said good-naturedly.

"Hafta let everyone know what's goin' on," she replied, slipping off a heavy backpack. "You probably figured it already. No power, a break in the gas line somewhere . . . and our big old generator gave up the ghost! On top of that the phones are dead. Walter's got a ham radio that runs on a battery pack, in case things get real bad."

Paul nodded. "Real bad."

"Anyway, the longest I remember everything bein' out was five, six hours, and that was durin' a terrible storm back in the late sixties."

"That's not comforting."

"First thing, did you turn off the gas valve on your furnace?"

"No."

"When it came on later, you woulda known. Go ahead and do that. I got some stuff for you." She opened the backpack. "A flashlight, some extra batteries, and candles, just in case. You got enough matches?"

"There's plenty on the mantel."

"What about your wood bin?"

"It's half full."

"I'll bring in more so it can start dryin' out."

"No way," Paul said. "You have enough to do. I'll get the wood."

"You sure?"

"Positive."

"Thanks, Mr. Fleming. Jeez, why ain't they all like you? Okay listen, we're gonna try to keep the paths as clear as possible so's everyone can get to Big House. We got a couple of portable generators, and the day room is heated up, so you're welcome there anytime. In case the power stays off, you might want to walk over before dark. Anyway, that's about it. Trust me, this is normal for up here. You get used to it."

"I thought the storm was supposed to be over today."

"That's what the radio keeps sayin', but who knows? Oh, there's one other thing."

"What's that?"

"Your lunch."

Nora Hardman went back out into the snow, which still fell steadily but without the force of the wind behind it. Paul ate his lunch by the fire and thought about being stranded in the high Sierras. Stranded? The colony had plenty of food and wood. There was a town nearby for additional supplies. The roads would be cleared within a few hours of the storm's end. In the event of some emergency, Walter McClain could summon help on his radio. When you thought about it, the situation hardly seemed menacing at all.

When you thought about it in comparison to the Thorburn party, it sounded like a vacation.

Stranded. They'd had no food or adequate shelter. There had been no roads for them to clear, even if they'd had the strength to do it, which they hadn't, for it had been sapped by many months of traveling across the American wilderness. No means of communication. Their only choices had been to starve or freeze. People in that circumstance would do anything to survive.

Anything.

The Donner party had proven that. It was a matter of record.

But what had John Thorburn and his people done? Were they just lucky, or had something else played a part in their salvation?

What had they seen through the trees on January 4, 1846?

Sherri Jordan's purple Volkswagen . . .

It was *the Indian, Mr. Fleming.*

. . . in the old livery stable.

Nasty storms. December . . .

A crackling log jarred Paul from his thoughts. He shook his head and swore at himself. Looking at the half-finished sandwich, he decided he wasn't hungry anymore. He recalled Nora Hardman's advice and brought in two armfuls of wood, spreading the logs out on the cabin floor. Finding no other jobs he could do, he got back to work.

At two o'clock the electricity came back on. Paul tried the gas, but it remained off. Outside, the storm had diminished to gentle flurries. A short time later even those had stopped.

By three — incredibly — the sun had broken through and the temperature pushed into the thirties. The snowplow sputtered up to the cabin. Paul twisted the valve on the furnace, heard the rush of escaping gas, and lit the pilot. If not for the walls of snow lining the path it would have been hard to imagine that a storm of three days' duration had just come to a halt.

At the end of the colony work day Paul did fifty pushups, three times that many situps, and a few other exercises he'd recently begun in earnest after catching a glimpse of himself in the mirror. He missed his bike rides, his morning jogs on the beach. There were sacrifices to be made for his art, but that didn't mean he had to sacrifice his body to gobs of Arthur Tyler's German chocolate cake.

He knew this experience was necessary; it had rejuvenated his creativity. But he was a southern Californian, no doubt of it, and in less than three weeks — after he picked up Jason and Bree — he would be home.

As he did deep knee bends Gail walked past his cabin, a sketchpad under her arm. She moved slowly, her gaze on the path. Paul saw her for only a moment through the fogged window. He wiped a larger hole. She was farther up the path, following it away from Leanna Creek to the sentinel pines, where for a moment she hesitated, then passed between them.

Her spot again, he thought. This was the first time in a couple of days that she could get out. But there must be a ton of snow on the clearing. The old log would be buried. . .

Gail emerged from the trees, walking fast. She nearly stumbled a few times, following her own deep prints back to where the path was clear. Paul watched, curious, as she stopped and glanced over her shoulder.

Finally she shook her head and continued along the footpath. He backed away from the window. She didn't look at his cabin when she passed.

Gail knew something seemed wrong about the clearing.

Would she be reluctant now to see him that night? He hoped not.

Paul started for Big House after five — seriously overdressed this time, but he didn't care. He phoned Jason and Bree after learning that service had been restored. The connection was not perfect, but they managed. He had less luck with Gary Marks, having to shout to be heard. Before finishing their conversation, they were disconnected.

Half the residents were in the day room, but not Mary Sherman. Paul wanted to talk to the woman and didn't think they'd have a chance at dinner, assuming Harriet Thorburn was back. In the library he saw only Kathy Parrish and a man at work. Dodging Jane Tyler's cold gaze — was the woman actually watching him, or was he crazy? — he walked through the library and into the outer corridor.

Mary had to be in her room. He climbed to the second floor, where a plain service door opened into a carpeted hallway as luxurious as the rest of Big House. Silver sconces without candlesticks hung on both walls. Six small, elegant crystal chandeliers lit the hall. Each guest door was painted a light shade of blue, with a brass number. The wallpaper throughout was a subtle floral pattern.

He knocked on the door of No. 203. Mary looked most pleased to see him. "Come in!" she exclaimed. "Just ignore the mess. Two things I never won any awards for were cooking and housekeeping."

"You sure I'm not interrupting you?"

"Not at all. Sit down."

She moved some books off a chair. Texts and papers lay strewn everywhere, even on the floor. The room was small and, contrasting remarkably with the hallway, appeared as spartan as his own cabin. The fireplace seemed more decorative than functional. Paul was glad he had decided to remain in No. 11.

"I was thinking about you and Michael when that last storm hit this morning," she said.

"Well, I survived it, and Michael's down in the day room."

She nodded. "I saw him before. You know, Paul, I'm starting to believe that he *does* sleep there!"

Paul grinned. "I was wondering if you dug up anything."

"About what we discussed? Not a whole lot. But it wasn't for want of trying. I spent a few hours on the Thorburn party and anything relevant to it. First thing I did was reread the diary of their seven weeks here."

"What do you think?"

"You know, if it wasn't for Jane Tyler's weird reaction, I would think you're way off base. I read where John Thorburn's diary was published with little or no editing, for the sake of authenticity, and I believe it. Some of the entries in the last couple of weeks tend to ramble. He suddenly gets closer to God, that sort of thing. So if he *thinks* he sees something, writes it down then forgets to amend it, that would be in keeping with where he was physically and emotionally.

"Aside from that, the Thorburn party incident is little more than a footnote in most of the texts. Some give it a paragraph or two, others a page. But in all cases their primary reference is *Trails of Promise*."

"Big deal," Paul said. "So where do you go from here?"

"Oh, I've hardly scratched the surface, dear boy! There are a lot more obscure works to delve into, and many of them are here, like you said. The only thing . . ." She paused.

"What?"

"That blasted librarian always seems to be looking over my shoulder! It got to where I was thinking of ways to throw her off the track. Then I thought, why should she care what I'm researching?"

Paul laughed. "Sounds like you're getting as paranoid as me."

"But that's the reason you're not pursuing it, right?"

"Yes," he admitted. "You're a better detective than I thought."

"Paul, what's this about?"

"I don't know. Really. I suppose that if I wasn't here, where it happened, I would hardly care. But I *am* here. My cabin is not far from where the Thorburns and McClains spent those seven weeks."

Mary nodded. "And you're feeling the ghosts, aren't you?"

"Feeling the ghosts?"

"Once, I led a research group on a field project. We retraced the entire route of Chief Joseph and the Nez Percé Indians in 1877 as they tried to escape from the U.S. Army and make it to Canada. More than fifteen hundred miles. There are paved roads along some of the path now: towns, people, billboards, smokestacks. But a lot of it was exactly as it had been over a hundred years ago. We rode horses, and sometimes mules. It was along those trails, especially when I was by myself, that the wind would carry the sounds of warriors in battle, the mourning wails of squaws, and the cries of their babies as their bellies went unfilled during the terrible trek. I was *feeling the ghosts*, Paul. Does that make sense?"

"Yes. But what I feel over there is . . . well, it's so unnerving. You want to get as far away from it as you can!"

"Paul, remember what happened in that cabin. People died; everyone was starving. Considering that, what you're feeling isn't unusual."

He shrugged. "It's something else."

"What?"

He looked at her. "Mary, the Indian tribe that once lived here — "

"The Washo."

"Yes. Could this area have held some significance for them? Any of the streams, maybe the lake itself?"

"It's possible. Lake Tahoe did, of course. It was the center of their universe. I'll check it out."

"I can do that."

"Nah, I'm having too much fun. Okay, enough of this. I allow myself two brandies a day and haven't had the first one yet. Let's go down."

They found Michael with Kathy Parrish and Robert Kingsley. "Good news," the cellist announced. "I'll be getting out of here tomorrow after all. Walter says the roads should be clear all the way to the interstate."

"It'll be a mass exodus from the mountain in the morning," Kathy said. "Four people are leaving, and no one else is expected up here until after Christmas. It's going to get even quieter."

Paul's dinner place was at the third table, between Thea Douglas and an empty chair. Sitting where he was, he couldn't help looking at Gail. Although dressed the same, she seemed . . . different. Something about the face, or maybe her hair. He wasn't sure. Their eyes met a couple of times, but unlike before she didn't turn away as quickly.

He wished dinner were over so he could be with her again.

Harriet Thorburn arrived on schedule. This time, as if trying to make up for having missed the previous evening, she started her reminiscences before the salad had been put down.

Thea groaned. "One more week of *this* and I can repair to the bosom of my many friends and many cats!"

"But you'll be back another time," Paul said.

She nodded. "I suppose you're right."

Gail left the hall only a few minutes before Harriet Thorburn ended the nightly ritual. Paul caught up to Michael in the day room after helping himself to a bottle of wine from a well-stocked rack behind the bar.

"What time are you leaving in the morning?" he asked the musician.

"Early," Michael said, rather emphatically.

"How about breakfast at six-thirty?"

"Sure, that's fine. But aren't you going to join us now? We have a little party planned."

Paul clapped him on the arm. "Sorry, but I'm on a roll and I want to get back to work. See you in the morning."

It was 28° outside, mild, no wind. Someone had graciously cleared off the snow and ice from the cars. Paul started up the Cutlass and let it run while he searched in the trunk for one of his books to give to Gail.

He hadn't expected to see her again until later, but she walked into the parking area with an armful of canvases. Her car, a teal-blue Nissan Sentra, was parked a few spaces from his. He watched her open the trunk and throw the paintings in. She noticed him, glanced around the parking lot, saw no one.

Gail waved, smiled, then closed her trunk and hurried back to the footpath.

CHAPTER EIGHT

The night felt good. Gail wanted to run forever but contented herself with a bracing jog to No. 13.

She felt different. The pain of Costa Nueva would never go away. But she had begun to understand that it was all right. Lyle and Todd would be part of her soul and her heart for the rest of her life. What she chose to do with that life was entirely up to her.

That morning she had awakened from eight hours of dreamless sleep and jogged to Big House. She'd enjoyed the early morning chill and moderate snowfall. Later, when the storm grew angrier, she had sat in front of the fire looking through the contents of a box she'd held onto for years, only opening it to put in more things. They were books, magazine articles, newspaper stories about Costa Nueva. Also, letters from sympathetic strangers — including one from the President — though only a few, for she had destroyed so many back then. She had spent an hour with the material, all she could handle.

But she would open the box again.

Drained, she had taken a nap. Some of the darker images had returned in desultory fragments, but mostly her dreams were of good times with Lyle and Todd. She saw them running again, smiling. All three of them smiling, which reminded her how it was done. That was the way she wanted to remember them, not face down on a floor.

Shortly before waking she had dreamed of Paul.

In the middle of the afternoon she finally set up the painting she was working on. This time it felt as if she were looking at someone else's work. She tried doing some things with the background, but it didn't feel right.

That was why she had decided to go to the clearing.

After those few days when she'd felt nothing there, it had begun to return. She had utilized the black motivating force, weak as it was, and at first it was all right. Then it had grown stronger at the same time that she was changing, until its effect on her seemed different from before. Where it had guided her hand in brushing the colors of her pain onto the canvas, now it became the *cause* of more pain, threatening to rip her apart.

That afternoon she had broken free before it could happen. She'd never go back there again. She swore that.

One part of her life was ending; another was beginning. It frightened her, but excited her too.

Paul had walked past ten minutes before. Despite what she'd told him, she couldn't wait. Throwing on her coat, she hurried outside.

He wouldn't mind. She knew that too.

Near his cabin, she felt it. Much stronger at night. She knew it from walks she'd taken during the first weeks of her residency. "No, damn you, no!" she told the night. "You won't stop me!"

And she went on.

Paul had felt it too. Not as keenly as Gail, but enough. He lingered in front of No. 11, staring up the path. Curiosity was stronger than fear. *What had happened there?*

Was he feeling the ghosts of more than just the death and despair that had been the aura of the Thorburn/McClain cabin?

The night seemed to mock his frustration. He went inside.

With Gail coming, Paul suddenly realized his cabin was a mess. He scrambled around, picking up clothes and throwing them in the closet, stacking books and papers, piling the dried-out logs into the bin.

A few minutes later Gail arrived. He had thought she might come early. He let her in and closed the door quickly.

She peeled off her coat. "Hi," she said, and smiled.

"You know, when I saw you smile in the parking area, I didn't recognize you for a minute."

"Sort of like Scrooge *after* he'd met all the ghosts, huh?"

He laughed. "Great analogy. Yeah, I guess so."

He hugged her. She gave it back without hesitation. They held each other, not saying anything for a few moments, finally separating.

Paul handed her a copy of *Summit of Fear.* "I found this for you."

"Thanks. Did you autograph it?"

"No, but I will, if you do the same to that." He indicated her sketch, which he'd hung on the wall with pushpins. "When your works are being auctioned at Sotheby's, I want to make sure I got my old age covered."

"Right." She smiled again then touched her mouth. "I better stop this, it hurts my face."

He stroked her cheek. "Don't, it looks great on you."

She looked at him, no longer smiling. "Oh, Paul!" she exclaimed, again embracing him. "Thank you. Just . . . thank you! I don't know what else to say."

"You couldn't have done it unless *you* wanted to," he said. "I think you know that."

"Nevertheless, I owe you a lot." She pulled free, reached for her purse.

"You don't owe me — "

"But I wondered if you'd settle for a Hershey's with almonds." She held up two bars.

"Consider it paid in full!" He took one. "That's great, my supply was depleted. Your rug, ma'am."

She sat in front of the fireplace. He poured two glasses of wine and joined her. She moved closer to him.

"Chablis and Hershey's," she said. "I'm not sure if white or red goes with chocolate. Are we gauche, or what?"

Paul laughed. "Who cares? You had a good day, didn't you?"

She nodded. "Yes. I didn't paint at all; I couldn't. Maybe I'm done with what you saw."

"Is that why you were putting the paintings in your car?"

"Partly. I was also making it easier on myself, since I'm leaving Wednesday morning. Less to load then."

"You're leaving Wednesday?" Paul couldn't hide his surprise. "I didn't know."

"It hadn't come up, I guess. Yeah, I've been here nearly four weeks. It felt like a lot longer — until now."

"Can I ask you something?"

"What?"

"How did you come to be up here?"

"I read an article about the Thorburn colony — what they do to encourage new talent, that sort of thing. What I liked most was what it said about the solitude in the mountains. I sent a note and got a questionnaire in the mail from Walter McClain, which I returned with some Polaroids of my work. He answered quickly, and I came up the following month."

"It wasn't easy for you to be here, was it?"

"After the first night I told Walter that I didn't want any part of Harriet Thorburn's dinner ritual. I . . . had already walked out, rather than deal with anyone. He said it was impossible, and I said fine, I'd leave in the morning. I guess he wanted me to stay, because he said that he would speak to her. The next day he offered the compromise, as you've seen it. I agreed, because I didn't want to go right back, and because I did feel comfortable in my cabin. The forest, the creek, all the mountains around. It started to snow the second week and that made it even better, sort of like . . . home."

"Did you talk to Harriet Thorburn?"

Gail scowled. "Walter insisted that an *audience* with her was required. It happened on the second night. He took me to her table. She was friendly enough, considering the trouble I'd caused. But she asked me questions, so many questions! I wasn't very cordial. One- or two-word answers; sometimes I didn't respond at all. A couple of times I thought for sure she would tell me to pack up and leave. But Walter, for whatever reason, was supportive, and I survived the interview. It had only been about fifteen minutes, but I swear it felt like hours!"

"Fifteen minutes? She talked to you for that long?"

"Yes. Why?"

"Nothing." He shook his head. "So you never spoke to any of the other residents?"

"They tried . . . like you did. Same result. After a while the word got out: 'Leave the crazy bitch alone.' Soon I was part of the woodwork. They hardly knew I was around."

"You don't believe that!" he snapped. "They talked about you, laughed when you walked out early . . ."

She shrugged, looked away. "It was my choice, and I had to live with it. Wasn't the first time."

"Tomorrow night's your last one here. If I talk to Walter and have him arrange it, will you sit with me at dinner?"

"Paul, no!" she cried, standing. He was afraid she would leave and immediately regretted saying it. "I can't, I — "

He took her hand. "Gail, I'm sorry. Please sit down."

Her body was trembling as she dropped cross-legged to the thunderbird rug. Still holding Paul's hand, she gazed at him.

"The head doctors would call my last twenty-four hours a breakthrough. Fine. But I can't take it any farther right now. There's still so much to sort out."

He nodded. "I understand."

"Everyone here has witnessed my behavior," she continued, "some for nearly a month. To change that suddenly on the last night . . . No, I'll sacrifice this residency, let them take home their stories about me. If — when I come back here another time, it'll be different."

"I believe that," he said, squeezing her hand.

"Besides . . ." She hesitated.

"What?"

"You still have more than half your time to go. I don't want you having to deal with anyone's comments about associating with me. That was why I didn't want them to see us together."

"I would have been proud for anyone to see you with me," he told her.

Gail looked into his eyes and knew that he meant it. She took his other hand. For a minute the only sound in the cabin was the crackling fire. Sometimes they glanced at it; mostly they stared at each other, trying to understand what was happening but hardly disturbed by the confusion they shared.

Finally she said, "Am I going to see you again? I mean, after Thorburn?"

"Is it what you want?" he asked.

"Yes."

"Me too."

Suddenly the thunderbird rug became their world, a stationary one, for everything else around them seemed to rush away. The fire, once near, became a faint star in the foreground of an infinite blackness. Their thoughts intertwined, and their souls, and they danced without moving, starting to become one.

Paul drew her closer. She yielded willingly. Her lips brushed his cheek with a feather's touch. She explored his face that way; he did the same. When it was again her turn she retraced her kisses, but more firmly, and he followed, going farther, under her chin, along her neck. She liked that and threw her head back and closed her eyes, hoping it would go on and on.

Then it was no longer enough. She took his head in her hands, found his lips with hers, crushed them hard. His tongue probed her cautiously. She let him know it was welcome. They thrust in and out eagerly, tasting each other, their hunger growing with each sampling. Finally, their hearts racing, they separated.

"Oh, God, Paul!"

"What should we do with this?" he asked.

Her face changed, and in it Paul read a fear not unlike what he'd seen in her work. It first surprised him; then he understood.

"You're scared, aren't you?"

Her mouth fell open but she didn't speak. She nodded rapidly; it reminded him of a child.

"We don't have to rush it, Gail," he said, touching her cheek. "It's okay."

The words finally came. "When a part of you that once died suddenly comes back to life, I'd say that's a reason to be scared. I'm all right now." She smiled. "See?"

They kissed again, harder than before, until even that could not satisfy them. Gail peeled off her sweater. Instead of the warm-up suit she wore white knit pants and a red pullover top, both of which outlined the curves of her body. Paul cupped her breasts and felt the nipples grow hard through the material. Gail undid the buttons of his Dickies shirt, then his belt. Her hand dropped casually to fondle his throbbing erection. He leaned his head back, his fingers massaging her breasts more vigorously.

They caught themselves and slowed the game down, delighting in every intricacy of what would be new only this one time. They laughed when Paul had trouble unhooking her bra in front. Then Gail struggled to restrain her hunger when his tongue laved the dark tips of her thrusting breasts. She pushed him away gently and helped him pull off his jeans. Taking his manhood in her hand, she studied it inquisitively, then touched the glistening droplets on the head and rubbed them gently over the sensitive skin.

Soon all their clothes were strewn along the perimeter of their small world. Gail stretched out across the length of the thunderbird rug. Paul, on his knees, admired the smoothness of her body with his eyes, explored it with his mouth. She made soft whimpering sounds and sometimes writhed when he touched special spots.

They changed places, Gail straddling him as she bent over to put her face near his. It was as if she had known him forever, he thought, for her tongue flicked into his ear, nearly causing his explosion before he was ready. He clutched at the sides of the rug, moaning, praying it wouldn't come yet. She felt his excitement, probed deeper. But he had anticipated that and rolled his head to the side. Then, to balance what was happening, he let go of the rug and put his hands on her breasts, first massaging them, then rolling the already hard nipples between his fingers.

"*Paul, oh, Paul!*" she gasped, stretching out beside him.

Reason and control were gone. Paul was over her, the tip of his manhood against the reddish brown triangle that was the gateway of her long-denied passion. Despite his urgency he opened her gently, his touch within the folds of her sex causing her body to tremble. She had been dry, but not now. He felt this, opened her more. She took his sticky-moist erection in her hand, first guiding it along the surface of the matted hair, then into her, taking all he had.

It hadn't been as long for Paul . . . but long enough. He thrust in and out slowly, deliberately, wanting it to happen but wishing it would go on forever. She encircled him with her legs, her fingers digging into his shoulders as her climax came in a silent burst of joy. His first pleasure was in watching her face. Then, before the tremors of her body could subside, he poured himself into her with a flood that he thought might go on and on, but finally ebbed.

They lay side by side, exhausted and happy, not spoiling the moment with words. Once again the fireplace was close by; the Wieghorst over the desk, the unused bed. Mostly back from the journey, they held on to what was left of it for as long as they could.

Finally Gail lifted her head from Paul's chest, looked at him, smiled. "Thank you," she said softly.

He smiled back. "You're welcome, it *was* my pleasure."

She was thoughtful for a few moments then said, "I think I might be ready now."

"For what?"

"Some help, someone I can talk to. Last night was a start, but I still have so much more to go."

"The fact that you recognize it may mean you don't have as far to come back as you think." He kissed her on the forehead. "I'm proud of you, Gail Farringer."

She put a hand to his cheek. "And you, you're a special person, Paul Fleming."

He shook his head. "No, not really. But I *am* your friend. By the way . . ."

"What?"

"No, dumb idea. I was going to recommend someone I know real well, a person I'm sure you'd be comfortable with, except that her office is in Irvine, not far from me. But it's a long way from Woodland Hills."

"There are some nice places to live in south Orange County. I'm not tied to the Valley. It was just another place to be. Sure, I'll give your friend a call." She rolled onto her back. "That is, if you don't mind having me for a neighbor."

He grinned. "It worked," he said to the wall. "She bought it."

She looked at him. "Oh *you* — !" she exclaimed, hitting him playfully but firmly in the stomach. He feigned agony, grabbed her, and they wrestled on the thunderbird rug. Then they kissed — long, deeply. Paul took a blanket off the bed, and they held each other beneath it, until the fire began to die. Gail glanced at the Baby Ben.

"I should be getting back," she said, and began to dress.

"You won't let me walk you to your cabin, I suppose. No one comes out this way."

"No one? What about that creepy handyman last night? I'll be okay. You get some more wood on the fire and stay warm."

When she mentioned Joe Landry, Paul suddenly thought of the clearing. He wanted to ask her about it — what she knew, what she felt. But the evening had been good, and he didn't want to ruin it.

"What are you going to do on your last day?" he asked, putting on his own clothes.

"Pack up what little stuff I have. Think, mostly, make some plans for when I get back. Maybe jog along the lake if the weather's okay. Will you come over after dinner?"

He nodded. "I'll write down some things for you: the name of my doctor friend, some people who can help you find a place, if you want to get started right away. If not, I can help you when I get back."

She finished dressing and slipped his book into her purse. They walked to the door, Gail stopping for a moment to peer out through the blinds.

"A clear night," she said. "I hope it stays like this through Wednesday."

"You'll be careful going back?" he asked.

She nodded, kissed him. "I can't wait to see you again," she whispered, and hurried outside before he could respond. He watched her run down the path, then closed the door and stood with his back against it.

"Wow," he said softly, shaking his head.

Nearly ten-thirty, and he was wide awake. He returned to his work, and a scene that had held him back now came out of his head faster than he could put it down on paper. An interlude in an otherwise violent, action-oriented story, a chance meeting between the lead character and a woman from his past.

Paul wrote until after one, then fell asleep thinking of Gail, wishing she were next to him.

Tuesday, December 10

There were no snowplows at dawn. The temperature was 20° and climbing. Waking early, Paul showered and hurried to Big House.

Robert Kingsley and another resident scheduled to leave that morning were loading their cars as Paul crossed the asphalt. "Aren't you staying for breakfast?" he asked the artist.

Kingsley laughed. "You think I would drive to Portland on an empty stomach? I'll be right in. Michael's already there."

Paul went inside, decided he was starved, and piled his plate with food. He joined Michael and Mary at the second table. Michael looked at Paul and made a face.

"Are you really going to eat all that?" he asked.

"Oh, leave him alone, Michael," Mary chided good-naturedly. "The fires of literary excellence must be fed, lest they burn out!"

"This is true," Paul said.

"Some fire," Michael said. "What is it, a fuel tank explosion?"

Mary groaned. "This is dangerous, Paul, he's actually starting to exhibit a sense of humor. The Phoenix Chamber Orchestra will never be the same!"

Michael laughed. "All right, peace. Anyway, do you believe I'm finally out of here? I must've looked out ten times during the night to see if it was snowing."

"Are you sure you can get down?" Paul asked.

Michael nodded. "Walter checked. The roads to Truckee are drivable, and the interstate is in good shape."

"Did you accomplish what you wanted up here?" Mary asked.

"That and then some!" Michael exclaimed. "Things weren't going too great for me. It was almost like . . . I was at odds with my own instrument or something. My performance was suffering, and I hadn't written a note of music in a year. But it was so peaceful up here, all the time in the world to think, practice, compose. This month at Thorburn was just what I needed. If I ever feel it happening again, I'll *beg* them to let me come back!"

"Quite a testimonial," Paul said. "And I sure do understand what you mean."

Robert Kingsley joined them, and they shared good talk over breakfast. Finally Michael glanced at his watch.

"Well, I really want to start down," he said. "I'll say good-bye here, since you're all still eating."

"I'm done," Paul said. "I'll walk you to your car."

Michael grinned. "I was right, you couldn't finish all that."

He shook hands with Robert Kingsley and endured a bear hug from Mary. Paul also said good-bye to Robert and agreed to meet Mary in the day room before dinner.

On their way outside Paul asked Michael, "When you had your audience with Harriet Thorburn, how long did you talk to her?"

"About a minute, if that much. She asked me a couple of questions, welcomed me to the colony then said good night." He looked at Paul. "Why do you want to know?"

"It's nothing."

They said their good-byes with vague promises to get together again, to call when one happened to be in the other's neighborhood. Michael drove off and was soon on the road down from Big House. The last resident scheduled to leave that morning was loading her car across the lot. It was, as Kathy Parrish had said, a mass exodus off the mountain.

Why had he asked Michael about his meeting with Harriet Thorburn? Paul wondered. He wasn't sure himself, but it was . . . something. Yeah, something crazy, like himself maybe. But why spend less than a minute with the personable musician and so much more time with someone as uncommunicative as Gail Farringer?

It was Harriet Thorburn's eccentricities. Had to be. This was a woman who, in the midst of an entertaining story about John Muir's visit to Big House, suddenly asked Walter McClain about a toilet that had overflowed.

Deciding he was right, Paul started back for No. 11.

The temperature had already risen eight degrees since dawn, with no wind. He lingered along the footpath. As well as the book was going, he felt no great desire to run right back to it. The morning was clear, the surrounding mountains impressive, especially Thorburn Peak, so sharply tapered that it resembled an Indian arrowhead.

Soon Leanna Creek had joined the path then twisted around the back of No. 13. Gail, in her warm-up suit but without a coat, sat on the step, a sketchpad open on her lap. She saw Paul and waved.

They were looking at each other when Nora appeared around the curve. Gail saw her first. She stood quickly and went inside. Paul, who had slowed, picked up his pace until he was near the woman.

"Strange bird, that one," Nora said, jerking a thumb in the direction of No. 13. "Yeah, we get 'em. I seen a few over the years."

Paul nodded vaguely. "I can believe that."

"I missed your cabin last night at dinnertime, so I was just out changin' your sheets and cleanin' up. Got your laundry too. It'll be ready tonight. Oh, I put all your papers back where they were, even the ones on the floor. I know how you people are about that."

"Thanks. See you later."

Nora watched him go then glanced at No. 13. Shaking her head, she continued on to Big House.

The disturbance from beyond Paul's cabin could barely be felt that morning. Still not ready to work, he strolled on to the clearing. Crossing Leanna Creek, he followed it for another ten yards. There, at the tributary's widest point, the icy grip felt stronger. But it held him in curiosity, not fear.

Was this the spot where the Thorburn/McClain cabin had stood? Maybe there, farther along. Who had died in it? Paul tried to remember. The McClains' baby. God, a baby! And the older McClain boy set off from there, to die eventually at Sutter's fort. The Thorburns had all survived, although the daughter — Leanna — would later die in San Francisco. Still, the families were freezing, hungry, at odds with the rest of the party, virtually isolated from them. This was a place of concentrated despair.

Emotions like that could linger for an eternity.

It bothered him now, being there. He crossed the creek and returned to his cabin.

For nearly an hour Paul stared at a blank page. The first words of the day came slowly, and it wasn't until late morning that he stopped glancing at the clock every few minutes. Once again he immersed himself in the story.

Still, by two-thirty a few more crumpled pages had hit the wastebasket. He decided that what he had written was crap, and stopped. Creatively speaking, it had been great for him at the colony; but ten straight days of working! Everyone had limits, and he might have reached his that afternoon.

After tomorrow — after Gail was gone — he would go down to Lake Tahoe, assuming he wasn't snowed in again. Not Sunday; he couldn't wait that long. Thursday, or Friday at the latest. He would clear it with Walter McClain.

Just having the option improved his outlook.

With the cabin walls beginning to close in on him, Paul decided to drive into Stillwell. It being Gail's last night, there were some things he wanted to pick up. He walked over to Big House in unseasonably mild weather, hoping it wasn't the calm before another storm.

Walter McClain sat in his office. He nodded at Paul over his reading glasses but didn't seem quite his affable self. Paul explained his plan.

"Well, I guess," McClain said. "I know you've been working hard. The only thing is, there's supposed to be more bad weather later this week. You might want to go as soon as possible. Just let me know tomorrow for sure."

"I will. One other thing. I know it's not four yet but I'd like to drive into town. Any problem?"

McClain waved a hand in dismissal. "What the devil, just go!" he said peevishly. "You'll excuse me, I have a lot of work to do."

Paul left. The man's behavior puzzled him. On the other hand, Walter McClain had lived there all his life — a long time — and had probably spent very little of it out of the mountains. He had been associate director for what, thirty years? And he'd probably done other jobs at the colony for a couple of decades prior to that. He couldn't be as dotty as Harriet Thorburn, but he had his ways.

S. Lakeshore Drive looked reasonably clear, aside from a few icy patches. Either way, Paul wasn't going to drive too fast. He passed no one on the way but was surprised at the number of vehicles parked downtown when he pulled in front of Fry Mercantile.

Carl Stillwell, the deputy, stood across the street, near Mountain Apothecary, engaged in a conversation with another man, whom Paul recognized as the critic from the Mule Deer Cafe his first day in town. They both looked at Paul, the deputy gesturing, the other still expectorating onto the sidewalk. Paul stared at them briefly then went into the store.

Jenny Fry was helping her only customer, an elderly woman, with some skeins of yarn. Paul wandered through the aisles, finding most of what he wanted. By the time he brought it up to the counter, Jenny was free. He thought she looked even more pale, which didn't seem possible.

"Hello, Paul, it's good to see you again," she said with little emotion.

"Hi. Are you okay?" he asked.

She jerked her head back. "Why? Don't you think I look okay?"

"I didn't mean — "

"It's my father again, he's very ill. I suppose he'll be dead soon, just like Mother, then what will I do?"

"I'm sorry. Has he seen a doctor?"

"Yes, a friend drove him to Truckee this morning. He has more medicine, but I don't know, I just don't know." She handed Paul his change and glanced around the store. "Oh, quickly, no one's here. I have to close for a little while and take some things to him."

She picked up two bags from the floor behind the counter. "Here," let me help you," Paul said, taking one. At the door, Jenny set the clock face on a WILL RETURN AT — sign to three forty-five, twenty minutes away, turned it around then locked the door behind them.

"Can I drive you, or do you have a car?" Paul asked.

"Oh heavens no," she said. "It's not far, and I enjoy the walk. Here, I'll take that."

The bag was heavy. "That's okay, I'll walk with you, if you don't mind. Just let me toss my things in the car."

She smiled. "Thank you. You're very kind."

Carl Stillwell and the other man had crossed the street and were smoking in front of the Mule Deer Cafe. They pinched their hat brims as Jenny and Paul walked past.

"Miss Jenny, how's your father doing?" the older man asked.

"A little better this morning," she replied. "I'm going to him now."

The deputy, who had been staring at Paul, said, "You still lookin' at old buildings?" It was more a challenge than a casual inquiry.

"How could you avoid it in this town?" Paul tried to sound cordial but was afraid he failed. He didn't like Carl Stillwell.

"Well, you give Dan my best, okay?" the other man said, spitting noisily. "Tell him I'll stop by tomorrow."

They walked past the Mule Deer Cafe, Paul glancing back once. "Who is that?" he asked. "Not the deputy, the other man."

"Jake? Oh, that's Jake Stillwell. He's Carl's father, also the mayor. I don't know if that's impressive, mayor of a town with a few hundred people. He owns the sporting goods store, bait and tackle and ammunition and that sort of thing. Also the Thorburn Lake Marina. It's busy sometimes, especially the week of the Fishing Derby, in the summer. But right now the town's practically shut down."

"Mayor Stillwell, Sheriff Stillwell," Paul said. "Sort of a monopoly. How many are there?"

"Just the three, that's all. Roy never married and Carl's mother died years ago. The Stillwells have always taken care of the town, the Thorburns the colony, from way back. Carl, by the way . . ." She paused, smiled. "He's courted me ever since back in school. Someday, who knows?"

Courted, Paul thought. Jenny Fry really did live in romantic novels.

They turned the corner and were on Alpine Street, across from Idlewood Livery. Paul glanced at it once then concentrated on Jenny, who recounted past liaisons with Carl.

Alpine ended one long block past the livery near the base of a steep hill. The Fry house, another of Stillwell's "old buildings," was the second one on Trout Lane, a short, narrow street to the left. The two-story frame house appeared deceptively small. An addition in the rear, constructed of native stone, extended almost to the bluff. There was a full-length shed-porch in front and a large brick chimney on one side. Twin doors in the ground, facing a vacant, snow-covered lot on the other side, led down into what Paul assumed was a storm cellar.

They went up on the porch. Dan Fry's racking cough was loud. Jenny took the bag from Paul.

"I'd ask you in, but . . ."

"I understand. Tell him I hope he feels better."

"Thank you."

Paul walked back to the middle of town. Carl Stillwell, alone, stood on the corner of Alpine and Washo, staring at him. What was it with these people? he wondered. While he hadn't planned on it, he slowed and began leisurely reading the nameplates on the facades of ancient stores, peering through the windows of an assay office and tonsorial parlor, bending down to study inscriptions on cornerstones. Okay, he was being an asshole, he thought, but if this was what Carl Stillwell expected, he'd give it to him.

Just stay away from the livery.

Stillwell watched him for five minutes, then shook his head and walked away.

Paul made one more stop at Mountain Apothecary, then started back. Thorburn Lake gleamed in the late afternoon sunshine, the snow-capped peaks reflecting off its gently rippling surface. He drove more slowly in order to enjoy it.

Another exodus was in progress as he neared the main gate. Thorburn's artists-in-residence, confined for days by the storm, were taking advantage of the break to drive into Stillwell. He passed seven vehicles, only two containing more than one driver. The last, an enormous ten-year-old Bonneville, belonged to Mary, who waved at him and rolled down her window.

"Back in an hour!" she yelled, slowing but not stopping.

Paul didn't feel like going back to the cabin; he wanted to be outside. After parking the Cutlass he strolled toward the buildings behind the mansion. While not indicating that they were off limits to residents, the information pamphlet had described the structures as being used strictly for storing supplies and other equipment. Still, they were as old as Big House itself, at least worth a closer look.

As Paul neared the smokehouse, Joe Landry emerged from it. Paul stopped. The man's cold gaze bothered him.

"Need somethin'?" Landry asked.

"No. I was just walking around," Paul said, "filling up some time before dinner."

Landry shrugged. "Got a ways to go." He gestured toward the smokehouse. "This is my place."

"You . . . live here?"

"Yeah. Always have."

Paul nodded. "Always."

Landry started off. "Got work to do."

Deciding to pass on the rest of the outbuildings, Paul spent the next hour exploring some of the colony grounds. He traversed a couple of the other paths then followed Leanna Creek to the lake.

A narrow trail along the edge of the lake led him to the far side of an inlet, where an abbreviated pebble beach ended at the base of a bluff. Already dusk, it was even darker there because of the many Jeffrey pines surrounding this finger of Thorburn Lake. There were no lights along the path either. Time to start back, Paul figured.

The sound pierced the silence of the lakeshore.

A baby crying in terrible pain. No, more feline than human. An unnerving cry that went on for a few long seconds then was punctuated by a clear *whoowow* and fell silent for a heartbeat, only to start again. It was nearby; it had to be. As strange and disturbing as it was, Paul felt drawn to it. He walked toward the pines, looking for whatever it was in the shadows.

Something darted from the trees across the pebble beach.

Low to the ground, dark, long. Too far away to see clearly. Moving rapidly, gliding, the mewling cry rising, finally ending with a last *whoowow* as the shape cut the surface of the water and disappeared below, not even causing a ripple.

"What the hell — !" Paul exclaimed. As if freed, he turned and tried to run but could only stagger away.

Mary's Bonneville was in the parking area. Others were just getting back. Paul had never been more pleased to see people. He went directly to the day room, but it was still sparsely occupied. His slot held no messages. Mary was not around. He found an isolated corner and tried to sort out what had happened.

An animal. Just an animal, that's all it had been. He didn't know what kind, not this city boy. The darkness, the shadows, being in a strange place — that would mess up anyone's perception. It was nothing, he decided. Nothing.

But it still troubled him when Mary joined him ten minutes later.

"What's with you?" she asked. "Bad day at the typewriter?"

"Yeah, it was." He smiled. "How'd you like beautiful downtown Stillwell?"

"I'm a small-town girl, so I'm used to it. But I did run into that girl you told me about, in the general store. Oh, that poor child . . . Spent the whole time I was in there reciting Robert Service out loud."

"Yeah, it's a shame. How did your work go?"

Mary shrugged. "I didn't find as much as I would have liked about the Thorburn party. There was this journal written by one Ezra Cage, a rather notorious mountain man of the time. He had nothing to do with the Thorburn incident, but he made a brief reference to someone who did." She took a small note pad from her purse. "I'll read it to you. My handwriting's lousy. Keep in mind I wrote it down verbatim.

"'LeBeau was good with horses and told good stories at night but I always thought the Frenchie was a little queer in the head. Like what he said about early this year when he went from Sutter's to go and bring those fool people down from the North Lake where they got freezing. He said they didn't look happy but looked like they was already dead but still walking around even though they was getting rescued. That is queer stuff and is why I'm not sure about LeBeau.'" Mary closed the pad. "Is that the kind of thing you're looking for?"

"How do you know he was referring to the Thorburn party?" Paul asked. "He doesn't mention the name."

"The date of his entry coincides with the incident. There were no other stranded parties recorded up here that winter. And the clincher is his reference to the North Lake. That was the old Indian name for Thorburn Lake."

"'. . . *looked like they was already dead but still walking around.*'" Paul shook his head. "What the devil does that mean? These people were being saved! And they'd already had food for a couple of days, whatever the Indian had brought. Why would they give that impression to the rescue party?"

"It might have had something to do with the illness that took so many of them right at the end," Mary said. "Remember how John Thorburn began his entry that day?" She drew upon her memory, which Paul realized was quite impressive. "'*We rejoice this day, but also grieve.*' Doesn't that fit?"

"The *illness* again," he said. "I suppose you're right."

"But you're still not buying it."

"I don't know if there's anything to buy or not. It was just . . . something I got interested in. Sorry, I didn't mean to snap."

"It's all right. Anyway, you were right about this area."

"What?"

"Next to Tahoe, the North Lake was the focal point for all kinds of Indian legends. There are stories of battles between gods and demons along the lakeshore and in the surrounding forest. Enormous firebirds swooped down from the sky and ripped up any mortals foolish enough to be around. A one-eyed, one-legged giant would hop down from Arrow Point — that's Thorburn Peak to us — to feed on human flesh. So would the wild men, who lived in the trees."

"Sounds great."

"The Water Babies were everywhere," she continued. "The lake, all the streams, puddles from rain — "

"The *what?*"

"Water Babies. Impish creatures that dominate Washo legends. Lake Tahoe was chock-full of them, of course, but this one must've had its share. They were supposed to lure Indians with their cry, then do something to them. It could be nothing more than a prank; they might even give the victim a gift, like a new song. But mostly an encounter with a Water Baby was unpleasant."

Paul felt his heart racing. "What did they look like?"

"That's hard to say. The descriptions are vague. They were also known to assume other shapes. But in their real form the best I can figure was that a Water Baby resembled a giant deformed otter."

"A giant deformed otter," he repeated, then broke up laughing in the way that Jeannie used to say reminded her of Steve Allen on his old television show. Mary joined him and for nearly a minute they were out of control.

When it finally subsided, Paul realized how much he'd needed the catharsis. Things had fallen back into perspective.

"The bottom line," Mary gasped, "is that whatever the truth or fiction of these legends, the Indians believed in them strongly. It's the *strength* of these beliefs, once so dominant here, that you must be feeling, along with what happened to the Thorburn party. You're incredibly sensitive."

He shook his head. "I don't think so."

"Remember I told you about feeling the ghosts? I'd always thought myself pretty receptive. Having an open mind helps, I guess. Well, before I drove into town I took a walk out your way, to where the Thorburn cabin had stood."

"You went to the clearing?" Paul exclaimed.

She nodded. "Walked around for a while, went up and down the creek. There was nothing."

"Nothing," he said vaguely.

"Surprised me too." She smiled. "I'm jealous now. Please understand, Paul, that I believe you. I *know* that you're feeling what you say. Maybe it has something to do with how long you've been out there. Whatever. Just accept it. Enjoy the fact that you're a little different from everyone else — which, being a writer, you might have already known."

"I *think* that was a compliment," he said.

"It was, dear boy."

"Thanks, Mary, thanks for everything. You don't have to bother with it anymore."

"Are you kidding? I'm having a ball! But we'll put it to rest for tonight anyway. I'm thirsty, and I know the extent of your gratitude is such that you'd love to go and pour me a brandy."

"You got it."

Put it to rest for tonight, she'd said. No, put it to rest, period, he told himself, because it was getting crazy. Finish up the residency, which so far had brought his career — and himself — back to life. Leave there with the nearly completed first draft of a new novel. Anticipate being with Jason and Bree.

And Gail Farringer.

Enough of the Thorburn party, the clearing, Jane Tyler, Idlewood Livery, the figure through the trees, purple Volkswagens, Nancy Thorburn's painting . . .

Water Babies.

Resolved, relieved, Paul carried the half-filled brandy snifter to Mary Sherman.

CHAPTER NINE

The lunch lady — Nora, was that her name? — greeted Gail in the corridor on her way to dinner. Gail responded with a vague nod and continued on to the main central hall. Had the woman, she wondered, noticed the interaction between Paul and herself earlier? What had she read in Nora's face when the woman spoke to her?

Did it matter?

She knew it didn't but could not help wondering. Despite what had happened, the work had hardly begun. That's what going back would be all about.

To learn how to stop hating.

Herself, mostly, for leading her husband and son to the slaughter.

The world, for carrying it out.

Gail suddenly realized that Nora was walking behind her. Glancing over her shoulder she said hello.

Nora smiled in surprise and crossed the hall. Gail went into the dining room.

Paul sat at the far end of the third table, next to a woman Gail thought was named Kathy. With the census down, residents were scattered through the room. Harriet

Thorburn could have bunched them together at the first two tables. But then, that was Harriet Thorburn.

On the other hand, had she done that, Gail would have looked even more absurdly out of place. As it stood, the nearest resident at her table was three places down.

Tonight she looked at herself through their eyes: not impressive, to say the least.

How badly she wanted to be sitting with Paul, talking to him, listening. For a moment she eyed the empty seat on his right. He had asked her, hadn't he?

No, she couldn't do it. Not to him. Whatever the stir it caused tonight, for her it would be over tomorrow. But for Paul the questions and comments about the crazy lady would go on until the day he left, and he would resent her for it.

One more night of this and then things would change.

She endured the ritual with difficulty. Usually she had a strong appetite and the food tasted good. But tonight, after picking around her dinner and leaving half of it, she hurried from the hall. She knew they were all watching; she knew *he* was watching. *Good-bye everyone, this is the last time you'll have to feel uncomfortable.*

I'm sorry, Paul.

All of her art supplies and a few other things had been loaded in her car. Everything was ready for the morning. On Paul's advice she had warmed up the Nissan. It nearly hadn't started; over a week had passed since she'd last driven it. Now she felt certain it would be fine tomorrow.

With night the temperature had plummeted. Gail stoked the fire and got a substantial blaze going. Then she waited, hearing in her head Harriet Thorburn's droning words going on at that moment.

Forty minutes later she was in Paul's arms, holding him tightly and not wanting to let go.

"I was worried about you," he said.

"It was a long night and I just wanted to be out of there," she told him.

"That I can understand."

"Did you have a good day?"

"Work-wise, no, but aside from that . . . yeah, actually it was real good. What about you?"

"I sketched some mountains, the lake . . ." She turned away, shook her head. "I thought about you all day. Oh, Paul, I don't want to leave you! Not now, just after . . . I mean — "

She cried softly as he held her. "Listen, lady," he said firmly, "this is the way it has to be right now. I'll see you in a few weeks, you know that. And just to make sure, I brought you a present." He reached into a bag he'd left on the desk and pulled out a blue road map. "Triple A, south Orange County, dog-eared but whole. My place is circled; so are some of the neighborhoods I like."

"Thank you," she said, wiping her eyes. "I'll use it." She glanced at the bag, looked at him. "What else is in there?"

"Ah, can't stand the suspense!" He stacked six Hershey Big Blocks on the desk. "You have a long drive back. That should get you there. And last, voilà!" He peeled the bag away. "Champagne. Robert Mondavi 1982, best I could find in Stillwell. Chilled in the creek for the past three hours."

She smiled. "It's perfect. Thanks . . . for everything."

She kissed him — gently at first, then with the urgency of her soaring desire for this man. He still held the bottle. She took it from him and put it down on the desk.

"Maybe you should have left it in the creek a little longer," she said in a husky voice.

They undressed quickly and came together in front of the fire. The next time their bodies were apart was two hours later, after they had exhausted each other making love and had, briefly, fallen into a gentle, dreamless sleep.

"Where are you going?" Gail asked, stretching.

"To pour the champagne."

"Warm champagne?"

"It was practically frozen; might not be too bad."

They each drank a glass. Paul was going to pour a second but Gail stopped him. "Not for me. The last thing I need in the morning is a hangover."

"Gail?"

"Yes?"

"Do you want me to stay with you tonight?"

She took both his hands. "Not yet, Paul. As much as I want to . . ." She trembled. "I'll regret it after I haven't seen you for a few days, but . . . not yet, please."

Her eyes were imploring him to understand. He smiled, kissed her. "It's all right," he told her. "One step at a time. Please don't be afraid of me, and don't ever worry about anything you might say. I'll never hurt you, believe that."

She nodded and rested her head on his chest. "I do. Thanks. But I want to see you in the morning!"

"What time are you leaving?"

"Early. Can you come over at six? We'll have a little time."

"Sure. I . . ."

She knew something was troubling him. "Paul, what is it?"

Reluctantly he said, "You'll be here tomorrow, won't you? When I come?"

"Of course. Why . . ."

"You won't leave before then?"

"Even if I just wanted to walk out on you" — she smiled — "I wouldn't drive these awful roads in the dark. I'll see you in the morning at six."

He nodded sheepishly. "Sorry, I — "

She touched his lips. "You don't have to explain. I think I understand."

No, he thought, *you couldn't. It's the crazy stuff again, it's vague entries in old diaries and Harriet Thorburn's audiences and one-legged flesh-eating giants and all of it that I thought was over with today. But I want it to be, so I'm not going to ask you about the clearing, which I know you feel even more than I do, because I understand it now, sort of.*

"I guess I'll start back," he said.

She held him tightly. "Stay a little longer."

Paul could tell another storm was coming. Maybe not that night or the next morning, but soon enough. It wasn't the chilled night air as he walked to his cabin, or the moderate wind that urged him along. There was something else, a *feeling*, which, he now realized, he'd experienced prior to other storms. He didn't pretend to understand how he knew, but he did. It disturbed him. New discoveries about yourself at thirty-six could be like that. He conceded that Mary Sherman was right about him.

Great, he thought, what should he do for an encore? Bend spoons? Find a serial killer for a frustrated police force? This was nuts.

But a storm *was* coming. He hoped it would arrive late enough for Gail to safely reach the interstate and get out of the Sierras.

The cold aura of the clearing felt weak; or perhaps, in his understanding, he was stronger. He stood in front of No. 11 gazing into the darkness, no longer experiencing fear, but pity instead.

"It's been over a hundred and forty years," he said softly. "Time to stop walking, find peace. Why can't you do that?"

The wind answered with a vague mocking laugh. Paul went inside.

Damn, why had the Dream returned?

This time it had begun as always before, minute details enacted clearly on the dark stage of her subconscious. The only difference tonight was her ability to switch it off before the worst could be consummated, to say "I won't watch this!" and draw herself from it, though not without effort.

Maybe she should have pleaded with Paul to stay the night. Had he been there, holding her, it might not have come.

No, not true. It would have, and he'd have seen her like this, sitting up in bed, her body shaking, cold sweat beading on her flesh. She wouldn't let it be that way.

Almost three a.m. Gail washed her face, calmed herself in front of the fire, slid back into bed. Outside, the wind made strange noises in the trees. There were other night sounds, some familiar, others less so. She seemed more aware of them than before. Perhaps she should lie there until it was time, avoid the fear.

But she was tired and sleep reclaimed her.

It was night but the clearing was lit by a great bonfire that sent flames half the height of the tallest trees, and by a bright moon that filled the sky in a place where none of the dense branches interfered. Paul stood in the middle, by the log, looking toward the lake, watching the dark figure through the pines. Tall, featureless, it came toward him, two long arms held tightly against its sides. Ten yards away it stopped, waited. Even in the light its face remained clouded in gray mist. Paul turned away from it.

Gail Farringer, in her gray warm-up suit, stood on the other side of the creek. If the figure beyond Paul disturbed her, she gave no indication. Without looking down she crossed the creek, each step finding the next stone, as if she had done it a hundred times before. Now on his side she stopped, held her arms out.

He wanted to go to her but couldn't move. He was unconcerned. She would know, and come to him.

Something crept out of the creek a yard from where Gail stood. A tiny hand groped for a hold on the bank, found it, pulled. The baby began its wailing the instant its head rose above the surface. Its pink naked body floundered on the ground for a moment, then it righted itself and, still crying, began crawling toward Gail.

Of course it cried, Paul thought. How cold it must be.

A second followed, then others, until there were six in all, each adding its cry to the din that rose above the crackling of the great fire. They were at Gail's feet, reaching up, and she wanted to take them in her arms, warm them, make the crying stop.

Then they were black wormlike things with no appendages or visible features, although the cries still rose from somewhere. They climbed on Gail, encircling her arms, legs, waist, twisting around and around. The warm-up suit fell to the ground in tattered shreds and she was naked, but the crying things wouldn't stop. Her blood darkened the snow and her flesh dropped off in long strips, like an apple being pared.

One of the dark things climbed on her face.

Paul watched, interested, still unable to move. From behind him came a strange rumbling sound that might have been laughter, but he couldn't be sure.

In the snow, to his left, he saw a shadow. Then another, on his right. Finally a third, which fell over him, and he felt cold, despite being near the fire. The shadows lengthened, reaching toward the creek, toward . . .

The thing that had been Gail raised two black sockets and saw what was coming. It was flung backward, like a leaf in a gust of wind, and fell beneath the surface of the creek, silencing the cries of the dark shapes that clung to her. Curious, Paul willed his body to move, then turned.

Wednesday, December 11

Four-thirty a.m. Why couldn't his nightmares come at a respectable hour? Like five minutes before the alarm went off.

The wind gusts were not as frequent as they had been earlier. Paul added wood to the fire and again lay down, hands crossed beneath his head as he stared at the ceiling. He would remain like that until it was time.

But the alarm jarred him awake at five-thirty.

He hated showers when it was still dark outside, which was the way it had once been, when necessity sent him to a job in the early morning rush hour. But there was a better reason today, so he finished quickly and dressed. At five minutes to six he left No. 11.

Gail's cabin was dark. Even with the blinds closed he could usually see slivers of light. She had overslept. No, she wouldn't do that, not this morning. He hurried to the door, knocked twice. No answer.

"Jesus, no," he whispered, fear welling inside him.

The door was unlocked. He slipped inside and shut it behind him. "Gail?" he called. "Gail, it's me."

He went to turn on the lamp but decided against it. Opening the blinds let in some meager light from the footpath. He looked around, expecting to see her roll over on the bed, mutter something. But the room was empty.

Nothing in the closet, the bathroom, not even under the bed.

Empty.

She was there, she had to be there, he told himself. She'd taken her things to the car and was on the way back. *Gail was still there!*

But he wasn't going to wait. He ran from the cabin, down the footpath, stumbling twice in his panicked rush, not giving a damn, finally bursting into the parking area.

Gail's car was gone.

She had left.

No, she wouldn't have left him. This wasn't Sherri Jordan.

On the other hand, maybe it was . . .

He understood now. In the moment that he knew Gail was gone, he understood. Not all of it; not about what had happened back then to make this so. That was the missing part. But he understood enough, and the fear he'd felt upon seeing the darkened cabin was nothing compared to what now gripped him.

He trembled. No one could see him like this. Alone; he had to be alone. Turning, he staggered up the path, his legs threatening to fold under him. Past No. 13, still dark, soon to be made ready for whoever would come next.

Sherri Jordan.

Purple . . .

Past No. 12, still empty, as it had been since the first day.

Gail Farringer.

Harriet Thorburn's audiences.

. . . the livery stable.

Sherri Jordan Gail Farringer.

To No. 11, closer to the place where it had happened.

Where something was still happening.

Strong again, taunting him with icy fingers in his blood. He sensed . . . anticipation.

"You bastards!" he cried. "What are you doing? Where's Gail? Where is she? *Bastards!*"

Harriet Thorburn's audiences.

Artists, writers, unique, different.

Kin always tell, easy.

Loners.

Sherri Jordan. Gail Farringer.

Inside now, on his bed, pounding a fist on the mattress. Put it together some way and see if it made sense. Get it out once and for all.

Sherri Jordan had said, *She practically pumped me for my whole life story.*

Gail Farringer had said, *It had only been about fifteen minutes, but . . .*

Why them?

Because they were loners. No friends, no family, no one waiting for them.

No one to give a damn whether they came back or not.

A few casual inquiries about Sherri, a perfectly good explanation by Walter McClain — Paul had bought it — and it's forgotten the same day.

And what about Gail? Maybe tonight, at dinner, someone might notice the absence of the weird lady, and ask, and be told that she'd left that morning, and say good riddance, and forget about it even quicker.

Artists, writers, alone on their creative quests.

Alone.

How many more like Gail and Sherri?

How many in over a century, since John Thorburn had begun the colony?

John Thorburn, historian, patron of the arts. Benevolent John Thorburn . . .

. . . and his legacy of death.

Because they were *all* dead, the nameless artists and novelists and sculptors and poets before now, those unfortunate enough to have had no one who cared.

And Sherri Jordan was dead. She had died that same night, because in the morning the clearing had been still. Whatever it was had been appeased.

Whatever it was. The missing part. The figure between the trees. The *illness.*

. . . *looked like they was already dead but still walking around.*

Dead. All dead — except Gail Farringer, because the clearing would have been silent had she already been murdered.

Gail . . . was . . . not . . . dead.

They had made a mistake. Gail *had* someone who cared. How ironic. Had they been seen together, had anyone known they'd become friends, Gail would have been spared. He would be saying good-bye to her right now, watching her drive off, anticipating the end of the month. But she had insisted their relationship be secret to spare him the alleged ridicule of other residents, and now they had taken her away to — wherever she was.

Wherever she was. Gail was still there, on the colony grounds, probably. He would find her and take her from here, and let others know what had been happening at the prestigious Thorburn colony.

Yes, they *had* made a mistake. They didn't know he would be coming.

They. Who were they? Descendants of the survivors. The names: Thorburn, Stillwell, McClain, Tyler, Fry, Hardman. But *all* of them? Nora? Jenny? Simple-minded Arthur Tyler? Paul had trouble accepting it. But until he knew otherwise, all of them were his enemies.

He was wasting time. First, get to a phone, call . . . who? Would anyone believe this? Then call Gary Marks, he told himself. Don't try to explain, just say there's trouble, that if he didn't check in at specified times to send help. Next, begin a methodical search of the colony. Assuming the worst, that whatever was going to happen would be late that night, he had that much time. But even with the dawn just breaking there were barely ten hours of daylight. He had to find her before dark.

He checked himself in the mirror, concerned that he wore his emotions. He found the flashlight that Nora had brought during one of the storms, shoved it in the large pocket of his down jacket, and went outside.

Snow had begun to fall.

It did not come down heavily, but the air was bitter cold and the wind blew hard, the driving snow stinging his face. He pulled up his hood and hurried to Big House, hardly glancing at No. 13.

Other residents were crossing the parking area on their way to breakfast. Just another day at the Thorburn colony. One of them was preparing to leave, hastily loading up his car to try to make the interstate before the weather worsened. Clenching his fists, Paul went inside.

Walter McClain was crossing the main central hall. Paul thought about grabbing him and shaking him until he told the truth about Gail. Right, that would really help her. He took a deep breath and nodded at the man.

"Good morning, Paul," said the associate director.

McClain's clothes were rumpled. He looked haggard. "You all right, Walter?" Paul asked.

"Had a little trouble sleeping last night." He shrugged. "Getting old, I guess. Well, looks like we're in for another storm."

"Is that what the forecast said?"

McClain nodded. "But they don't think it'll last too long. Maybe you'll get your trip in yet."

He went on to his office. *Yeah*, Paul thought. *I'll bet you had trouble sleeping last night.*

The day room was empty. Paul picked up the receiver of the pay phone and listened. No dial tone. Although this phone should not have required it, he tried putting in a quarter. Same result.

"You won't be getting anyone, Mr. Fleming."

He jumped, spun around. Nora stepped back to avoid his elbow.

"What did you say?" he snapped.

"Hey, didn't mean to scare you," she said. "Phones've been dead since last night. Might be a while to get fixed if it keeps snowin' like this."

"Blast it!" He slammed the receiver down.

Nora looked at him curiously. "Who'd you want to call this early anyway?"

"What? It's . . . my publisher. Back in New York. It's later there."

"Oh, yeah." She nodded. "Well, they'll probably be workin' before long. You have a good day, huh?"

The woman went about her business. Paul returned to the central hall, angry at himself for the way he'd handled the confrontation with Nora. He would have to do better than that, or they might start wondering.

On his way to Big House he had made the decision to look for Gail first in the outbuildings. There was already a thin layer of snow on the asphalt when he crossed the parking area. Seeing no one around, he hurried to the farthest structure, a small storage shed. He slipped behind it, found a clean spot on a grimy window, and peered inside. Freestanding metal shelves were pushed up against the walls. They were mostly empty — a few rusty cans, some boxes, little else.

The next two buildings, similar in size to the first, yielded nothing. Staying concealed was a problem. Paul kept each structure between himself and Big House, when he could. But there were also footpaths. Once he hid behind trees when Thea Douglas walked past on her way to the mansion, complaining loudly about the weather.

The old stable came next. He stole inside through a rear door, closed it, began looking around. He smelled gasoline and noticed two snowplows in front, near the double doors. No horses had been boarded there for a long time, although assorted tack still hung on the walls. Cords of firewood were everywhere.

He was looking through the stalls in back when the double doors opened. He dropped to the floor, jarring his shoulder and nearly crying out. He waited, afraid his frosty breath would give him away. He heard two voices; one belonged to Joe Landry.

"You want I should start on the parking lot?" the other asked.

"What the hell else?" Landry said. "Here, take this one."

The machine would not start. It sputtered a couple of times, whined then was silent.

"Goddamn son of a bitch!" Landry swore.

"What you gonna do, Joe?"

"Fix the fucker, what do you think? Take the other one and get outta here! After the lot make sure you do all the way down to the gate."

The second machine started and was soon outside. Landry kept up a stream of foul language as he dragged a heavy tool chest across the floor. Paul looked around, making certain there was nothing the man could need anywhere near him. Now he could only wait.

Ten minutes later — it seemed longer — Paul chanced a look. Landry had parts of the engine scattered on the floor and was dismantling it further. His work had just begun.

Shit, Paul mouthed, leaning back.

Landry worked on the engine for over an hour. Once he injured a finger and paced around the stable, cursing louder. Paul hoped he would leave to take care of it, but he kept working.

Finally done, he drove the plow outside, leaving the doors open. Paul waited another minute then left through the back. Although he hadn't seen everything, he felt certain Gail wasn't in the stable.

Snow was slicing down hard. He crept stealthily to the next building. There the only choice was a single door facing Big House, for the cube structure had no windows.

He counted on the falling snow to give him the few moments he needed.

The building was a freezer, something he hadn't realized despite all the times he'd passed it on the way to the footpath. He gripped the handle, hesitated, then opened the door and satisfied himself that nothing out of the ordinary hung next to the sides of beef or stacks of boxes.

All that remained was the smokehouse. Joe Landry's place. He probably had nothing to do with this, but Paul had to make certain. In the distance he could hear the drone of at least one snowplow. The handyman could be back at any minute.

The door was locked, but one window felt loose. He managed to raise it an inch, slip his fingers under, and open it all the way. It was not a big window. He went in headfirst, quickly shutting it behind him.

Joe Landry's living quarters were two small rooms and a closet-sized bath, the whole thing no bigger than Paul's cabin. He had come in through the bedroom, a dark, depressing cubicle that looked as if it had never been cleaned. Grimy clothes were scattered on the floor. He caught a faint smell of gasoline, a stronger one of urine. The walls, where visible, showed peeling layers of paint; the rest was covered with pictures of women, cut out of magazines. Women having sex with men, with other women, with dogs, and by themselves using a variety of exotic aids. There were even some of men and small children.

"Sick bastard," Paul muttered, looking in a closet. Other than more clothes, it contained boxes of the magazines from which Joe Landry had clipped his wallpaper.

The front room, a kitchenette with a couch and television, was as filthy as the bedroom. Dishes with food stuck to them sat on the table and in the sink. The smell was of garbage and whiskey.

A ring of keys hung on a nail over the sink. Looking at the barely legible tags, Paul realized they opened many of the doors on the colony grounds. But what about the risk of taking them? Landry might report their absence quickly, and the descendants would be warned that something was wrong. Still, having them would be invaluable. . . .

The smell began to overwhelm him. Resisting the urge to vomit, Paul took the keys, slipped out the front door, and ran across the parking area.

Big House was next.

The work day had started. Residents were not usually afoot in the main building, unless they needed to use the library. Paul had to remember that in case he ran into any staff, at least on the first floor. Upstairs he would be on his own.

A plan, some sort of sensible plan, he told himself. He couldn't just open every door. The message center. A room number was next to each resident's name. Not only would he learn the numbers in Big House, but also the cabins. He would search them next, assuming Gail was not in the mansion.

Assuming he made it that far.

Walter McClain was crossing the hall on his way to the staircase. Paul watched from the corridor until he was gone then hurried to the day room.

A resident with whom Paul had little more than a nodding acquaintance sat in one corner, writing on a steno pad. She barely noticed him, although he glanced at her a few times while copying down the numbers of unoccupied rooms and cabins. He pocketed the scrap of paper, studied the colony map for a few moments, then left quickly.

Arthur Tyler carried a heavy box across the central hall. Paul could not avoid him. The big man smiled but, obeying the colony rule, said nothing. Paul changed direction toward the library and was almost there when the cook disappeared into the dining room. Turning, he crossed the hall to the corridor, his heart pounding heavily, hurting his chest. And he had barely started, he thought.

There was no one in the corridor or on the service stairs. He ran up two steps at a time, slowing near the top. If Gail was in Big House, it made more sense to keep her on the unoccupied third floor. He could search the guestrooms later, if necessary.

A sign on the door said STAFF ONLY in block letters. The door was locked. Paul found the right key and opened it slowly, grimacing when it creaked. He slipped in quietly.

The dark third floor was nearly identical to the one below. Most of the doors were not only unlocked but ajar. It all but eliminated them, because they would not have been open with a prisoner inside, not even up there.

Still, he looked in every one, on the chance that Gail's captors were either smug or thoughtless. Some of the rooms were empty, not even a rug on the hardwood floors. There was furniture in others, ranging from ornate pieces to the most dismally plain, although all of it was quite old. He noticed a few chests, as well as flat, tightly nailed wooden crates, the kind in which paintings were shipped.

One room behind a closed but unlocked door was different. An oval rug covered the middle of the floor, and two Queen Anne easy chairs sat on either side of a tall lamp. The walls were covered with paintings. Someone's sitting room, perhaps, sanctuary from the daily routine below.

A large chest stood next to one of the chairs. Memories were probably stored there. Paul decided to have a look. John Thorburn's eyes watched him from the largest painting there, above the stone fireplace. Paul knew it was him, for the portrait had been used on the cover of one edition of *Trails of Promise*. He stared at it.

"What happened up here, great man?" he asked bitterly. "You took something to your grave, I know you did.

Whatever it is, they're going to kill Gail over it. I wish I could make you talk, you son of a bitch!"

The chest was open. Paul had guessed right. It was filled with clothes and shoes from other eras, old books, large framed photographs, albums filled with smaller snapshots of what must have been the Thorburns through more than a century, packets of letters, and other memorabilia. Normally Paul would have been fascinated looking through something like that.

Not today.

Still, he continued digging until he reached another layer beneath the clothes and linens. Here were items of greater value, not only as antiques: jewelry boxes, varying in size and shape. One of them, Paul swore, had been forged from solid gold. All had precious stones inlaid. This was the cherished collection of one of Harriet Thorburn's ancestors.

Nancy Thorburn's collection. Her chest. *Their* chest. That was why Paul continued to rummage through it, although he wasn't sure what he was looking for.

Until he found it.

On the bottom was a sheaf of paper wrapped in thin supple leather and tied with heavy twine. A faded but legible two-line inscription said *Journal, 1845-1846, J. Thorburn.*

His diary. As he had written it, along the trail.

And here, in the mountains.

No time to treat the historical treasure with the respect it warranted. Snapping the twine easily, Paul laid the diary on the floor. If there was an answer, he knew just where to look. He flipped halfway through; the slightly yellowed pages were sturdy, with a linen-like texture. The first date he saw was in November, when they'd arrived at the lake. He kept turning the pages until he found the entry he wanted.

January 4, 1846.

He already knew the words: *Jordy Fry said he saw a figure through the trees in the direction of the pass. Tyler thought he saw it too. Maybe our Salvation is near.*

Paul was at the bottom of the page. He flipped to the next one.

The entry for January 4, Sunday, went on.

Three-quarters of the way down that page the entry for January 5, Monday, began. Unlike the brief entry in *Trails of Promise*, this one ran through all of the next page and part of the following one.

And unlike the published diary, there was one dated January 6, Tuesday.

John Thorburn's missing journal entries.

Sweating, Paul slipped off his heavy jacket. His mouth was dry. Although reluctant, he knew this had to be done. He turned back to January 4 and began reading.

> *We had no trouble finding the man. It seemed as if he was waiting for us. He had nothing with him, no pack, no animal, but he seemed to be in no difficulty, so we assumed he must be from a party of others who were nearby. We asked many questions, but all he would tell us was that he had come alone. Then he started walking toward the lake. Tom Hardman confided in me that he found the man very disturbing. I felt that way also. You could not look him in the eyes without wanting to turn away.*
>
> *Later, Mr. Black — this is what Nancy called him, since he never told us his name — looked around our pathetic camp. I think he was amused by the suffering. He took me aside and said that every one of us would perish unless we accepted his help. But there would be a price, which he named. I told him he was mad and would have chased him off, except I realized that he would do whatever he wanted. Afterward I saw him talking to the Stillwell brothers. Knowing the character of these men I am not surprised that they were more receptive.*

That was the remainder of the entry for January 4. Paul continued reading.

> *January 5, Monday — Very cold, but the sun is up. Mr. Black was in camp again this morning. No one knew where he had gone for the night, but it had not been in any of the cabins. He said that he would prove himself and told us that an Indian would be coming with supplies. If this happened, he insisted, we would have to believe him.*
>
> *A Digger Indian came into camp at noontime. He brought food and blankets, which we have divided. I thought this to be a coincidence, and I told Mr. Black. He spoke to the Indian, who then left. A while after he told us that the Indian would return with meat. Again, he was right. The Indian dragged in the carcass of a bear.*
>
> *How could we doubt him now? The Stillwells were willing to go along with whatever he wanted. I was not. From what he had told us I believed that this man, although himself evil, was only a servant of a greater Evil. We needed to drive Mr. Black away, before whatever it was came, then hope for rescue, or the end of winter. How could we pay such a price!*

The price again, Paul thought. And the entry for this date read differently from the book.

> *Mr. Black spoke to me and said it must be done tonight, or there would be no other chance. After that he would leave. Our food would last for a week or less. And more storms were coming, he promised, terrible ones. None of us would leave the mountains alive. Tonight; that was all the time we*

had. I said that I would meet with the others near my cabin and talk about it. This seemed to satisfy him, and he left.

Perhaps my mind has grown feeble from hunger, and I'm imagining things that cannot be. But if it is true, then the Lord God help me for what I may be party to this night!

It is after dark now. All of us have eaten well. Patrick McClain has begun a large fire outside. I can see the first of the families coming up from the lake.

That was the end of the January 5 entry. Not a word about any illness. Paul wasn't surprised.

The last missing entry was illegible in some places. It had been written in what must have been a trembling hand. Blotches of ink were like crushed insects on the page. Paul filled in words that seemed to fit.

January 6, Tuesday — It is the afternoon now, sun shining, cold, quiet. I am supposed to be a man of words, but how can I find any to describe what happened last night, a few yards from where I'm sitting? After all the people were here, I went out and spoke to them. It was an unpleasant surprise to learn that most already knew of Mr. Black's proposal, because the Stillwells had been spreading the word through other cabins. They were aware that, in order for the majority of us to survive, others would have to die.

The price, Paul thought. Jesus, they had to sacrifice some of their people!

There were those who scoffed at the whole thing. Louis Gibbs, for one, and William

Parkhill. They thought Mr. Black to be some trickster with another motive, such as acquiring our possessions. Joseph Krueger and Franklin Smith, God-fearing men, knew Mr. Black for what he truly was and wanted no part of any agreement. The Stillwell brothers and Tom Hardman were willing to do anything for survival. That left the McClains, Tylers, and the peddler man, Fry, all without an opinion yet. I would have expected that of Noah Tyler, who had been my teamster, for he was a simple man, although very loyal.

So we talked about it, and argued, and the women had their say also. But since none of us could truly understand what this was all about, we arrived at no conclusions and became more frustrated. Then Parkhill's son — a boy of ten or eleven but with so much wisdom! — said what was the most sensible thing of all. He didn't like this Mr. Black, he said. We should make him go away, and then the Digger Indian, who was still around, would either take us out of the mountains or continue to bring us enough food to last until spring. Simon — for this was the boy's name — knew he could make the Indian understand.

I believed him, truly, and so did some of the others. But Edward Stillwell scoffed at us for listening to the words of a child, and it began again, until I thought it would grow violent.

Mr. Black appeared then, looking smug, as if he were feeding off the rage off our helpless band. Everyone stopped talking. He raised his hands and said something about the time having come. Right then I knew that there had never been a choice at all.

The Stillwells and Hardmans moved toward Mr. Black, pleading to be saved. Jordy Fry followed. Then, more reluctantly, the McClains went. Patrick looked at me and shook his head. I could see the fear in his eyes.

Nancy, holding our children's hands, urged me to step back, which we did, along with the rest. We moved closer to the fire, perhaps for its warmth and safety, although at this time it gave neither.

Those surrendering to the evil were around Mr. Black in a half-circle. He stared at them silently as he unraveled the scarf from around his face and tossed it away. Then he removed the rest of his clothes and stood naked. One of the women — Lavinia Smith, I think — screamed when she saw his body, which was disfigured with deep scars. Leanna squeezed my hand so tightly that it hurt, but I did not say anything.

It seemed to please Mr. Black that we were so repulsed by him. He looked from one face to another, then turned and gazed across the clearing in the direction of the lake. His back was equally scarred. He was saying something, but the words had no meaning.

Then we heard a sound that was like the wind blowing, only there was no wind. It grew stronger, so loud that it was deafening. Still, we felt nothing, and the fire was not affected.

Something was happening in the clearing. I couldn't see at first, then I noticed something in the snow. They were shadows, three shadows, moving toward us as they lengthened. But this made no sense, because nothing cast them. Still, they were coming.

Mr. Black turned around. He was grinning. Our fire reflected in his eyes. He yelled at those closest to him to fall on the ground before the dal-yawii (I think this was what he said), to acknowledge their greatness, because only then would they be spared. The terrible sound of the wind grew even louder as Edward Stillwell and his family dropped to their knees at Mr. Black's feet and were followed by the rest. The shadows were closer, and I wavered, but stood where I was.

Then, across the clearing, we saw what was casting the shadows. Nancy screamed something about not letting our children die. She joined the others around Mr. Black. I could not be without my family, so I ran forward too. Noah Tyler, with his wife and baby, followed. The others remained by the fire.

I felt a terrible coldness inside as the shadows reached us. Mr. Black urged us to lift our eyes and see what cast the shadows in the snow, but I only looked down. Strangely, most of the screams came from those on the ground near me, not the brave souls awaiting their fate by the fire. I knew shame then.

Mr. Black continued uttering sounds as the shadows fell over our meeting place. The coldness within seemed enough to destroy me. They were closer now. There was a smell about them, like death. I shut my eyes, cried out for Nancy and the children to do the same. They were around us, studying, probing, then past, to those at the fire.

Oh, the screams and the pain! I wanted to cry out to God, not for myself, having forfeited the right to ever again ask His help after being a part of this, but for the others. Not even He could have heard me above the agony, and the rushing wind, and — now — the laughter of Mr. Black.

They were being murdered — the Smiths, Gibbses, Parkhills, Joseph Krueger and his son. Why did it take so long? On and on, as though the pleasure was in prolonging it. Nancy's hands were over her ears as she screamed. I opened my eyes a little and peered behind me. The snow was *stained with blood as close as a yard away. Of those who had chosen to stand against the* dal-yawii, *I could only see young Simon Parkhill. He too cried out, but with a sound of defiance in his voice as he swung a branch over his head. Then something, huge, dark, came at him, and his cry was silenced by a terrible cracking noise. I shut my eyes again.*

It went on almost forever, but finally ended. The last of the screams that fell silent were from our own throats. We looked up, though not yet behind us. Mr. Black, again clothed, stood over us like some benevolent preacher man. Past him, the clearing was still. He gestured for us to rise, but no one did. No one could.

Tom Hardman asked him if it was over. Mr. Black said that it was, that in two days a rescue party would find a way through the pass and take us out of the mountains. He warned us to bury our dead before then, and not just in the snow.

Our dead. Amanda McClain was the first to turn around. She screamed and fell into Patrick's arms. We . . .

This part of the entry, at the top of the next page, was illegible. Something moist had smeared the ink before it could dry. A third of the way down, Paul was able to read it again.

. . . buried all of them this morning, deeper than the others. We saw nothing of Mr. Black until we were done. He said that he was leaving but would see us again. I demanded to know what he meant, since this business was over. He told us it would never be over, not for us, not for our children or their children, not ever. The dal-yawii, *he said, were not that easily satisfied.*

*I told him that once away from these
mountains not he nor his shadows could hold us.
He laughed then, and said that there would be a
sign, and that we would be back here to stay. Then
he went off into the forest, the way he had come.*

A sign, Paul thought. The deaths of the Hardman child,
and Thorburn's own daughter.

The entry for January 6, Tuesday, ended with a single
line well before the bottom of the page.

*Whatever happens in the future, no one must
ever know of this.*

The January 7 entry, beginning on the next page, had
been reprinted verbatim in *Trails of Promise*. Paul read the
words that John Thorburn had forced himself to write:

*. . . because of the terrible illness that befell us so
near the end.*

Sickened, Paul dropped the diary.

So the Thorburn party had returned to the North Lake,
had built a town in the path of the pioneers and gold
seekers, had started an acclaimed artists' and writers' colony.

*Had murdered scores, possibly hundreds, through the decades as
part of an unending payment for their survival.*

Sherri Jordan had died in the same manner as the brave
Parkhill boy and the others.

Just as Gail was going to die.

He extracted the pages with the missing journal entries
then put everything back into the chest. Donning his jacket
he made certain the room looked undisturbed then slipped
out into the hallway. It did not take him long to complete
his search of the third floor. He found nothing.

Paul's head throbbed. He needed to talk to someone, to
share the secret of the Thorburn colony, because the

thought of it was threatening to drive him mad. Mary Sherman was the only person he could reach, perhaps the only one who might believe him.

Briefly abandoning caution, he ran down the steps. Another resident, her arms laden with books, had just come upstairs and was almost to her room on the far end of the second floor. He watched until she was inside then strode to Mary's room. He knocked twice but did not wait for an answer. The woman was alarmed when she saw him.

"Paul? My God, look at you! What is it?"

She took his arm to guide him in and made him sit. He caught his breath, stared at her.

"Something's wrong, something's really wrong," he told her. "You have to hear me out."

She nodded and sat on the end of the bed, across from him. He spoke for five minutes, wishing he could be briefer. The woman listened, not interrupting but shaking her head as she tried to comprehend what he was telling her.

"Dear Lord!" she finally exclaimed when he stopped. "It's not possible."

"I have proof." He pulled out the pages of John Thorburn's journal. "Read them. Do you have something for this headache?"

"Yes, in the bathroom."

He found a bottle of Tylenol, swallowed a couple of tablets with three glasses of water, and closed his eyes for a few minutes while Mary read the entries. She was shaken by the time she finished and handed them back.

"The monsters!" she snapped. "Paul, what do you want me to do?"

He glanced out the window at the falling snow. "I was hoping you could leave here, maybe bring help, but — "

"Not a chance," she said. "I was down at breakfast late and heard them say that the roads were already impossible to drive. And the phones aren't working."

He nodded. "I know. Damn this place!"

"Okay, so we can't get out of here yet. The most important thing is to find Gail. Tell me what your plan is, so I can help you."

"Mary, I can't ask you to get involved in this!"

She shrugged. "I'm already involved, dear boy. This can't be allowed to go on. Tell me."

He detailed his plan, which now sounded ludicrous, considering the weather and the limited time. Mary was aware of that.

"I agree with you that she has to be found before dark. Okay, I'll finish searching Big House. I belong here, so my wandering around won't raise too many eyebrows. In the meantime you can check out the cabins." She looked out the window. "Lord, I don't envy you that. Will you be all right?"

"Don't worry. You'll look for Walter McClain's radio?"

"Of course."

"Mary, listen," he said firmly, "I don't want you being the SWAT team or anything. If you find Gail but can't help her without risk, just leave it alone. Okay?"

She nodded. "I don't have a death wish. We'll need a time to meet." She checked her watch. "It's nine-forty. Can you be back here at one?"

"No, too late. I'll cover the grounds quickly and meet you at noon."

"Paul," she protested, "it's not long enough — "

"It'll have to be!" he snapped. "Mary, if she's not here, at the colony — "

"Then you go into Stillwell." She shook her head. "Christ, Paul."

He wrote down the numbers of the unoccupied rooms on the second floor and removed all the keys for Big House from Landry's ring. Mary opened the door and looked outside.

"It's clear. Paul, be careful."

"I only have to worry about the snow. You have *them*." He clutched her hand. "You be careful too."

He left. Mary watched him enter the stairwell then gathered up the keys and the list of room numbers.

CHAPTER TEN

Snow fell hard outside. Paul saw no one. A day like this was good for staying where you were — like inside a warm cabin. At least one risk was minimized.

Thin trails of smoke rose above Joe Landry's filthy quarters. He had abandoned the futile task of trying to plow in the face of the storm. Paul wondered if he'd noticed the missing keys. No time to dwell on that.

Four cabins were on the first path that Paul chose, only one of them occupied. The farthest, No. 7, was where Michael Whitney had stayed. Regardless of the storm, Paul walked the covered path cautiously. No one should be out in the storm, but he could take nothing for granted, the stakes being what they were.

No. 10 stood closer to Big House than he had guessed. The door was unlocked. No doubt all of the empty cabins would be accessible — except for the one where they held Gail.

There was no one in No. 10. He hurried out and continued along the path. It took nearly five minutes to reach No. 9. These cabins were spaced widely apart to accommodate anyone who made music: "Noisemakers," Michael had said.

Allan Kroll, once-renowned composer-conductor, occupied No. 9, his home away from home. Considering the weather, it was a wonder the man could make it to Big House for his meals. Didn't they pick him up or something? Smoke rose above the snow-blanketed roof, and there was the sound of a piano from inside as Paul went past. At least he was working.

No. 8 and No. 7 were also empty. Michael's former cabin, near the outer fence, was over a quarter-mile from Big House. Paul understood why the musician had joked about spending so much time in the day room.

The map at the message center showed a narrow trail along the fence that encircled the grounds. Utilizing the wrought-iron bars to keep from sinking too deeply, Paul trudged through the snow until he came to the end of another footpath. There were three cabins, two with residents, the third empty.

He wound up back at the edge of the parking lot, behind the stable. The force of the storm had abated, but snow still fell in light, steady flurries. Joe Landry and his helper were taking advantage of the break. The ill-tempered handyman plowed a swath through the lot on his way to the main gate; the other worked on clearing the asphalt. Paul chose the nearest footpath.

The cabins along there, two of which were unoccupied, yielded nothing. He retraced his steps to the parking area. He'd been listening to the distant drone of the snowplows and hadn't expected to see one, until it rounded a curve fifteen yards away. He dove off the path into the trees. The snow saved him from being jarred any harder than he was. He rolled down a bank, sank deeper then lay there, hoping the driver wouldn't notice the footprints, or care, if he did.

The sputtering plow went past. Paul waited another minute then pulled himself out of the drift. He climbed the bank, slipping twice before pulling himself up and over with the help of a handful of rabbit bush. The cleared path was his only consolation.

Nature had been toying with the region. Any respite from the storm was an illusion. Within a few minutes the snow again fell heavily, propelled by a swirling wind. From meager shelter behind a storage shed, Paul watched Landry drive the plow back into the stable. He could almost hear the string of obscenities. The second plow returned a minute later. They closed the double doors. Landry trudged to the smokehouse, the other man to the service entrance of Big House.

Had Paul considered how cold he was, how exhausted, he might not have continued. The next path had been cleared before the storm's resurgence. Kathy Parrish was in No. 17, the first cabin. The rest — three of them — were unoccupied, according to the message center. Paul searched them, slamming the last door shut in his growing frustration.

There was probably a shorter way to the next path, but he couldn't risk it through the forest in the storm. Again, he started from the parking area. But this one had not been cleared all morning. Residents were in No. 20 and No. 19, but not No. 18, the farthest one out.

The failures took their toll. Paul was freezing, could barely feel his toes. His muscles protested each plodding step through the drifts. His head throbbed again. Once he stumbled over a rock and could not make himself get up. The snow held him, like a blanket. He felt peaceful, safe . . .

But they were going to murder Gail! They had murdered Simon Parkhill and Sherri Jordan and so many others in-between and now they were going to murder Gail. He couldn't let it happen. Not even the snow — *December kin bring some nasty storms* — could prevent him from finding Gail before they sacrificed her to the fears they had inherited from their ancestors.

He got up and willed his body to No. 18. Empty. Only one path remained: his own. No. 12. How ironic if they were holding her there. No, not likely; but he had to make sure.

The snow held him back like a giant hand as he struggled to square one — which was how he thought of the parking area. Then it swirled around him as he started up the familiar path. He glanced at No. 13 but gave no thought to stopping. Had they been holding Gail there, he would have found her earlier that morning. . . .

No. 12 was empty. Unless he had missed something on the map, Paul had to concede that Gail was not being held in any of the colony's outer buildings. That left the rest of Big House.

And Stillwell.

He needed rest, warmth. What good would it do Gail if he fell in the snow again and couldn't get up? His cabin was close. Just a few minutes . . .

The last yards to No. 11 were the longest that he had walked all morning. His numbed fingers frustrated him as he tried to unlock the door. Finally inside, he turned up the thermostat then crumpled atop the thunderbird rug, where he shivered uncontrollably.

Get up, dammit!

He rose and slowly stripped down to his shorts and T-shirt, then pulled a blanket from the bed and wrapped it around him. His toes were numb but not discolored. He massaged them, walked around the cabin. Soon he could feel them. Relieved, he sat on the bed and huddled in more blankets. He stared at the Wieghorst and concentrated on staying awake.

But fatigue lured him. He might have succumbed but for a noise that penetrated the haze. It came from outside, on the porch. Paul knew what it was.

Lunchtime.

Five minutes past twelve. He hadn't thought about time all morning. Mary expected him at noon. He had insisted he would be there.

"Shit," he muttered, throwing off the blankets. He dressed warmly, pulled on three pairs of socks. Two minutes later he was ready.

He returned to Big House in the heavy snow. The thermometer at the service entrance read 5°.

"Hello, Paul, what brings you out in this nasty weather?"

Walter McClain, cordial but curious enough to ignore the Prime Directive, approached him in the corridor. Paul forced a smile.

"Some research that couldn't wait," he replied. "You know."

The associate director nodded. "See you later."

They passed each other, McClain watching Paul. Was he suspicious? Paul wondered. But why should he be? Paul couldn't take that chance. The man could check with Jane Tyler to see if he'd been there. He hated to lose a minute, but he had to go to the library.

He strode quickly across the central hall. The librarian eyed him over her glasses. He nodded as he walked to one of the nearest shelves, where she'd seen him working before. Two others were in the library. He sat down with some books, opened them, made notes. His gaze was seldom off the clock.

Twelve-thirty.

It was killing him, but it might buy him the rest of the day. He spent ten minutes there and left. McClain saw him coming out of the library. He had made the right move.

"My God, where have you been?" Mary exclaimed as he rushed into her room. "I was worried."

"Did you find her?" he asked brusquely.

"No. Then you didn't either."

He shook his head. "Not a damned thing! How far did you get?"

"I checked all the unoccupied rooms. Even closets. The only thing on the second floor I couldn't get into was

Harriet Thorburn's quarters. But she always goes downstairs in the middle of the afternoon. I'll try it later."

"You be careful doing that," Paul warned. "What about the first floor?"

"Almost everything down there is accessible to anyone. I poked around in a few odd places. Nothing. But I know where Walter McClain's radio is."

"Where?"

"In a small closet behind his desk. But that's the problem. He's either there or he keeps his office locked. And we don't have the key."

"If we need to, we'll find a way in. You did good, Mary. Thanks."

She shrugged. "Big deal. We didn't find Gail."

"It's not over yet!" he snapped. "They didn't take her far, I'm sure of it. We know where she's not, so it's either the old lady's rooms — or Stillwell."

"Little towns, Paul, can get awfully big when you're looking for something that no one wants you to find."

He nodded. "I know, but I'm going anyway."

"If you find her, get her out of there and down to Truckee or wherever as fast as you can."

"What about you? I was going to come back —"

"Don't be foolish. They're not going to do anything to me. I'm perfectly safe here. Just make sure you bring the blasted cavalry tomorrow!"

"I will." He turned to leave, then looked at Mary. "If I can't find Gail now, I'll be back . . . because I sure as hell know where she'll be tonight."

He raced down the stairs and out the rear door. The temperature had dropped another degree. Looking wistfully at his buried Oldsmobile, he walked around to the side of Big House and started toward the main gate.

Most of the road had been cleared during the one brief lull. The new snow rose above his ankles, but there were mounds on either side over five feet high.

The road beyond the main gate was obliterated by drifts. Each step became part of a tiring process: extract a leg from one deep hole, make another, and do it again. He fell once, not realizing he had strayed off the road to the rim of a bank. It winded him, and he lay there for a few moments, struggling for breath.

Slowly. Go more slowly. The road intersected S. Lakeshore Drive. Soon Thorburn Lake — gray and brooding, not the blue jewel he had seen on the first day — was on his left. There, with few trees for shelter, the wind threw whips of snow at his face and chilled his body through the layers of clothes.

Paul thought: *How did your daddy die? Oh, he froze to death. And he didn't even like snow that much.*

What if he couldn't find Gail in the town? He had already told Mary he would return to the colony. But how? Right now there was some question about reaching Stillwell. And if he got back later, then what? Show up at the appointed time, dripping guns like Rambo, or Ripley hunting aliens? His fans would have been disappointed, because Paul hated guns, knew little about them other than what he briefly absorbed in research for authenticity.

Besides, what good would weapons be against whatever was in the clearing?

Okay, give up, he told himself. *With that kind of motivation, why not lay down here in the snow and the hell with it! Or even better still — assuming you can stand a little more effort — turn around, go back to the colony, forget this bullshit. Finish out your four weeks, go back to the career, the kids. Have a nice life. Come back someday and do another residency. . . .*

He was near the lake when he realized that he now stood still. He couldn't remember why he'd stopped, or when. Disgusted with himself, he glanced across the lake at unseen enemies and shouted "*No!*" A faint echo mimicked him. The wind replied with a puzzled howl; those who dwelled below the surface of the lake remained silent.

Satisfied, Paul started walking again, and walking, and walking . . .

Ahead, less than half a mile, the small town waited.

Paul continued walking, and walking, and walking . . .

Ahead, less than a quarter-mile, the small town waited.

Paul continued walking, and — staggering . . .

Then, the wind sighed something like *you've won for now* and relented as Paul looked up and realized that he neared Washo Street.

Snow piled up on untended streets. The Mule Deer Cafe was closed; so was Fry Mercantile and Dooley's Garage, even the Nugget Bar. Someone moved around inside Mountain Apothecary. But that was because the woman who owned the store lived above it and had nothing better to do that afternoon, the cable being out and probably causing her to miss *One Life to Live*. The flashing light at Washo and Alpine was a meaningless beacon in the gray-white gloom.

He was concerned about what he had to do, mostly of being seen and having it all come to a premature end. Even if he could avoid people, the task seemed overwhelming. The small town had grown large, as Mary had said, and there were precious few hours of daylight left. It was one-fifty. Nearly an hour to get here from the colony!

Nor could he continue until he had a few minutes out of the storm. He was freezing, exhausted. He had worked hard and now paid the price.

An alley ran behind the stores on the west side of Washo Street. He hadn't noticed it at first. The entrance from S. Lakeshore Drive was hidden by mounds of snow pushed off to the side when part of the road had been cleared earlier. The drifts in the alley itself were deep. But it gave him a better option than Stillwell's main thoroughfare.

Paul left the road and trudged to the first building. A sign on the door read DELIVERIES, but nothing had been delivered there in years, for the door was nailed shut.

There was a window, mostly covered by boards. He looked inside, saw the cannibalized interior of a bathroom. Shards of broken glass covered the floor. No shelter there, since it was just as cold within. He moved on.

The next store was another long-abandoned shell. A narrow driveway ran along the side. He walked cautiously to the front, peered up and down Washo Street. Nothing. Stillwell was blind to his presence. Its citizens were somewhere else. Somewhere warm, dry.

But Paul remained in the shadows. Back to the alley, past more derelict buildings, until he came to Poplar Street. To his right, Poplar dead-ended near the base of Whiskey Hill. He turned left and hurried across Washo to the alley that ran behind the stores on the next block.

He had already made Fry Mercantile his next goal.

A CLOSED sign hung in the window. He'd noticed it before. Even if that was a mistake and someone was in the store, it would probably just be Jenny. Her father wouldn't risk his illness to this kind of weather. Just Jenny Fry and . . .

Gail?

Would they trust their prisoner to the strange young woman who recited poetry and took day trips to Hallucination? But if Gail were bound and gagged, maybe drugged, then would it matter who was watching her?

Bound and gagged. This woman had witnessed the murder of her husband and child. For the first time in five years she had faced it, admitting to herself that — maybe — there was some sort of life to live. How did she feel now? What was her opinion of the world? A world with places like Costa Nueva and Stillwell and the Thorburn Colony?

Stop thinking, about it, or you won't do her a damn bit of good! Whatever they'd already done to Gail was nothing compared to what they planned to do.

The heavy door at the back of Fry Mercantile was locked and bolted from the inside. A single small window hovered a foot over Paul's head. He looked around for a way to climb up. There was a dumpster a few feet down the alley, probably shared by a few businesses. It was half-full and heavy, despite being on wheels. He managed to push it under the window. He climbed up, tried to open the window: locked.

Break it! Damn the risk, time was too valuable.

He found a brick doorstop near the back of the Mule Deer Cafe and used it to smash out one of the panes. The glass shattered in a few large pieces. He picked out the ones that had not fallen inside, then unlocked the window and climbed through.

Fry Mercantile's back room was mostly for storage, with a small office and bathroom. The only other door led into the store. He checked up front quickly, saw no lights on. The store was empty.

He covered the broken square of glass with an end flap from a corrugated carton. For the first time since leaving Big House he was out of the storm and able to rest. The room felt warm to him, even with the thermostat turned down. He sat in a worn armchair, put his head back, and shut his eyes for a moment, letting his tired body soak up the warmth.

Stillwell, California, probably didn't have a phone book; maybe two poorly mimeographed sheets of paper. But a Rolodex sat on an old metal desk. He flipped through it, noticing that the Frys used it to keep a record of what their customers owed. He found Walter McClain's card first. The associate director's address was neatly printed in the upper left-hand corner. Not that it mattered, for McClain's A-frame on Whiskey Hill was the only other house he knew, aside from the Fry place on Trout Lane. It was the addresses of the rest — Hardman, Tyler, both Stillwells — that he wanted. He found them all and pocketed the cards.

He was hungry and helped himself to a quart of milk and a bag of Chips Ahoy. He finished half of each.

Ten minutes there. Too long. He cleaned up the broken glass and left by the same way he had come in.

The alley ended at Alpine Street, across from Idlewood Livery. Paul first sidled along the old storefronts to Washo, where he looked up and down. Still deserted. He dashed to the door of the livery and peered in.

Something was there again, under the burlap cover in back. Although he had expected this, Paul could hear his heart pounding as he ran around the door in the alley. But the oversized door was sealed with an enormous padlock, the kind that on television even bullets shot from high-powered rifles couldn't open.

In spite of this imposing deterrent, the door did not seem that sturdy. It rattled when he shook the knob. Maybe he could break it down. The idea seemed ridiculous. In movies, people broke down all kinds of doors. Even in his novels some of his characters did it. But for real? He held the knob with both hands, gave an exploratory shove with his shoulder, then leaned back and rammed it. The rotting wood in the frame splintered; the door opened so easily he nearly fell.

He was in an area that had once been used for storing tack. A wide doorless opening led into the stable. He raced to the rear stall and grabbed the tarp but decided against yanking it off. His hand shaking, he looked underneath . . .

. . . at Gail Farringer's teal blue Sentra.

"*Bastards!*" he cried. "*You goddamn crazy bastards!*"

Both front windows were open, keys in the ignition. The car was empty. He removed the keys and started to open the trunk, then hesitated. Although it made no sense, what if Gail's body was in there? He trembled, not from the cold, as he played the discovery scenario over and over in his head. Finally he raised the trunk and saw only her belongings.

Her paintings were stacked under three pieces of luggage. A couple of sketchpads had been thrown in last. He absently flipped the pages as he imagined one of *them* loading the bags then driving her car to the livery. Who had done it? McClain? One of the Stillwells?

The sketches were recent ones. One of Big House, another of the lake, a third of Thorburn Peak . . .

And a half done portrait of Paul Fleming.

He stared at it in disbelief. Had *they* seen it? Did they suspect his relationship with Gail? Maybe they had been watching him since he began his crusade, following his steps, laughing at his persistence, wanting to see how far he would get in their world. Playing with him, ready to step in as soon as he was close and say *Nice try, asshole, now we'll take you to her.*

He tore the sketch out, folded it many times, and shoved it in his pocket. Whatever they did or didn't know, it wasn't going to stop him. Leaving the trunk exactly as it had been, he put the keys back and smoothed the tarp over the Sentra.

Outside, he wedged the door from underneath so it would stay closed. He weighed his choices. The residences of Jake and Roy Stillwell were on Snowcrest Way, the same as Walter McClain's A-frame, which put all three on Whiskey Hill. The Fry house was nearby, and farther down Trout Lane were those belonging to Nora Hardman and the Tylers. The three of them were at the colony; so was McClain. The Frys were undoubtedly home.

Paul chose Whiskey Hill. He guessed that one of the Stillwells would be responsible for watching Gail.

The storm was relenting. Light snowfall, less severe wind. It was past two-thirty when he reached the far end of the alley and turned onto Placer Street.

A machine's sputtering roar broke the long eerie silence. The town made ready to clear its streets. From the corner of Washo and Placer, Paul saw Carl Stillwell emerge from the sheriff's office, across from Dooley's Garage and not far from where he stood. It was fortunate that the deputy went in the other direction. Paul watched him walk to Mountain Apothecary then hurried to the other side of the street after Stillwell had gone in.

Placer Street curved left behind the back of the deserted Liberty Mill, which took up the entire block. It then turned sharply right and wound up the side of Whiskey Hill. The tree-lined street was now called Snowcrest Way. Houses sat back from the road, at the end of long drives. Paul read the address on the first mailbox and kept walking.

Snowcrest Way grew steeper. It was slippery beneath the thick layer of new powder. He fell a few times and once slid back a couple of yards. Finally he came to 74 Snowcrest Way, the home of Jake Stillwell and his son.

Gray smoke poured from a brick chimney on the side of the conventional ranch-style home. Utilizing the cover of trees, Paul plowed through deep drifts and circled around to within five yards of the back door. He hid behind a stack of wood and studied the house, noticing low, horizontal windows at ground level, mostly covered by snow. A basement. Maybe the rest of California couldn't have them, but that rule didn't seem to apply up here.

He heard a sound from somewhere inside. It was vaguely familiar. He crept closer to the house and peered in a basement window. Jake Stillwell was cutting wood with a power saw. Most of the tiled cellar had been converted into a workshop. Stillwell was intent on his hobby. Paul could have watched him for a long time without the man looking up. But he moved on, peering through each window, until he had circled the house.

The mayor apparently had nothing to hide. Gail was not there.

He took the long way back to the road, diving for cover once when a Bronco four-by-four rumbled down the hill, its heavy tire chains clanking loudly. Paul couldn't see the driver. When the Bronco was gone he started back up Snowcrest Way, mindful that people who lived in this environment didn't need a two-day thaw to resume their lives.

Sheriff Roy Stillwell's house, a hundred yards farther up, was an old two-story brick colonial with a large barn in back. The driveway and part of the street had recently been cleared. Paul guessed the lawman was in town, but he nevertheless approached cautiously.

This one, he knew, would have to be searched from inside.

A large picture window in the den overlooked the partially visible town and Thorburn Lake. On clear days Roy Stillwell had an awesome view from his stuffed armchair. *I hope you got to enjoy it yesterday, Sheriff, because if I have anything to do about it your life is going to change.*

The window was locked. Paul went to the next one, much smaller. Inside was a room of about eighty square feet, its only furniture a tubular side chair. Two black file cabinets stood against the near wall. A utility room, seldom used. He tried to raise the window, which was unlocked but stuck. He worked until it gave way then climbed in.

Crossing the room, Paul realized he was tracking snow. He pulled off his boots and left them in a corner, then brushed more snow off his clothes. Ready, he searched Roy Stillwell's house.

His caution was unwarranted on the first floor. All of the rooms were empty. He tried the phone in the kitchen. The line was dead.

The basement was nothing more than a storage room, about the size of a walk-in closet. Cases of Coors beer in bottles were stacked against the walls. Paul looked for doors leading into other chambers, but there were none. He went back upstairs.

Second floor. All of the doors in the hallway were open, except one. A linen closet. Gail was not there. Paul swore at himself for guessing wrong again.

Downstairs, a door slammed.

Paul backed away from the top of the stairs and ducked into what was apparently a seldom-used guest bedroom in the front of the house. From the window he saw Roy Stillwell's squad car parked a few yards from the door. He hadn't heard it pull up.

Too late to worry about that. The sheriff was inside. Paul opened a closet door and entered an oppressive darkness that smelled strongly of camphor. He waited, listened.

Stillwell was in the kitchen, making himself something to eat. The refrigerator door opened and closed a few times; dished clinked. Music came on: Randy Travis. Sometimes the sheriff sang along, even with food stuffed in his mouth.

Twenty minutes in the closet; twenty minutes that felt like twenty hours as Paul thought about his boots in the room below and wondered if Stillwell would find them. The man had to be going back to town; he had just stopped home for a bite. He would be out of there soon, and Paul would follow —

Roy Stillwell started up the stairs.

His footfalls sounded like the beating of a drum. He reached the top and sounded so close Paul thought he was in the same room. But he had gone past, to a bathroom near the end of the hall. From the sounds that followed, it was likely he would be occupied for a while.

Paul slipped out of the closet, carefully shutting the door, then peered out into the hallway. The bathroom door, open, was on the same side. Stillwell continued his business loudly as Paul crept to the stairs, then ran down. Back to the utility room, where he snatched up his boots and climbed out the window, pushing it down after him. With the boots in hand he ran behind the barn, keeping it between himself and the house until he was into dense woods, forty yards away, where he stopped.

His feet were wet and freezing. Nothing he could do about it, other than pull the boots on. Using the cover of the woods, he trudged back to Snowcrest Way in snow at times waist deep.

The road was now little wider than a driveway as it neared the top of Whiskey Hill. There was only one house left.

Walter McClain's A-frame.

An impressive home on half an acre of land, all for a man who lived by himself and spent most of his time somewhere else. No vehicles were parked there, and the snow along the driveway had not been disturbed, aside from the tracks of a small animal. Nor was there any smoke from the tall chimney. Still, Paul approached warily, for there was little shelter. He glanced back at Snowcrest Way a few times.

McClain told residents at the colony to keep their doors unlocked, but his house was sealed tighter than a bank vault. After checking every door and window, Paul dug around in the snow-covered shrubbery along the base until he found a large rock. He carried it to the kitchen window and hesitated for only a second before shoving it through the glass. It was nearly three-thirty; no more time to be discreet.

He enlarged the opening then listened. The breaking glass had not roused anyone. He climbed inside the attractively paneled room and explored every square foot of the house. For the third time he was frustrated on Whiskey Hill, although not surprised.

Before leaving he helped himself to some dry socks from Walter McClain's dresser. At three-forty he started down Snowcrest Way.

Harriet Thorburn was late.

Mary usually saw her on the first floor between two and two-thirty. But today she hadn't appeared on the great staircase until three-twenty, while Mary was crossing the main central hall from the day room. She had found a lot of reasons for being downstairs during the workday and, like Paul, worried about arousing suspicions. But other than Jane Tyler, who seemed to treat everyone with equal indignation and distrust, she had not encountered any of the descendants more than once.

Mary cursed age and weight as she tried to climb the service stairs faster than normal. Breathless, she approached the door that separated the guestrooms from Harriet

Thorburn's private quarters. She opened it with one of the keys that Paul had given her.

Another corridor. Mirrors on both walls in fancy scrolled frames. The end wall, twenty-five feet from where she stood, was covered by a large, colorful Indian rug. Two pairs of double doors were opposite each other, halfway down. Mary chose the set on the left and tried the knob. It was unlocked. She opened the door an inch and made sure no one was inside before she entered Harriet Thorburn's drawing room. Two chairs and a love seat wore brightly flowered chintz coverings, which matched the draperies. Dozens of framed photographs filled the tops of two Golden Oak sideboards and the mantel of a small stone fireplace. A harp stood in one corner, next to an ancient music stand. A comfortable room; but Mary spent little time there.

A door in the right-hand wall led into Harriet Thorburn's large bedroom. Mary wondered if the frail woman felt lost in the middle of the mahogany poster bed that dominated the chamber. A Queen Anne highboy was undoubtedly priceless. In fact everything there, Mary decided, was incredibly old, except for a portable television sitting on top of a side table.

But knowing what she now did about this descendant of John Thorburn, Mary felt strange standing there. *Crossed hands on a pillow*, she thought. She glanced at the vanity and suddenly thought about Vera Miles's Lila Crane character walking around Mrs. Bates's bedroom in *Psycho*. It made her shudder. Gail Farringer was obviously not there. She wanted out.

The door opened behind her. There was a click; light filled the room. Mary turned, then froze.

The way down Whiskey Hill was not easy. Paul stayed off the road for fear of suddenly confronting a vehicle. One did pass: Roy Stillwell's squad car, which Paul watched from a clump of skeletal trees.

Snow fell lightly again as he reached the bottom of the hill. Four o'clock. The colony day had just ended. He might not be out of place walking around Stillwell now, he thought, as he neared the intersection of Washo and Placer. Then he remembered the cars buried behind Big House. No, stay in the shadows. It was the only sure way.

He hid in the doorway of an empty store and checked the activity on Washo. There were a couple of vehicles by the Nugget Bar, which had just opened. Closer to him, Roy Stillwell's squad car and a Chevy Blazer were parked by the sheriff's office. Looking at them, Paul knew where he was going next.

He assumed both lawmen were inside. Jake Stillwell was home. The colony staff more than likely remained at work.

That eliminated all the descendants except Dan Fry and his daughter.

Gail was in their house. He would bet on it.

One loose end was tied when Carl Stillwell stepped out of the station. He opened the front door of his Blazer, took something from the glove compartment, looked up and down the street, and went back in.

How was he going to cross Washo? Paul wondered. What if one of them came out again? Exposure, though brief, could not be avoided. Still, he had to chance it.

His gaze on the sheriff's office, he stepped off the curb. Washo Street had been cleared but remained slippery. Without realizing it he was practically running to the other side.

Mostly there, his feet gave way. He fell backward, hard. The impact stunned him. He lay there a few moments then crawled up the curb, over the sidewalk, to the corner building. He stopped there, his back against the brick façade, and shook off the haze that blurred his vision. His neck hurt from the fall, and he stretched it, hoping to ease the pain.

Move, dammit! The sheriff's station . . . move!

He pulled himself up, staggered to the alley, then hurried past the back of Dooley's Garage and other stores to Alpine Street. He remembered to check the door of Idlewood Livery. It was still wedged tightly.

Someone walked along Alpine Street from the direction of Trout Lane: Salazar, from the restaurant. Paul hid in a doorway and watched him pass. The heavyset man reached Washo Street and turned the corner. Satisfied that no one else was around, Paul left the alley.

The Fry house stood out ominously on the deserted Trout Lane. A few days ago he had helped Jenny carry groceries to her sick father. Now he approached their house like a burglar, using doorways, trees along the edge of the curb, and finally the fence of the house next door for cover. No one lived there. Windows were boarded up; the roof was in terrible disrepair.

Paul decided to take advantage of the house being deserted. He passed through a broken gate in the picket fence and crept stealthily to the side of the house. There, next to a large, decaying woodbin, he felt safe from exposure for the first time in a while.

Smoke poured from the chimney of the Fry house. Maybe just one was home, if the other had decided to open the store for the rest of the afternoon. The windows, all with light-colored shades drawn, revealed nothing.

Farther along the side fence a couple of slats were missing. Paul couldn't fit through. As he started to widen the opening, he heard a noise. A cat scuttled atop the garbage cans in a sheltered niche on the side of the Fry house. He watched as the hungry animal squeezed under the lid of a half-opened can. The lid came loose, clattered against the next can, and fell to the snow. The cat froze then began rummaging.

A shade went up. Jenny Fry opened the window. The animal jumped from the can, knocking it over. There had not been much inside. Jenny yelled "Shoo!" and beat her hand against the sill until the cat ran off. She watched it disappear around back, then closed the window and pulled the shade.

Paul waited for her to take care of the overturned can. After three frustrating minutes he decided she wasn't going to come out. Removing another slat allowed him a wide enough opening. His gaze on the house, he crossed the snow-filled yard. He stopped once behind the trunk of a young Ponderosa pine then went on until he knelt under a window.

His back pressed against the side of the house, he caught his breath. This was crazy, he thought. Even if he got inside without being seen or heard, how was he going to move around and look for Gail?

The basement. There were windows at his feet on either side. Small, but enough to fit through if he could get one open. The nearest was caked with soot from the inside. He crept to the other. Through a narrow opening he could see a portion of the Frys' dreary basement. No lights were on, only the furnace's red glow from an unseen corner.

Some luck: one of the small panes was broken. A rag had been stuffed in, waiting for the glass to be replaced. Paul worked the rag free and buried it under the snow. Putting his hand inside, he unlocked the window and pushed it in slowly, quietly, despite the urgency he felt.

Four-fifteen. It would be dark in less than an hour.

He squeezed through and lowered himself to the cracked concrete floor, then shut the window. It seemed oppressively hot. Cartons with names of diverse products were stacked along one wall. Jars of nuts, bolts, and nails lined shelves. There was a workbench, gray with dust and spider webs. Across from it, a rusty old bicycle lay on its side.

Farther in, past the wood staircase to the kitchen, was the hidden corner. As Paul moved toward the red glow, it suddenly flared brighter. A loud chuffing noise startled him, until he realized the furnace had turned on. He circled the base of the stairs, looking up at the kitchen door. From above came Dan Fry's terrible racking cough.

Paul stopped, peering into the niche. A cot ran lengthwise against the wall, opposite the furnace. Gail Farringer, dressed in a heavy sweater despite the heat, lay on it, either asleep or . . .

No, not dead. Her hands and feet were bound; a belt was secured around her waist and under the cot. She was gagged with a red bandanna. Her boots were on the floor near the furnace.

Still, until he knew for sure, Paul's heart raced. He leaned over her. "Gail?" he whispered.

Her eyes snapped open. She saw him, and they widened. The garbled sounds she made through the gag were too loud. He put a finger to his lips. She understood, nodded.

The knot in the bandanna was tight; it must have been hurting her. He loosened it, and she moved her jaw painfully.

"Thank God you're here!" she gasped. "Paul, *what's happening?*"

"Later," he said, looking up as Fry's cough echoed through the house. "We have to get out of here!"

The other knots were hard to work loose. Paul had a small pocketknife on his key chain — not sharp, but it might take too long to find something else in the basement.

While Paul worked, Gail whispered in a halting voice, "They came . . . early this morning. I don't know how many, but . . . they were in my cabin before I was awake. They tied me up, put me . . . in a *sack!*" She bit her lip. "It was Arthur, the cook! Big, gentle Arthur carried me out and put me in someone's trunk. They . . . drove me here."

He cut the last strands of the rope around her wrists. She threw her arms around him, and they held each other. Then Paul said, "I'd better finish."

"That . . . woman has been down here a few times," Gail continued. "She sits here, says crazy things, strokes my hair. She feeds me, too, but won't answer anything." She touched his arm; her hand was trembling. "Paul?"

"Yes?"

"They were going to do . . . something awful to me."

"It won't happen now. There." He threw the piece of rope on the floor. "Hurry, get your boots on."

As she did, Paul realized Fry's coughing was louder. He looked up. The door was open. Jenny stood on the stairs, a third of the way down, looking over the rail.

"Paul, what a nice surprise." She smiled. "I didn't know you were friends." Louder, she called, "Dad? We have another visitor."

Reacting quickly, Paul circled to the base of the stairs and climbed them two at a time. Jenny backed up. The stairs were uneven; he stumbled once. His only thought — perhaps their only chance — was to get to Jenny.

Then Dan Fry was next to his daughter. Paul looked into the barrels of the man's shotgun and froze.

"Why'd you come here?" Fry wheezed. "You can't know what you stuck yourself into." He sounded apologetic.

Paul glared at him. "Wanna bet?"

Fry glanced down at Gail. "Jenny's gonna tie you back up. You let her, or I'll blow his friggin' head off. Understand?"

"Yes," Gail said coldly.

"You, get your belly up against the rail and your hands out over the side," he ordered Paul. "Don't even breathe while Jenny's goin' down."

Paul did as he was told. Jenny passed him, still smiling. As she reached the bottom, her father exploded in a paroxysm of coughing. The shotgun was aimed at the steps. Paul whirled around and grabbed the cold metal with both hands, trying to yank it away. But Dan Fry had once been a strong man. Even now, racked by illness, he was the equal of his younger aggressor. They wrestled with the gun. Paul finally pulled it free but nearly lost his balance. The shotgun flew from his hands, down past Jenny, and struck the hard basement floor. Both barrels were discharged with an ear-splitting roar, the metal spray ripping a hole in the wall.

"*Damn you!*" Fry yelled, reaching for Paul with both hands as blood trickled from his mouth. Paul sidestepped the lunging attempt, and, still coughing, Fry tumbled down the basement steps. There was a disquieting sound when the floor checked his fall. His body thrashed for a moment.

Then the coughing stopped.

Jenny knelt by her father's body, poking it in hope of finding some life. Paul started down the stairs, then halted when she stared up at him.

"You killed him," she said dully, then wailed, "*You killed my father! Oh no, he's dead!*"

She stood and screamed. Paul clenched his fists, uncertain what to do. Gail spun the woman around and drove a fist into her face. Jenny moaned then went down, her fall broken by her father's body.

"Let's go!" Paul shouted.

He grabbed Gail's hand. They ran up the stairs and into the kitchen. Paul noticed Jenny's purse on the table. "Wait a minute," he said, opening it.

"What are you looking for?" Gail asked.

"Car keys. Ah, here we go."

"What about your car? How did you get to town?"

He rolled up a shade halfway. The snow was falling harder than a few minutes before.

"It's been like this all day," he said. "My car's buried at the colony."

"You *walked* to town?"

"Yeah."

"To look for me?"

He shrugged. "Listen, you better find a coat or something before we go out."

She kissed him, only for a moment, but hard, then hurried into the living room and found a closet near the front door. Paul checked the phone. Dead. He looked out the window. Trout Lane was deserted. Apparently no one had heard the gunshot.

Gail was ready. She handed him a pair of heavy gloves. "You left yours in the basement," she said. "They were torn anyway."

"Thanks."

They went out the front door and ran to a large shed that doubled as a garage. Paul raised the door. The only vehicle was a five-year-old Ford pickup. It appeared ready for the road: no chains, but the tires were studded. They climbed into the cab, and he started the engine. It protested then finally turned over. He let it run for a minute.

"This is crazy," he said. "I'm not sure we can get out of here. The road out of Stillwell is probably buried. Maybe we're better off finding someplace to hide until we know it's clear."

"Then why don't we?" Gail asked.

He slammed a fist on the dashboard. "Because these are crazy, desperate people! Wherever we hide — in town, at the colony — they *will* find us. Right now they're not expecting this, so we have an advantage."

She nodded. "Let's try it."

He forced the pickup through the deep snow in the driveway. Trout Lane and Alpine Street had been cleared once, but the slick surface was covered by another inch of powder. Luckily the studded tires bit deeply and held. As long as it stayed like this, he thought, they might make it.

Their element of surprise was suddenly gone.

Carl Stillwell's Blazer turned onto Alpine Street.

"Shit," Paul muttered. "Gail, hold on!"

"What are you going to do?"

"He doesn't know who we are yet, so he won't be expecting anything. We're going to ram the bastard."

Paul maintained his speed as the Blazer neared. When the vehicles were five yards apart he could see Carl Stillwell's ruddy face. The deputy stared as he realized that neither of the Frys was in the truck.

"*Now!*" Paul yelled, shifting and accelerating. The tires first caught the ice then skidded when he jerked the wheel to the left. But even without full control the effect was the same, the vehicles being so close. The pickup plowed into Stillwell's door with a frightening crunch of metal against metal. A headlight shattered; the front bumper, already loose, fell off. But the worst of the damage was to the Blazer.

Paul cut back to the right. The vehicles rubbed lengthwise for a second, finally separating. He slowed and regained control.

"Are you all right?" he asked Gail.

She nodded. "I'm fine."

They looked back. The Blazer had come to a stop against the curb in front of Idlewood Livery. Carl Stillwell opened the door, which nearly fell off. He staggered away from the vehicle, stared at them, then crumpled to the snow.

"Was he in your room this morning?" Paul asked.

"Yes. He held me while Arthur tied me up. He . . . hurt me."

"I'd like to drive back over his face."

"So would I, but let's just go!"

They turned onto Washo Street. The wind from off the lake pushed the snow hard behind them. Paul watched the sheriff's office until they crossed Placer Street. Half a minute later they were beyond the last of the town's buildings.

But on its only run of the day the snowplow had given up halfway to the Aspen Creek bridge. A mound of snow several feet high blocked the road. No one was driving in or out of Stillwell that day.

"So we do it on foot," Paul said. "Are you up to it?"

"Yes, but what about you? I noticed you limping before."

"I'm fine. Come on!"

He wasn't fine. His ankle throbbed from a fall on Whiskey Hill; his neck was sore. *Screw it*, he told himself. He'd worry about it when they were somewhere safe. He'd take Gail away from this madness, then — as Mary had put it — they'd come back with the cavalry.

Mary. By now she'd found nothing in Harriet Thorburn's quarters and was safely back in her room. But *was* she safe? Were any of the residents safe from these people, all of who would soon be aware that the end was near? What would they do in desperation? Paul tried not to think about it.

A sign, barely above the top of a drift, read ONE-LANE BRIDGE AHEAD. It was near, although with the snow and descending night they could not see farther than ten yards.

"Paul, listen," Gail said.

He heard it too. From behind, a motor. They went faster, Paul gnashing his teeth against the pain. Then another sound: the rushing water of Aspen Creek. Ice had formed all along the sides, but it was wide, and open water ran through the center of it.

On the bridge now. Holding tightly to each other, they slowly forced their way through the deep snow.

A gunshot, fired high above their heads, echoed somewhere. Barely visible behind them, Roy Stillwell called out, "That's far enough. We don't want to hurt you."

"Gail, run!" Paul yelled, putting himself between her and the sheriff. Stillwell said something like "Damn fools." Then a bullet hit one of the trusses near Paul's head. He jumped aside, landed awkwardly, and struck a waist-high guardrail. His momentum carried him over, and he plummeted to the surging water below.

"*Paul!*"

His head grazed a large rock in the middle of the creek. A numbing chill captured him as the water rose around him, penetrating his clothes. He felt the current moving him along, then . . .

Nothing.

CHAPTER ELEVEN

Someplace dark but warm.

A familiar place, with a familiar smell and a familiar feel under his bound hands.

The thick softness of the thunderbird rug.

Paul was a prisoner in his own cabin.

Why were the lights off, the fireplace dead? Maybe he was blind, or his head hadn't cleared enough, or they had something over his eyes. No, he could dimly see outlines of things. And as he became used to the darkness he knew that someone sat in a chair by the door.

"Paul? Paul, can you hear me?" Gail's voice.

"Yeah," he said with difficulty. His mouth felt like straw.

"Thank God!" she exclaimed. "You were out for hours. Paul, they have us at the colony again."

"I know." He tried to move. Everything hurt. "Jesus, what happened?"

"You better keep it down," a man cautioned, and punctuated the warning by spitting loudly on the cabin floor. Their jailer was Jake Stillwell.

Paul, like Gail, wore different clothes. He started to remember things as his head cleared.

"The creek," he whispered. "How did I get out of there?"

"That sheriff was going to let you drown," Gail said bitterly. "The bastard! He said it didn't make any difference."

"Then . . . you . . .?"

Three quick knocks sounded on the door. Stillwell got up as Walter McClain entered and switched on the light, nearly blinding Paul and Gail.

"So he's back," McClain muttered. He crossed the room and stood over them. "We had no idea you were such good friends. You take her from the Fry house — killing poor old Dan in the process — and she pulls you out of Aspen Creek! More than just friends, I think. Oh, if we'd only known, then none of this would be happening."

"McClain." Paul glared up at the man. "You son of a bitch!"

"Actually, I'm glad you didn't drown. It's been so long since we've had two at the same time."

"Two for *what?*" Gail asked.

McClain smiled grimly at Paul. "I don't understand how, but *he* knows. Don't you, Paul?"

"You won't get away with it this time!" Paul snapped. "I'm not like Gail, or Sherri Jordan, or Christ knows how many others you murdered! It's *over*, don't you understand?"

"That will be my problem," McClain said. "A traffic accident on your way to the casinos, something like that. Terrible tragedy. Such a well-known, talented writer. But accidents happen, Paul. No one will suspect anything different." McClain turned to go then looked at him again. "Tell me, how *did* you figure it out?"

"Go fuck yourself."

McClain smiled. "I really do want to know. Since you did it, who's to say someone else won't in the future? I'll make a deal. It doesn't matter to *them* who they get. Tell me everything, Paul, and you'll be the only one. Gail will die quickly, without pain. If you know the truth, then you understand what you'll be saving her from."

Paul wavered. Gail looked at both men, then cried out, "No, Paul, *no*! If I'm going to die, then I'll die with you. But don't give him the satisfaction of knowing anything. *Please!*"

Paul stared hard at McClain. "There's your answer. Now get the hell out of here."

McClain spun on his heel and looked at Jake Stillwell. "Everything will be ready soon. Watch them carefully till then. Any problems . . . take care of it however you want."

He left. Stillwell checked their bonds, then switched off the light and again slumped down in the chair. Paul's body shook with rage from the confrontation with McClain. Gail could feel it.

"Paul?" she whispered. "Paul, please, it's all right."

"*Nothing's* all right! They're going to — "

"No, stop," she said firmly. "I changed my mind. Paul, I don't want to know."

He nodded. "Maybe that's best. Gail?"

"Yes?"

"You could've died jumping into the creek."

"You could've died trying to find me."

"McClain said we must be more than just friends. I think he's right."

"I *know* he's right. Paul, listen. Can you hear me?"

Her voice had dropped. "Barely," he said.

"Good, then he can't hear us at all. There's still some time left. I can't just wait for them to come and kill us."

"Do you have a plan?"

"A lame one. I can still move my fingers. If we were back to back, maybe I could untie you. But with him sitting there . . ."

"If I get on my side, you can reach."

He started rocking, then moaned, as though in pain. Stillwell sat up. "What the hell's wrong with you?"

"My arm hurts from laying on it!" Paul yelled. "Jesus, ow!" He rolled onto his side. "That's better."

Stillwell was alert for a few seconds, then relaxed. They waited, to be sure. Then Paul felt Gail's fingers. Her body shielded the frantic movements of her hands from Stillwell, even if he could see across the small room in the dark. So subtle were her actions, Stillwell suspected nothing.

But the knots were too tight, her access limited. She worked at it for fifteen minutes, growing more frustrated. Finally she gave up.

"Sorry, Paul, I can't do it."

"I've been thinking of something," he said, "but it's more desperate than brilliantly conceived."

"That's where we're at now. What is it?"

He eased onto his back without a stir from Jake Stillwell, then explained his plan to Gail.

Jake Stillwell wished the night's business was finished. He had never cared much for it, but like his father had always told him and Roy, "You gotta do what's gotta be done." Not profound, but concrete. Still, he wished it were over so he could be back in his basement. Especially since this one was not going so smoothly. If only Ms. Thorburn hadn't felt so poorly last night, it would have already been over.

They had been quiet for a while. Now he could hear them talking again. Softly at first; then, in growing fear and anger, their voices rose.

"Why the hell am I dying for you?" the man yelled.

"For *me?*" the woman cried. "I didn't ask for your help. You could've stayed out of it!"

"I don't want to die!" he whined. "Where's McClain? We can make a deal!"

"Coward!" the woman shouted. "You make me sick!"

"Hey, shuddup," Stillwell warned, "or I'll stuff something in your mouths."

They ignored him, the man saying loudly, "McClain! I want to talk to you! Let me go and I'll tell you everything! Take *her*, like you were going to! *McClain!*"

"*You bastard!*" the woman screamed.

Stillwell was on his feet and across the room. "Goddammit," he snapped, "I swear I'll — "

Gail thrust her legs out in front of him. Stillwell fell hard, his head just missing the brick ledge around the fireplace. His shotgun, not cocked, dropped harmlessly to the rug. Although dazed, he tried to get up quickly. Paul, already in position, drove both heels into the man's face. Stillwell groaned, then was quiet.

Both knew what they had to do. They worked silently, untying each other's hands. Gail managed to stand, then bent and slipped the ropes off her legs. Paul did the same on the floor. They finished at about the same time. Gail's gaze remained on Jake Stillwell, but the man did not move.

"Let me help you up," she said to Paul.

"I'm okay." He scrambled to his feet.

Their captors had touched nothing in No. 11. Even the rough draft of his new novel lay scattered on the desk, as he had left it. Inside the smaller of the two desk drawers he found his Swiss army knife, a gift from his father on his tenth birthday.

"Let's hurry," Gail whispered as Paul snatched up Jake Stillwell's shotgun.

"Put some more clothes on first." He hurried to the front window and peered out between the blinds. "Wouldn't do us any good to get out of this and then freeze to death in the damn woods."

The clothes they had worn earlier were strewn across the cabin floor, still damp from the plunge into Aspen Creek. Paul's down jacket, which he had changed at noontime — a hundred years ago, it seemed — was on the bed where he had left it. He gave it to Gail then helped himself to Jake Stillwell's large hooded coat, heavy with extra shotgun shells and the man's gloves in the pockets.

"Come on," he said, again checking the footpath. "It's clear."

Baby Ben read 12:45 when they stepped outside.

The clearing was alive with anticipation. They felt it there, in front of No. 11. It affected Paul as it always did. Gail was overwhelmed.

"Not that way!" she exclaimed. "Oh no, I can't!"

Paul understood. "The trail to Big House is out too. They'll be coming soon, if they're not on the way already. Let's get across the creek. We'll follow it to the lake and take our chances there."

Leanna Creek was nearly three yards wide where it wound past the cabin. Plenty of stepping stones, Paul knew, but not easy to find in the dark. He hadn't thought of bringing a flashlight. Too late now.

They crossed warily, concerned about their visibility from the footpath. Paul slipped once, the icy water numbing his left leg. The opposite bank was steeper. They scrambled up, paused for a moment then hurried on.

Snow had stopped falling hours ago. The sky was clear, and there was no wind, but the temperature had to be in the teens, or less.

The internal chill eased its grasp as they moved farther away from the place where the Thorburn/McClain cabin had stood. Despite the danger, they were both relieved.

Dense manzanita, rabbit bush, and quaking aspen slowed them; so did the deep virgin snow. They could see the footpath on the other side for a time but finally veered away from it.

Even harder going now. One deep drift took Gail up to her waist. With poor leverage, Paul could hardly help her out. More time lost.

Thorburn Lake, finally. The creek was narrow and forceful where it emptied into the broader body. There they found the path that skirted the lake. Paul took Gail's hand then suddenly stopped.

Arthur Tyler's great bulk filled the trail a few yards away.

"Uh, sor-ry but . . . you can't go no more," he said.

Arthur appeared to be unarmed. Paul raised the shotgun. "Get out of our way, Arthur," he warned. "I *will* use this."

"You *won't*, Mr. Fleming, not unless you want this woman's head blown off. Now put it down!"

Jane Tyler, both hands on a service revolver, emerged from the trees on Gail's left. Jake Stillwell, shivering in a blanket he had thrown over his shoulders, followed.

"You do like she said," Stillwell told them. "Janie can hit anything she can see."

Reluctantly, Paul obeyed. Arthur retrieved the shotgun and handed it to the older man.

"We can't wait anymore," the librarian said to her brother. "Go tell them that Jake and I are bringing these two out."

"O-kay." Arthur looked at Paul and Gail sadly then left.

Stillwell approached the pair. He was rubbing the side of his face where Paul had kicked him. "Take the coat off, now!" he snapped. "The gloves too."

Paul felt the man's rage and quickly unzipped the heavy coat and pulled off the gloves. Stillwell snatched them away and threw him the blanket, then tied their hands — too tightly — in front of them.

"Jake, you lead," Jane Tyler said. "You two, single file behind him."

"Janie, you watch out for 'em," Stillwell warned.

"Don't worry about me."

Paul expected the way back would take them along the parking area behind Big House. Not that it would help them much. But the trail they followed was neither along the creek nor directly toward the mansion. It was narrow, thick with snow, but easier than the way he and Gail had come. A few minutes later they were again on the familiar path, between Gail's cabin and No. 12.

Both Stillwell and the librarian were behind them now. They were urged forward quickly, past the deserted No. 12, past Paul's cabin, where earlier the snowplow had finished its work long before reaching the sentinel pines. Their footprints in the deep snow became the first. If others were already in the clearing, they had a different way of getting there.

Gail's anxiety grew as they neared; she shivered uncontrollably. Paul stayed close, trying to keep his body against hers.

Closer to the pines they could see a glow in the distance, through the trees. A small fire, Paul thought. No, hardly a small one. As they neared, he could see a mound over five feet high just across Leanna Creek, its flames crackling as they groped for the night. A strange illusion, to have perceived it as small.

Two people stood close to the fire, adding more wood. Paul recognized Nora Hardman's red coat. It was a moment before the other hooded figure turned: Jenny Fry, her face bruised where Gail had hit her. The woman had lost her father that day and was now about to take part in murder. She saw Paul and Gail, smiled, waved.

"Stop here," Jake Stillwell ordered when they were a few yards past the fire. "Guess they aren't ready," he said to Jane.

"It won't be long," the woman said.

There was some warmth from the blaze, although Gail continued to tremble. Her gaze darted around the clearing, never remaining long on anything. Paul felt her fear grow.

"I can still give in to McClain and spare you this," he said.

"No . . . way!" she gasped. "Just . . . take my hand."

It was hard, but they managed to link fingers. Gail breathed deeply, exhaling through the mouth. Soon the trembling lessened.

But the terror of their surroundings would not go away. It was alive, this place, some living, throbbing entity. The darkness was its lifeblood, the branches of the pines its arteries and veins, the angry fire its heart. They were intruders there — infectious things — and in time the organism would protect itself, as it always did.

More people were coming. They emerged from the trees near where Leanna Creek again penetrated the forest. Two of them carried something. They walked like litter bearers at opposite ends of what appeared to be flagpoles, each maybe fifteen feet long. The man in front limped badly.

Carl Stillwell and his uncle carried the poles to where Paul and Gail waited at gunpoint. The deputy, his head bandaged under his Stetson, glared at Paul as they lowered the poles to the snow. Paul noticed that one end of each was threaded, as if they were giant screws. Roy Stillwell knelt by Jane's feet and dug in the snow. When he had dug deep enough he rolled away a large rock, then brushed the earth off a hinged metal flap, about the same diameter as the poles. His nephew did the same at another spot a yard away.

"We won't even have to untie 'em," Roy said. "Bring 'em over."

Jake Stillwell pushed them forward and forced them to their knees. Grimacing in pain, Carl lifted one of the poles then guided the threaded end between Paul's arms and into the hole. He didn't try to be careful. Twice the cold metal knocked against Paul's wrists. With his uncle's help he lowered the pole a couple of feet into the ground, then began turning it. They screwed it in another half a foot before meeting resistance, and were grunting as they tightened it.

Paul caught the deputy's eye as he worked. "Done this a few times, have you?" he said.

"You shut your mouth, mister," Carl exploded, "or I swear — "

"Carl, enough!" his father said. "Just get it done."

They inserted the other pole, trapping Gail, then backed away. For the first time Jane lowered her pistol. She and the

Stillwells walked over to the fire. There the six descendants spoke in hushed tones, occasionally gesturing in the direction of the prisoners.

"Tell me one thing," Gail said to Paul. "Will it . . . take long?"

He shook his head. "I don't know."

Once, Paul's eyes found Nora's. The woman's face was lined with anguish. She didn't want to do this, he thought. Maybe she had never wanted to. But that hadn't stopped her before, and it wouldn't now, because she *was* one of them, and this was their legacy. Still, if he could somehow reach her . . .

After a moment she shook her head and turned away.

The dancing flames made the trees surrounding the clearing seem alive. Yet aside from the fire and the flow of water in the creek, they were engulfed in silence. Not a bird or animal. Nothing.

Arthur Tyler emerged from between the sentinel pines and lumbered across the clearing. His sister looked at him admonishingly, as if he had done something wrong. Then all the descendants turned toward the trees where the Stillwells had earlier appeared.

Harriet Thorburn held Walter McClain's arm. Their entrance was the same one they performed every night in the dining room. Slow and regal, not even the terrible Sierra chill enough to quicken their steps. They walked past the other descendants to Paul and Gail, stopping a yard away. The old woman, heavily clothed, stared at Paul.

"So, here's our complication," she said, her expression like that of a stern parent with a troublesome child. "We had another once, didn't we, Walter?"

"Yes, but not like this," McClain replied. "That one was an accident."

"I remember now!" she exclaimed. "It was 1951, in . . . February, I think. Weather like this. That fine artist from Idaho. Excellent work. But the poor fellow had trouble sleeping. Used to take walks at all hours. Wound up here one night, when he shouldn't have."

"Entertaining story," Gail said scornfully. "Why don't you tell it at dinner sometime?"

"We took care of it," she went on. "But afterward it was a dilemma. The man had a big family, friends . . ." She tilted her head, suddenly remembering something. "Not an accident, you say? He *knows*, then?"

"Yes," McClain said.

She took two steps toward Paul. "*How could you know?*" she shrieked. "*How could you understand?*"

She began slapping him. A fire grew in her eyes, and it was more than just her creeping senility. Raising an elbow, he tried to ward off the blows. She managed to scratch his face with a long fingernail, drawing blood. Paul bit his lip against the pain.

"*Leave him alone, witch!*" Gail cried. Using the stake like a child's maypole, she swung around and struck the woman in the chest with the heels of her boots. Harriet Thorburn went down in the snow. Some ran to help her; Jane Tyler and Carl Stillwell headed for Gail, the librarian again raising her pistol. McClain stepped in their way.

"Get back, now!" he ordered. "Janie, put that damn gun away! Is she all right?" he asked the others.

Brushing away Nora's and Roy Stillwell's helping hands, the matriarch stood. Some of the madness seemed to be gone. She looked at McClain.

"It's time," she said.

The nine surviving descendants of the ill-fated Thorburn party formed a widely spaced straight line, their backs toward Paul and Gail and the fire. They were transfixed on a single spot in the forest — not by the sentinel pines or the place where most of them had entered the clearing, but somewhere else, the trees in the direction of the lake. Paul stared past Harriet Thorburn, who stood in the middle, to see what they waited for. The moon was in its first phase and gave meager light. Still, the figure that appeared was clearly visible.

The same figure their ancestors had seen in the forest nearly a century and a half ago.

They had called him Mr. Black then.

Now his name was Joe Landry.

Paul knew him, even with a scarf around his face and shadows of the forest in his path. He walked slowly toward the disciples, stopping in front of Arthur but looking past the big man at the prisoners.

"We're ready," Harriet Thorburn said.

Landry shook his head. "No you ain't."

He waved Arthur to him and spoke briefly. The cook nodded and trudged off toward the sentinel pines.

"This is irregular," McClain said. "What's wrong?"

Dismissing the question with a curt wave, Landry walked toward Paul and Gail. McClain stayed close behind the dark man. Landry's gaze was on Paul when he stopped.

"I'm glad it's this one," he said. "Don't like him much." Landry took a step toward Gail and began unraveling his scarf. He looked her over, his eyes undressing her.

"I woulda liked some time with you before this," he said, then shrugged and turned away.

Motioning for McClain not to follow, Landry walked to the fire, circled it once then went to the edge of the creek. Paul watched him standing there, staring into the water. What was he doing? What was he *seeing*? Paul glanced at the descendants. Landry's actions seemed to puzzle them. Apparently this was not the way.

Then Landry gestured toward the sentinel pines. Everyone looked. Arthur Tyler emerged, a large burlap sack slung over his shoulder. Despite his strength he bent under the weight. Landry ordered him to empty the sack in front of Paul and Gail. Arthur pulled the knot.

Mary Sherman, bound and gagged, tumbled into the snow.

"Oh Christ, no!" Paul exclaimed.

McClain looked at Harriet Thorburn, then Landry. "Why is she here?" he demanded.

"Caught her an hour ago, sneakin' around in your office. Second time she was somewhere she shouldn't be today. Used a screwdriver to break in. But she had keys for the rest of Big House. *My* keys." He looked at Paul. "Some of which we found on him. I remembered they was chummy too. Figured she knew what's goin' on."

"What was she doing in Walter's office?" Harriet Thorburn asked.

"Couldn't tell."

"Why don't we find out?" the sheriff said.

"It doesn't matter!" the old woman snapped. "She'll die too. Get her up."

McClain turned away, his shoulders sagging as he walked back to the fire. "Look at him!" Paul shouted to the descendants. "He knows you've gone too far this time. Don't you, Walter? Here's *another* accident you'll have to explain!"

"You shut your mouth," Jake Stillwell warned.

Jane Tyler cut the rope from Mary's ankles while Carl Stillwell retied her hands around Gail's pole. They removed her gag last then backed away, most drifting over to McClain. Landry walked back to the creek, separating himself from the others. The descendants appeared to be troubled and were speaking among themselves in a way that reminded Paul, ludicrously, of a football huddle.

Mary was shaky. "Are you all right?" Paul asked.

She nodded. "Yeah, great. Hello, Gail. Hell of a place to meet, isn't it?"

"I'm sorry this happened to you," Gail said.

"My fault. So stupid, getting caught like that! Twice in one day, no less."

"What do you mean?"

"I got into Harriet Thorburn's rooms and was looking around when a maid — that cute little Mexican girl — found me. I did some fast talking, convinced her I was up there to see the old woman. She took me back to the sitting room, said that's where I had to wait. I would've gotten out of there after she left, except that Ms. Thorburn showed up. So I interviewed her! Told her I needed background for my work. She was cooperative, but I think she was suspicious."

"So you got through it," Paul said. "What did you do then?"

"Wasn't much I *could* do. Like you, I figured everyone was watching me. And there wasn't anywhere left to look. So I waited, hoping you'd found Gail in town and gotten out of here. It was harder than hell not knowing what was happening.

"Then, a little while ago, I was looking out my window and saw some of them on the path to your cabins. That didn't make sense, so I followed. It wasn't easy; I had to hide a few times. But I finally saw where they were headed, and I heard one mention your names. I knew what was going on.

"This time I had to get into McClain's office and use that radio. But he was still there, and others were around. It took a while, especially having to break in."

"But Landry caught you before you could do it," Paul said.

Although the descendants were far enough away, Mary dropped her voice even more. "Wrong, dear boy. I got through."

"Oh, Mary!" Gail cried.

"Talked to the sheriff's office in Tahoe City, told them as much as I could in a minute without sounding too crazy. Mostly I tried to make them understand that the danger up here was immediate."

"So the cavalry *is* coming," Paul said.

Mary shrugged. "But I don't know if they'll make it in time. The roads are buried, and the few available helicopters in the area were sent to an avalanche at one of the ski resorts." She shook her head. "Sorry. I think Jessica Fletcher would've done better."

"Mary, you did great," Paul said. "But we may not need the cavalry for anything but cleanup."

"What do you mean?" Gail asked.

"You'll see. They're coming!"

Their huddle over, McClain and Harriet Thorburn led the others back to where they had first waited for Landry. Their uncertainty of a few minutes earlier seemed overcome by strong-jawed determination. The dark man turned away from the creek and walked several yards past them, toward the center of the clearing. He faced the nine descendants and the prisoners, his hands raised. For a moment there was silence, a choking, unnatural silence so intense it seemed as if no sound would be heard should someone try to speak. Even the fire blazed mutely.

There would be no more silence after that.

Landry's voice rose. No. The voice came from inside him, but it wasn't *his* voice. The singsong chanting of an ancient shaman, uttering words that Time had forgotten since the death of the Indian. Loud, eerie; then louder. Landry — Mr. Black — began peeling off his clothes, tossing them to either side. He was naked now, his leathery body covered with deep crimson scars from hundreds of self-inflicted knife wounds. Bending, he dug under the snow and withdrew a dagger of such polished steel, it reflected the fire with blinding light. He cradled it in two hands, holding it out toward the disciples.

"Christ," Mary said, staring in horror and disgust at the ravaged body.

"What is he doing?" Gail cried.

"It doesn't matter," Paul told her. "This is as far as it goes!

"*Listen to me!*" Paul shouted. "It's over! Do you understand? There are others who know about you and are on the way! *This . . . is . . . over!*"

The descendants turned, gazing in confusion at the prisoners and at one another. Carl Stillwell finally said, "He's lying. They didn't have no chance to tell anyone."

Paul looked at McClain. The associate director was pallid. "Ask *him*! He knows it's true!"

"What's he talkin' about, Walter?" Roy Stillwell asked.

McClain sighed. "The radio. She got to the radio."

The descendants, like a herd of cattle, gazed dumbly around. Jane Tyler cried, "Then it *is* over. We have to get away from here!"

"And go where, Janie?" McClain snapped. "You know we can't ever leave the mountains, not for long. No, we're staying."

"But we can let them go," Nora said. "We don't have to do this no more!"

"No, *we have to finish it!*" Harriet Thorburn screamed. "They have to know we kept our part till the end!"

The sheriff nodded. "Damn right."

Nora held out her hands. "But it ain't gonna matter now if — "

"You shut your mouth, woman," McClain warned. "Don't forget you've been a part of this since you were a kid. We'll play it out — *all* of us!"

"*Walter, for God's sake — !*" Paul cried.

"Another word from you," Harriet Thorburn said, waving a gloved finger at him, "and we'll not only cut out your tongue but your woman's too. Now get on with it!"

Defeated, Paul shook his head and tried not to look at Gail or Mary. The descendants turned to Landry, who had waited silently during the confrontation. He smiled without humor, amused by what had transpired among these *people*, all of whom he loathed. Then he started chanting again. His eyes changed, growing blank as he swayed to his own rhythm.

Not all the descendants watched the scarred man. Nora glanced behind her a few times at the prisoners. Arthur did it once, until his sister pinched his arm and made him look ahead. Jenny, drifting even farther away from reality, looked everywhere, sometimes smiling vaguely, especially when her gaze lighted on Paul or Gail.

Landry held the dagger over his head in both hands. He brought it down slowly, the point toward him. No patch of his skin was unscarred. The tip penetrated leathery flesh below his neck. Paul stared in disbelief. Mary and Gail cried out, the older woman struggling against the urge to vomit. Still chanting, Landry cut a vertical gash down his chest. He withdrew the blade and spun around, though not before Paul saw blood pour from the wound. It darkened the snow between Landry's legs, a circular stain that grew to several inches across before it stopped dripping.

Like oil on water the stain slid across the surface of the snow, leaving no mark behind, until it was absorbed by a drift in the middle of the clearing.

Landry's monotone grew louder. Now a second voice joined his. Harriet Thorburn's shrill cry sounded like the imitation Sherri Jordan had done for Paul his first night at the colony.

Sherri Jordan, who had also witnessed this scene.

The old woman ripped off her clothes as she joined the dark man, her shriveled body oblivious to the cold. She took the knife from Landry and laid it ceremoniously in the snow.

Harriet Thorburn, who had inherited the legacy from her famous ancestor, had become a participant . . .

Because she enjoyed the role.

The wind rose. No, the *sound* of wind, for they felt nothing, nor did the fire jump or a branch sway. It roared toward them, like the rush of an oncoming train, until some of the descendants had to cover their ears. The prisoners did not have that luxury.

"Look!" Mary cried. "My God, *what is it?*"

A small dark shape emerged from the creek. Another sound assaulted the clearing. Paul had heard it before: the pathetic keening from the lake. The thing crawled up the bank, red eyes aglow in the firelight, black fur glistening from the icy water. Baring its mouthful of teeth in a mocking smile, the Water Baby draped itself across a log to watch.

A second and third came up, their infantile wails joining the first. Landry saw them too, opened his arms then waved brusquely, as if in dismissal.

These, Paul knew, weren't what Landry had summoned or what the descendants awaited.

"Paul, I can't stand this!" Gail screamed.

He tried to move the pole, pulling against it, pushing it with his shoulder. Nothing. Gail used her teeth on the rope but stopped. There would be no time to finish.

It had begun.

The descendants, except for Harriet Thorburn, turned around and knelt in the snow, their eyes down. Beyond Landry and the old woman, near the place where his blood had vanished, were three dark spots. Small, but growing larger. Extending lengthwise, slowly, steadily, toward the place they had touched many times before.

The pair awaiting the shadows waved their arms and continued to chant an unnecessary summons. McClain, the Stillwells, and the Tylers swayed to the bland rhythm. Nora, powerless, shook her head.

No one expected Jenny Fry to stand up.

The young woman stared at the shadows for a moment then faced the others. Something was different about her when she spoke. "What is our debt to *them*? Lives, give them *lives*. And if we don't? Then we pay with ours!"

"Jenny, stop it," Carl warned.

"I'll pay!" she cried. "I don't care. They put this on us, our parents, and the ones before them. We never wanted it. So let's pay. Let's have it written off!"

"Jenny!" Carl exclaimed. He stood.

The shadows crept closer.

"Paul, Gail, they won't hurt you," she called, walking toward them. "I'm — "

Jenny's eyes grew wide then rolled back in her head. Blood erupted from her mouth. She toppled in the snow.

The knife Harriet Thorburn had pushed into the base of her skull was left there. Twisting around, the old woman confronted Carl Stillwell, towering over her. The stunned deputy wanted to reach Jenny. Harriet Thorburn shoved him away.

"*Get down!*" she shrieked. "*All of you, stay where you are!*"

Carl obeyed, but his gaze remained on Jenny. Harriet Thorburn warned the rest of them with a glare and rejoined Landry.

The shadows had crept to within a yard of the pair.

There was still nothing in the clearing that could have cast them.

Carl's body shook as he sobbed. Nora glanced at the prisoners. Jane Tyler seemed as spellbound by what transpired as the matriarch. She no longer was aware of her brother, who looked around inquisitively, his mouth agape. McClain, pale as death, stared at Jenny.

The shadows spread out as they passed over the descendants.

Paul stared at Nora. The agony in the woman's face was clear, but again she turned away.

The shadows fell across the gap that separated Paul, Gail, and Mary from the others.

They were touched by the darkness, and a fierce cold, like nothing they'd known before, froze them inside. Mary pulled against the ropes in a frenzy that left the flesh on her wrists raw.

"Mary, stop!" Paul shouted, futilely resisting the fingers of ice that raked his insides. "Please, stop it!"

Those that cast the shadows appeared.

The wailing of the Water Babies grew in delirious anticipation. Windsound roared beyond reason. Landry shook like an animal shedding water. Harriet Thorburn danced around him with spastic jerks, like a grotesque marionette. The descendants, their backs turned, knew what was there.

"*No!*" Gail screamed. "*OH MY GOD NO!*"

They grew like noxious weeds in a sequence of time-lapse photography, rising tall above the clearing. Three snaking things, enormous, each thicker than the bole of a lodgepole pine. They were . . . spinning, Paul realized. Like waterspouts or cyclones. *Black dust devils.* The top of each was wider than the base, the whole shape conical. They were not, however, swirling circles of dust, not wind and not water, but . . . things of flesh. Dark, slimy, their whirling occasionally shedding loathsome, scaly bits into the snow. Paul stared, but in spite of their size he could not distinguish a recognizable feature in any of the masses. At the end of their emergence they stood half the height of the pines. The spinning stopped and they became still, as though surveying what awaited them. Paul thought they swayed slightly; that might have been a trick of the firelight.

They began moving across the clearing.

The snow shielded whatever it was that propelled them along the ground. They came slowly, undulating in a perverse mockery of a dance. Again they began to spin, and although close together their individuality was apparent. They bent in the middle, their wider tops twisting down cobra-like just above the snow, hovering there like obscene gaping mouths.

Harriet Thorburn, frothing like a rabid creature, reached a frenzied pitch as one of the dark orifices became the background for her gyrations. Landry stared at Paul, who *felt* the handyman's words, because there was no way they could have been heard.

The dal-yawii *come for you,* mushege. *Greet them, and see if it will make the pain less. But I think not.*

Then a laugh — shrill, taunting. Harriet Thorburn, grinning, raving.

The shadows covered the mountains and forests and quarter-moon as the *dal-yawii* snaked past their servants.

Mary fell awkwardly to her knees, her eyes blank, for the moment spared from the sight of what approached. Gail tugged against the ropes and screamed without being heard.

Paul couldn't look away from the *dal-yawii* as they neared the descendants.

He saw something in each of the wide black maws.

Heads. Human heads. Or humanlike. Bunched tightly together in places, like clusters of grapes. Men and women, some children. Faces of unspeakable pain and suffering, mouths open in silent warning screams, dark tears of blood streaming down from wide, eyeless sockets. Colorless, unrecognizable faces . . .

No, color in one. A larger face, new, not yet absorbed by any cluster. The color was on top: the hair, the blond-red punkish hair . . .

Paul, the mouth was saying. *Paul.*

Something else in the blackness: birdlike mutations with blood-red feathers spread wide, razor talons at the end of thin legs. Large talons, gleaming white mostly, but with dark stains that centuries could not wear off. Terrible faces with malignant coal-black eyes above broad, hooked nebs that clattered obscenely, like nestlings waiting to be fed.

Things from Indian legend that had once cast the shadows of their bloated wings over a terrified world.

Things from nightmares.

Paul thought, *This isn't going to be quick.*

Nora stood. She staggered to Jenny Fry's body and began pulling out the knife. No one reacted immediately to what she was doing. She wrenched it free and stumbled toward the prisoners.

Windsound diminished; so did the Water Babies' keening, now with an inquisitive undertone. Landry pointed a finger at Nora as she neared the stakes. His mouth formed the words *Stop her!* Harriet Thorburn — his creature — obeyed.

While the other descendants remained on their knees, Carl Stillwell stood and put himself in the old woman's path. His hands were raised, as if he were directing traffic on Washo Street. The matriarch glared at him.

"Get out of my way!" she screamed. "You're as spineless as every Stillwell before you!"

She made an animal noise and ran at him, hands curved like claws. Stillwell cuffed her on the side of the head, driving her into the snow.

The windsound lessened more.

Nora reached Gail first. Trembling, she cut Gail's wrist along with the rope; not deep, yet painful. Gail winced but did not cry out.

Her hands free, Gail grabbed the knife. Nora looked at Paul.

"Sorry, Mr. Fleming!" she cried. "You was one of the good ones. Sorry for all of it."

She backed away. "Nora!" Paul shouted.

"Sorry . . . for *them*!" She gestured toward the descendants.

Gail freed Paul as Nora turned and faced the *dal-yawii*, her hands out. Carl Stillwell bent over the fallen matriarch.

"Ms. Thorburn," said the deputy, "I — "

She kicked him in the genitals then clambered to her feet and charged Nora. Her eyes danced with madness.

"*Stupid bitch! You'll die too now, you — !*"

Gail stopped the old woman before she could reach Nora. The knife penetrated Harriet Thorburn's heart. Eyes bulging, she reached for Gail's throat. Gail shoved her away; the blade slid out as she fell back. Her bleeding, shriveled body thrashed for a moment, then was still.

The windsound lessened even more.

Some of the descendants staggered to their feet. Others cowered more deeply in the snow. The *dal-yawii* reared, like trapped beasts. In the confusion that gripped the clearing, Paul hurried to Gail and took the knife from her trembling hand.

"Get to the trees, quick!" he yelled. "I'll help Mary."

She shook her head. "I'm not leaving you."

Together they ran to the other woman, who looked around, trying to understand what was happening.

Nora took another step toward the *dal-yawii*. "*No more Thorburns left!*" she cried. "*No more Frys. Just the Stillwells and Tylers, McClain . . . and me! Take us, and let this be over!*"

"No-oo!" Jane Tyler shrieked, standing. "You can't speak for us!"

Nora glanced over her shoulder at Paul. "Sorry," she said again, and walked toward the spinning black things.

"*Nora, don't!*" Paul cried.

One of the flaking abominations spun forward to meet her. Windsound rose, again threatening to shatter their senses. The Water Babies' cry mocked the helpless humans. Nora was swept up into the black maw, her feet lifted from the snow. Inside, the clusters of heads lamented soundlessly. The talons of the bird-things raked the air, scraping together, then found something that was — at first — less yielding.

They ripped Nora Hardman apart.

It was done with surgical skill. When her body was returned almost reverently to the snow, only small rivulets of blood poured from the stumps where her limbs and head had been. The arms and legs, equally bloodless, were dropped a few seconds later.

Nora's head was not returned.

"*Let's go!*" Gail screamed.

"Mary, can you walk?" Paul asked.

"Sure, yeah," the woman gasped, trying to stand. "Just help me — "

She toppled, nearly dragging them down with her. They held her more firmly and tried to lift her up.

The *dal-yawii* met and came toward them.

Carl Stillwell had crept through the snow to Jenny's side. Now he ran across the snow, putting himself between the *dal-yawii* and those who had been prisoners.

"Not them, no," he said calmly to the nightmare creatures. "You're gettin' your due."

The *dal-yawii* hesitated.

"*Carl!*" his father cried.

The deputy glanced at the others. They were standing. "Pa, Uncle Roy, don't fight it no more," he said, but it was doubtful anyone heard him.

He ran at the horrors and threw himself into the first one.

This time the bird-claws tore at him with fury, abandoning the earlier precision. His screams penetrated even the windsound as blood and pieces of flesh and darker bits of organs erupted from the black orifice, staining the snow, spattering Paul and the women.

They saw Carl's large torso strike the snow. A part of one leg remained. So did most of his head — although without a face.

Death aroused the *dal-yawii*. Two of them twisted around the bonfire, which had grown blindingly bright. The third reared above Landry, imitating the way its servant stood rigidly, his eyes closed, still chanting.

Paul felt the words again: *See*, mushege. *See the* dal-yawii *collect an old debt.*

The *dal-yawii* snaked through the clearing in the darkness of their own shadows. Not caring anymore, Jake Stillwell dropped to one knee and waited to follow his son into oblivion.

He didn't wait long.

The Water Babies' cry was more like laughter now. Roy Stillwell tried to run for the trees but never got close. The screams of his death were the longest yet. Strips and gobbets of his ravaged flesh darkened an area five yards across.

"*No, not me!*" shrieked Jane Tyler to the one that twisted above her. "*Take them! Them! Let me live and I'll keep repaying you! Let me — !*"

Her brother encircled her with one massive arm, lifting her like a child's doll. She kicked and pummeled him; Arthur ignored it. The big man looked at Paul and the women and shook his head.

He carried his sister to the *dal-yawii* then joined her.

"*Leave me here, dammit!*" Mary cried to Paul and Gail. "*Just go!*"

But the *dal-yawii* surrounded the three, daring them to try. They were safer in the eye of the carnage.

Walter McClain stood alone. Firelight danced in the beads of sweat across his face. He still tried to comprehend the death of the woman he had served for over half a century; he was looking down at her when one of the *dal-yawii* took him.

But even something from Hell can be glutted by blood and death. It held him for a moment then vomited him out. Walter McClain emerged whole.

No, a trick of the angle from where Paul and the women watched.

Nearly whole.

His right arm was missing, along with part of his face and most of his scalp. The distortion on one side of his mouth left a death's-head sneer.

McClain stayed on his feet.

Raising his one arm, he waved an unsteady finger at Paul. "Your fault!" he shrieked, staggering toward him. "No trouble before now. I'll kill you! Kill . . . you!"

The *dal-yawii* undulated around Paul and Gail but left McClain alone. Mary, still kneeling in the snow, looked at the things and might have wondered if they were amused by this confrontation.

"Walter, *stop!*" Paul warned.

McClain covered the remaining yards quickly, grabbing Paul around the neck before he could react. His strength was surprising for a man practically dead. Paul tried to push the arm away; Gail grabbed McClain from behind, trying not to look at his ravaged, dripping face.

"*Kill you!*" he exclaimed in a liquid voice as blood gushed from his throat.

Finally wrestling him free, Gail threw McClain into the snow. He rolled over twice then tried to scramble to his feet.

Two of the *dal-yawii* fell upon him at the same time. No piece of what they returned to the snow seconds later was too large to be held in one hand.

The last descendant of the Thorburn party was dead.

The *dal-yawii* reared upright, in formation. They appeared greater in size. Again, maybe an illusion. Behind them, Landry's hands were raised in triumph.

Windsound diminished, like a train fading beyond the outskirts of a town. The Water Babies' cry was the same until the dark shapes retreated into Leanna Creek and, one by one, were silenced. Landry backed across the clearing, toward the trees where he'd first appeared, his face blurry in the darkness. Paul and the women heard his voice.

"*The* dal-yawii *are satisfied. The old debt is paid. Now they go back. Remember what you saw here,* mushege. *Remember it.*"

Then the forest took Mr. Black.

The *dal-yawii* followed their servant but stopped in the center of the clearing. Windsound rose again, briefly, as they twisted into the earth. Their shadows followed; they were three pine trees on the snow, then three broad stains, then three small circles, then . . .

Nothing.

Not a sound in the clearing other than the crackle of the dying fire. But enough signs that the *dal-yawii* had been there from the death and blood and pieces of bodies left in the snow.

Gail and Paul held each other. Mary managed to stand, and they let her in. There were no words yet; they shared the silence.

Finally Gail said, "There will be a time — soon — when we'll have to explain this."

Mary nodded. "We will. Paul, Gail, I . . ." She hesitated.

"What?" Paul asked.

"The way I acted here . . . Dammit, I'm sorry!"

"Mary," Paul said. "You risk your life for us, then apologize . . ."

They heard a sound, far off. The whirring of a helicopter's blades, probably near Big House.

"So the cavalry got here," Paul said.

"Too late." Mary shook her head. "Looks like we'll be explaining sooner than we thought."

The fire was nearly out. Gail shivered uncontrollably. "I want to be away from here!" she exclaimed. "Paul, please, let's go . . . *now*!"

"Wait a minute," Mary said, indicating the trees. "What about Landry? He's — "

"Gone," Paul said. "He's gone. With . . . *them*, maybe. I don't know. Whatever, we don't have to worry about him."

"Not now, anyway," Mary said, and shuddered.

She started for the creek. Paul held Gail as they followed. "When we're done with this," he said, "I mean away from here and everything, I . . ."

"What?" Gail asked.

"I don't want you to be alone. *I* don't want to be alone! Shit, I don't know *what* I mean!"

She tried to smile, couldn't. "I do," she said. "We'll talk about it later."

They kissed briefly then followed Mary across Leanna Creek. Gail kept her eyes straight ahead; Paul glanced behind him . . .

. . . at the remnants of the bodies in the snow, of the descendants who perhaps had found some kind of peace in their final act.

At the shadows of the nightmare they had lived.

Remember what you saw here, mushege. *Remember it.*

He and Gail followed Mary between the sentinel pines, to the footpath.